THE CASTAWAY LOUNGE

THE CASTAWAY LOUNGE

JON BOILARD

DZANC
BOOKS

DZANC BOOKS

5220 Dexter Ann Arbor Rd.
Ann Arbor, MI 48103
www.dzancbooks.org

Library of Congress Cataloging-in-Publication Data

Boilard, Jon.
  The Castaway Lounge : a novel / by Jon Boilard. -- First edition.
     pages cm
  ISBN 978-1-938103-01-8
  1. Bars (Drinking establishments)--Fiction. 2. Murder--Investigation-
-Fiction. 3. Choice (Psychology)--Fiction. 4. Massachusetts--Fiction. I.
Title.
  PS3602.O47C37 2015
  813'.6--dc23
                              2015000618

First U.S. edition: July 2015
Book design by Michelle Dotter

This is a work of fiction. Characters and names appearing in this work are
a product of the author's imagination, and any similarity to real persons,
living or dead, is coincidental and not intended by the author.

Printed in the United States of America

10   9   8   7   6   5   4   3   2   1

I wrote this book for my brother, Carl.

"But I keep under my body, and bring it into subjection: lest that by any means, when I have preached to others, I myself should be a castaway."

— 1 Corinthians 9:27

Saws and axes forged and filed in New England mill towns cleared forests in Ohio. New England ploughs broke prairie sod; its scales weighed wheat and meat in Texas; its serge clothed businessmen in San Francisco. Its cutlery skinned hides to be tanned in Milwaukee and sliced apples to be dried in Missouri. New England whale oil lit lamps across the continent; its blankets warmed children by night and its textbooks preached at them by day. New England guns armed troops and its lathes, looms, forges, presses, and screwdrivers outfitted factories far and wide. But harsh winters took their toll on the bottom line, and one by one the mills moved south. With these mills went jobs. With these jobs went people. Finally the Great Depression of 1929 sent the remaining millers into bankruptcy, leaving in its wake generations of the desperate and the damned.

1986

PART ONE

"You can't change who you are unless you change what you do."

— Jenny Two Drinks

CHAPTER ONE

Applejack sits in the truck and watches Hoyt light his uncle's pond ablaze using matches and a gas can that's supposed to be for his lawnmower. The fire smokes and burns, somehow smells like birch bark, doesn't do much else but kill mosquitoes and catfish. A cold wind strips leaves from the trees across the way where early swamp maples bend and a picket fence snakes along the hillside. Good enough, Applejack says through the open window. The two men drive around with cigars, stop at the Conway Inn to drink beer and play cards with the Jablonski brothers, whom everybody in town calls the mental twins. Hoyt wins ten dollars and they go to the Castaway Lounge for amateur night, billed on the marquee as *five beautiful girls and one ugly one*. A new blonde named Suzanne sure isn't the ugly one. Applejack takes her out back behind the curtains and gives her a fistful of money. Once he's settled in the chair Suzanne makes a face and says he smells like her daddy's old mechanic shop. He tells her, yeah, he just got done wrenching on his MGB. His hands are so dirty she won't let him touch her and he wishes he'd showered. But she does a pretty good job to a couple songs by Hank Williams Jr. and by the last line of "Whiskey Bent and Hell Bound" she has dropped her bra, slipped down her panties to a tease, and turned, looking back at him over her shoulder.

Jesus fucking Christ, Applejack thinks.

It's way more than he has paid for.

He gets cleaned up the next night and goes back and she's there again. She doesn't recognize him. He reminds her and she says she's sorry, must have been nervous or something. They talk a bit and then she has to go on the main stage. Applejack orders a beer and sits up front. The waitress delivers him a foamy jelly jar. Even though it's only her second night, Suzanne moves around like a real professional and makes a lot of tips. After the set, Applejack buys her a drink, Jack Daniel's with a splash of tap water, and she settles in his lap.

She grew up in Bernardston. He knew a couple of her cousins from knocking heads with them in high school football. They played dirty and talked trash on the line. She tells Applejack she wants to be a teacher and plans to someday learn how at the University of Massachusetts in Amherst. From behind the bar Stavros is giving them funny looks so she gets up and makes the rounds. When she returns Applejack asks if she wants to join him for something to eat after her shift.

A little grub, he says.

Twenty minutes later she goes to clock out, changes her clothes, and comes back.

Well, Applejack says. You sure look like a schoolteacher now.

Suzanne's eyes narrow, wondering is he fucking with her. She decides he isn't and they leave the club together, holding hands, and get into his car, parked beside the pines.

The BP Diner is open all night. It's mostly truckers in there at this hour. They get a booth and he orders biscuits and gravy. She orders a short stack of blueberry pancakes. She plays some of his favorite Elvis Presley on the jukebox and she about knows all the words. Boy Country sees Applejack from across the diner and despite the fact that he can barely keep his legs under him from drinking too much vodka, he comes over and tries to be some kind of joker. Applejack slides across the vinyl seat and stands up out of the booth, puts his hand on Boy Country's shoulder and leads him a couple steps away.

I get it, he says, making a face like they're in cahoots over his secret plans for this babe. Boy Country smiles, puts his chin against his chest, looks at his shoes. Applejack turns Boy Country around, gives him a gentle shove to send him on his way. All right, Boy Country says as he heads out the door.

Nothing seems to faze Suzanne. She says she has an apartment in Bucktown but she doesn't want to go there just yet. She wants to show Applejack where the flying saucer picked her up the first time. It was Mark Wesoloski's cornfield, out past the drive-in movie theatre.

They park on the side of the road and Applejack can hear the shush of the river as she describes the experience to him. She doesn't remember everything because that's the way they wanted it, and what she does recall is like trying to piece together a dream. Things kind of move around, she says. She told her story on *Oprah Winfrey* and that's when her daddy threw her out of the house. She asks Applejack if he thinks she's crazy and he tells her he can think of worse things than crazy.

CHAPTER TWO

Mike Mercier pours himself a cup of yesterday's coffee and makes a face as he drinks it. There's a woman sitting in a foldout chair near his desk. Her ankles are crossed and her purse is in her lap. Janice McElvey keeps the books for several local businesses. Mercier sees her in town, at the pharmacy, Frontier Service Station, the tailor, someplace almost every day. Mercier has known her and her ex since high school. Janice ended up leaving the man because he never did change his violent ways, even after she birthed him two sons and a daughter. It's her daughter, Kristie, that Janice wants to talk about today. Mercier sits behind his desk and regards her.

You sure I can't get you nothing, he says.

No, Janice says. Thank you.

He takes another sip, makes another face, and puts his cup on a stack of papers.

Janice shifts in her seat, nervous. Most folks get like that in the town's only police station, such as it is. They sit in a small open area that serves as the office. There's a bathroom in the corner and a drunk tank out back that'll sometimes play host to two or three guests, but this morning it's only Scotch Padykula, who is just waking up. He hollers every few minutes, mostly the incoherent ramblings of an inebriant.

Mercier waits for Scotch to finish a fresh rant and then turns toward Janice.

So, he says. Tell me about Kristie.

They call her Peanut. She's gone missing.

Missing.

Janice nods her head.

Since when, Mercier says.

I ain't seen her since May.

Mercier sneaks a glance at the calendar on the wall.

So a couple months already, he says.

That's right. Figured maybe she'd run off again and was giving her time.

How old is she now.

Seventeen next month.

Jesus Christ, Mercier says, smiling.

He remembers her crawling around in diapers and he says as much, but Janice makes it clear she isn't in the mood to reminisce just now. Mercier says of course and apologizes. He looks at his cup of coffee, oily black and cold. He won't drink it, figures he'll put on a new pot when Janice is gone. Or maybe cross the street to the pharmacy, get ham and eggs for a change, drink coffee somebody else brewed.

Janice clears her throat and leans forward, separates her ankles. Mercier looks at her and sits up straight. His wood chair creaks.

She still working over to the pharmacy, he says.

Yeah.

Does she have a boyfriend or anything, Mercier says. I was just thinking.

I know what you were thinking hey.

Or maybe she's with Thomas, he says.

I already checked with him and her brothers.

Mercier heard that her ex-husband and the boys lived way up in the hills now. All right, he says.

She's gone missing, Janice says. And I think something bad happened.

Why do you think that.

It's just a feeling I got. Janice starts to cry.

Mercier thinks oh shit here we go. He gets up from his chair to find her a tissue. There's a box of them somewhere, and by the time he finds it under some papers next to the coffee machine, he feels more like a damn fool than any kind of gentleman. He brings the box to her and she takes one out and he half sits on the corner of his desk. Janice blows her nose.

You all right now, Mercier says.

Yeah.

He waits for her to collect herself, figuring she's got more to add. Janice clears her throat again and Mercier folds his arms across his chest.

You think it could be that flying saucer, Janice says. Like that took that other one and brought her back, she adds. I saw it on *Oprah*.

Mike Mercier closes his eyes, lets out a breath, and shakes his head. That's all anybody wants to talk about these days. Ever since that dancer went on the television and ran her mouth about getting abducted by aliens or some such nonsense. Now if your chicken coop is raided it must be Martians—never mind the fox turds and bloody feathers. Mercier opens his eyes again and Scotch lets loose a string of obscenities from the back, something about another stale bologna and cheese sandwich, an apple with a brown spot, something else about the Kingdom of Heaven. The lawman stands and apologizes to Janice, smiles, tells her to hold that thought.

A long-abandoned sawmill—red-brick and angular, plywood-covered windows, curse words and crass reckonings like ancient hieroglyphics spray-painted on its massive walls—sits rotting alongside the river that fueled it until alternatives to water power were developed in the twentieth century. Across South Main Street,

Grandma's is packed, so Applejack and Hoyt sit on stools past
the pool tables near the crapper. Hoyt's combing the crowd but
Applejack doesn't really give a shit, he'll fight just about anybody.

Applejack has been throwing hands with grown men twice his
size since he was a teenager. His father, at first unemployed and
eventually unemployable, had recognized something in his son—
the high threshold for pain, the indomitable spirit, the makings of a
real killer. He would parade him around town to the local watering
holes, pitting him against other layabouts equally desperate for
quick cash. From the jump the kid won more than he lost, besting
infamous tough guys and established like-to-fighters with bulldog
ferocity and the resolve of a pugilistic prodigy. After years of giving
and taking beatings, getting knocked in the head with fists and feet
and kneecaps, he gets migraines that sometimes bang around inside
his skull for days.

There's a girl Applejack knows from a couple towns over and she
winks at him so he goes into the alley with her. He drops his trousers
and leans into the cool mason work. He closes his eyes as Tina's hair
brushes against his bare thighs. He blows smoke rings that float over
her head like temporary halos. A dog-sized raccoon digs through a
trashcan while another stands guard hissing at them. The breeze off
the river smells like chemicals and fried food from Grandma's kitchen.
It's the Fourth of July and the Blue Angels buzz the Berkshires in
perfect formation. The sound of their engines shakes the valley and
becomes the only thing, though Tina's still on her knees in the dirt.

When he goes back inside, Hoyt has it all set up. A bowlegged
boy with a U.S. Navy tattoo on his bicep will exchange blows
with Applejack. The boy sees his opponent for the first time and
underestimates him immediately. It's a common mistake.

They go outside into the alley and Tina is still there, talking to
some other yahoo now and the raccoons are gone, leaving behind

the upended barrel. The rowdy crowd, including a half-dozen young flattops wearing bright white crackerjack uniforms, follows and forms a semicircle around the fighters. Applejack takes off his T-shirt and sticks it in his back pocket, wraps his knuckles in duct tape, and inserts a plastic guard into his mouth, works it until it settles. The big lug shadowboxes on the brick wall, as though that can help him at this point, as though there is any way truly to prepare for Applejack's brand of ass-kicking. A coyote starts barking near the bridge and that gets a whole gang of them going. They have to hurry before the fucking cops come.

CHAPTER THREE

William drips paint thinner onto his sleeve and huffs it like that. Honey does some too. They sit in the dirt in the carport. William's daddy stands in the backyard, playing his acoustic guitar. Everybody who lives in Whitebirch Campgrounds comes over to drink beer from a keg when he jams like that, convincing the old man he should be getting paid for making music, filling dance halls. William and Honey listen to him strumming and picking and singing, finish what's left in their red plastic cups. Then William closes his eyes for what seems like several days and when he finally opens them they all three jump into his daddy's Silverado and drive out to the culvert. Honey falls asleep on the ride.

William's daddy regards the girl's head in his son's lap.

Be careful, he says.

Oh, William says. She's all right.

With females in general, I mean.

William's daddy understands a thing or two about women. People in town started calling him *the Cock* back when he was still shitting yellow, and he has worn the nickname like a badge ever since.

Honey wakes up when they get to the ridge. An eagle perched on a dead branch in a nearby sugar maple tree spreads its wings and falls into a glide toward them, so close she can feel the thrum of powerful vibrations in her ear, feel the air ripple over her skin. William's daddy takes off his shirt and he is thick and strong and Honey doesn't even bother to look away and she smiles at him. Oblivious to the flirtation,

William helps get the equipment out of the back, though his daddy does most of the heavy lifting. Honey smokes half a cigarette and watches them.

I'm bored, she says to William.

Go for a swim.

Fuck you. William knows damn well she didn't bring her bathing suit.

Well shit, he says. Just leave us do this thing.

The stone entrance of the culvert is cracked in places and they have been hired by the township to patch it. William's daddy scrambles down the wall of the gulley and William follows him. The last bit of mountain snow runoff has the river running pretty good. They remove their shoes and socks and pants. Their legs are whiter than the rest of their bodies. The water pulls hard but they maintain their footing. William's daddy ducks into the craggy shadows of the tunnel as William stumbles over a beaver hut. Honey laughs at his clumsiness.

Oh, he says. I see how it is now.

She makes a face at him and he smiles up at her.

William's daddy clears away rubble and removes wobbly rocks, cleans off the old cement from the wall and from the loose stones by lightly tapping them with a blue-handled hammer. He checks for unsettled masonry and removes it, not concerned with large chunks of cement that remain firmly attached. He uses a trowel to knock off debris and then brush away the dust, piles the unbound rock, allowing for a clear and safe workspace. William watches his father and mixes the cement in a ten-gallon bucket, using a busted-off shovel handle to stir the mixture until it's the color and consistency of oatmeal. He takes a break and leans on the shovel handle. His father stops working, too, and looks at him.

Son, he says. Come over here.

He shows William how to wet the stones on the damaged portion of the wall with a big-pored sponge to prevent them from leaching too much water from the new cement.

This shit here keeps the cement from cracking. He pronounces it *see-ment*.

He fills in the open areas using a trowel and then reinserts the cleaned stones, using a wooden stick to properly sculpt the fresh cement. On the high side, the wall's base has been altered by the ground shifting. William's daddy allows for the likelihood it'll happen again and digs down some with a shovel to establish a strong footing, about six inches deep and eight inches wide. He steps it to allow for changes in the grade. William helps wedge larger support stones in place low in the elevation, saving the better-looking stones for the visible wall.

Put some cement in the footing there, William's daddy says. Like this.

William gets the bucket and applies the sludge with a trowel and his father firmly presses the footers into place, continuing this process until they are level. He stretches a string between two stakes to check that the borders are flush, taps the stakes into the ground. William's daddy uses more or less cement to join the stones and grow the wall to meet the undamaged portion. He examines the face and dimension of each stone, placing each one carefully, explaining to his son the delicate practice of fitting the stones and cleaning the mortar joints between them. Then William's daddy uses a handheld whisk broom on the wet cement to create a brushed effect—a bit of vanity, as though anybody is going to appreciate his artistry way out here.

When he's finished, he stands back and puts his hands on his hips.

That should do her, he says.

William begins collecting the tools and placing them in the empty bucket. The trowels and the shovel and the hammer. The roll of twine, the wire brushes and sponges. Up in the truck Honey's head is pressed against the closed window on the driver's side, and it seems as though she's gone to sleep. He can hear a soft buzzing inside the cab. She has the radio on. Goddamn it, he thinks. William's daddy will be pissed because she'll kill the fucking battery like that.

Boy, William's daddy says. Come over here and see this shit.

Something in his tone gives William pause.

William's daddy has gone deeper into the darkened tunnel. William joins him in there, his eyes adjusting to the gloom, and there's another low hum in his ears—a thousand black horseflies swarming what appears to be a disembodied human head nestled between a couple same-sized rocks. William's legs get weak and he tries to turn away but his father wants him to keep looking. He can barely tell from the features that have been exposed to the elements, but it's a woman's head, judging by the long auburn hair wrapped around those rocks, holding it fast. A coyote has just been picking at the eye sockets, and that old trickster stares at them, showing its teeth, curling its mottled lip.

Where the fuck's the rest of her, William's daddy says. He throws a stone that ricochets and he whistles. The reddish-brown coyote puffs up its white-buffed throat for a few seconds and then scampers out the other end of the tunnel and off into the dusky woodlot.

CHAPTER FOUR

Old Squaw Reservoir sits still and black at gloaming, reflecting a bright orange moon on the rise. A rainbow trout breaks the surface as it jumps for a fly and the water ripples outward like a skull-cracked windshield as the fish disappears. The branches of the Swift River feed the reservoir, which is surrounded by trees and rugged red rock and then fields of green and gold as far as the eye can see.

Applejack squats in a small aluminum motorboat he took from the ranger station. He has never much minded appropriating things that don't belong to him, and besides it wasn't even locked up, so he sees it as a donation. He kills the motor to just float a while.

His head hurts.

He closes his eyes and moves to the soft rhythms of the water. His senses settle and it feels like sleep but better.

When he was a kid, Applejack loved the hamlet of Mill Town and the surrounding county—the big river, the rolling hills, the farms, the wilderness of the valley. The reservoir was a body of drinking water born to quench a mighty thirst in Boston, hundreds of miles away. But it meant more to him than most people, then or ever since. He'd hunt the watershed lands and fish and just walk, cavorting, swinging a big stick at tall grass.

Today, though, he wonders how a place that can seem so like heaven is the same one where all hell breaks loose.

Applejack opens his eyes again.

His thoughts turn to Peanut. She comes into his mind more instead of less as the weeks pass since that night in May. The night nobody wants to fucking talk about. Nobody wants to remember.

But he remembers all right.

He puts a cigarillo on his bottom lip and cups his hand around a blue Zippo to light it, sits forward with his elbows on his knees, inhales and holds the smoke in his lungs. A country road cuts east and west just past the tree line. Applejack's far-off gaze follows the road to a rusted old tractor abandoned in a tobacco field, a tall maple casting a shadow on a faded red barn. A busted wood sign lying on the dirt shoulder is supposed to be welcoming all who pass through Mill Town. Then some rude automobile engine rumbling and backfiring messes with the serenity. It sounds like gunplay. Applejack laughs at the old Ford Econoline swerving down the middle of the blacktop stretch past the Reservoir Road access gate, spitting gray smoke from its exhaust pipe, facing a mighty struggle to reach its next destination.

Even from this distance, Applejack can hear small dogs barking inside the van and can just about picture the porcelain Jesus Christ figurine swinging on a thin silver chain from the rearview mirror. The van turns into the empty lot of the shoebox-shaped Castaway Lounge and its headlamps illuminate an extension ladder and a brand-new billboard leaning against a broad-based tree out front.

Looking at the cinderblock building, Applejack marvels at how small and unassuming it appears from the outside, and how when he is inside those four walls something happens and it becomes massive and all-consuming and inescapable, a sour-smelling labyrinth of rooms and hallways and secret encounters, too like the only place in the world.

The parking lot at the Castaway Lounge was full, mostly pickup trucks and old cars made by Ford and Chevrolet and a handful of Japanese-brand ATVs, and parked along the tree line was a candy-apple-red Ranchero right behind a primer-painted Cadillac Eldorado. Music inside the bar was loud and male voices were drunkenly counting backward from ten and catcalling. Stavros's office door was closed to the muffled noise of the bar. Archibald Salvo, a man known around town simply as the Selectman, was sitting across from Stavros. A twenty-year-old bottle of scotch stood on the wooden desk between them and they each had a glass in hand.

You know, Stavros said, I only take this down for you.

The best of the best, the Selectman said. He took a sip and closed his eyes, made a sound deep in his throat that said better than anything that he approved the pour.

I like the new sign out front, he said. Almost didn't recognize the place. Really.

The Selectman opened his eyes. Yeah, he said. Almost drove right past.

Oh, I'm sure you'd find your way back.

The Selectman laughed. Only 'cause you always take such good care of me, he said.

Stavros raised his glass to the Selectman. Gone to give the joint a facelift too, he said. That's the plan anyhow.

All at once, you mean.

Nah, we'll just go bird by bird.

Good enough, then, the Selectman said. And you outdid yourself with new talent.

Glad you approve.

Like the United Fucking Nations, he said. Niggers and spics and everything.

But a little crowded tonight.

Yahoos coming to see strange pussy, Stavros said. Word gets around.

That wears off hey.

Stavros twisted the cap back on the bottle of booze. Hopefully not too much, he said. I got to get this place back in black.

Oh yeah, the Selectman said. Or what.

Shit, Stavros said. You don't want to hear my problems.

Banana Nose already sent you to Siberia way the fuck out here. For a guy like you, the Selectman said, what's worse than a life in Mill Town.

Stavros put his feet on the desk and struck what he considered to be a thoughtful pose with his hand on his chin. The bottom of his left shoe was worn nearly through.

Dead in Mill Town, he eventually said. That'd be way fucking worse.

He wouldn't ever, the Selectman said. Would he.

Stavros coughed into his elbow. The prick said this is my last chance.

No shit hey.

After all these years, Stavros said. All the shit I done for him.

The Selectman took a tug and made a face. Well I don't know nothing about that, he said. I'll swear it on a Bible.

Stavros laughed.

'Cause you're not a wop, the Selectman said. Is that the thing though.

Well, that sure don't help.

Can never get made. On the outside looking in.

Right, Stavros said. And he's got some nephew or something, Rodney, needs a place to start.

Ah, and so this is as good as any.

Right.

Who's the kid.

His old man's from around here.

A local boy, then.

Used to box, Stavros said. Fought at the Centrum.

A real tough guy.

Yeah. And about as smart as you'd expect.

The Selectman laughed and shook his head, finished his drink, shifted around in his seat.

Stavros finished his drink, too. Don't worry about tonight, he said. I got you all set up.

A gentleman and a scholar.

Just sit tight and enjoy the show for a while. And then later we'll do the other thing the way you like it.

A true patriot if ever I saw one.

Well, Stavros said, I doubt you ever fucking saw one.

A black limousine pulled into the lot and parked behind the Ranchero. Its engine shut down hot and ticking; Hoyt Bowers drove the limo for the local funeral home and he'd commandeer it from time to time, like when Stavros said he needed a fancy ride for one of his private parties. Hoyt and Jill Sanderson both got out on the driver's side and she jumped on him for a piggyback. Applejack and the new girl called Peanut got out too, his arm around her waist holding her up, helping her walk. He felt bad for her, young as she was and already heading deep into this shit swamp. But Stavros wasn't paying him to worry about girls or to think about anybody's future; he was paying him to be a loyal foot soldier and to deliver the goods, whatever they might be. In this case, Stavros knew somebody who wanted a virgin and so Jill had scoured the county.

All four made their way to the front door.

Better sober up some before Stavros sees you, Hoyt said.

Fuck that Greek fuck, Jill said back.

The girls entered the club through the front door, busting into the main bar area, and rushed past Nick Bean, who was supposed to collect the gate. He tried to catch Jill's eye but she ignored him. She'd ignored him since they were kids, but what he felt was more than some teenage crush and he was nothing if not a patient man. He figured she'd come around. Jill held Peanut's hand and they beelined for the dressing room.

Fucking Stavros is looking for you, Nick said after them. He jabbed a finger at Hoyt, figuring he'd been fooling around with Jill again. Applejack and Hoyt greeted Nick with handshakes and half hugs and headed right for the raised, roped-off section in the back. Nick cracked his neck side to side but stayed at his post.

Applejack and Hoyt passed the Selectman sitting open-legged in a chair near the center stage, talking to a Puerto Rican girl until he put his hand on her ass and she knocked it away, stormed off, left him staring after her.

Jill rummaged through her small locker in the dressing room, grabbing at handfuls of fabric and inspecting them, sniffing them. Four other girls in various states of undress were gossiping, talking shit to each other, putting on body lotion and glitter, getting ready to get the eyes going, the hungry hands groping, the money handed over. Finally Jill found what she was looking for and held it up to Peanut.

Perfect, Jill said. You can be a cheerleader.

I don't know.

Oh shit, Jill said. I knew hooking up with them two cats was a fucking mistake.

He's so nice. What's his name again.

Applejack.

Peanut giggled. You need a good breakfast, she said, that's a fact. Start it out with Applejack. Her voice drifted off as she forgot the words.

Come on now, Jill said. You got to rally for this money thing.

Another girl came in, the same one the Selectman had been playing grab-ass with. Jill saw her and smiled.

Oh fuck yeah, she said. Camilla, get your brown ass over here. This is my girl Peanut.

Camilla nodded at Peanut, wondered where Jill even found these fucking country kids she brought in to audition. Peanut was so out of it Camilla asked can she even stand up for a couple minutes, much less dance and shake her moneymaker.

We had a few drinks to loosen her up, Jill said. But you know how Stavros is.

Yeah, Camilla said. Him and his rules.

You got something for her that'll make her right, Jill said.

What, Camilla said, for the nerves or for the drinking.

I don't know. Whatever the fuck.

Fucking amateur hour, Camilla thought. But she dug through her purse while Jill helped Peanut get undressed.

Stavros stormed into the dressing room. He wore a black cotton T-shirt that hugged his thick frame. The girls didn't flinch; they were used to him busting in on them. Except Peanut—she tried to cover up.

Stavros looked at Jill. What the fuck, he said.

Look what I brought for you, Jill said. Ain't she a doll.

He inspected Peanut like she was a horse at the Franklin County Fair: pulling her lips to check her teeth, cupping her tits, slapping her ass cheeks. He leaned in closer and sniffed, made a face, looked at Jill.

All right, he said. You girls been drinking, though.

She's just nervous is all.

You know the rules. No drinking before.

Aw, Stavros.

Jill touched his forearm gently, trying to distract him. What'd I tell you, she said. She's wicked hot.

Yeah. She's a real fucking tomato.

And a cherry tomato, like you wanted.

Stavros clapped his hands together twice in rapid succession. Get your asses on the floor then, he said. Make me some fucking scratch tonight and then I got that private thing for you later.

Stavros followed his stomach out of the dressing room and Camilla gave him the finger once he was gone. She pulled some pills from her purse. Watch yourselves, she said. Some real pinche scumbags out here tonight.

CHAPTER FIVE

William and Honey drive to Hamp in his daddy's Silverado that he's just washed. She laughs at the fuzzy dice dangling from the rearview mirror. She's wearing a black miniskirt, a wife-beater tank top with no bra, and those plastic sandals that she has a funny name for. Her lips are shiny with raspberry-flavor gloss and she has her hair back in a high ponytail. There's a bit of traffic on Route 5 and it takes them nearly forty minutes to get downtown and find parking behind Fitzwilly's, which isn't too bad for a Saturday night. It's a real college town and Honey gets self-conscious around all the coeds. A group of girls passes them on the sidewalk, smacking bubblegum and laughing.

Honey catches them looking at William and him looking right back. She gets enough of these empty-headed dolls in her classes at UMass.

Fuck those preppy bitches, she says. I seen you looking hey.

Easy, tiger.

He pulls her close and she pretends to fight him off.

Madder than a wet hen, he says. So you're the jealous type, then.

Fuck off.

You think I'll ever go to college, he says once Honey settles down.

I don't know, she says. Not like this, anyhow. She makes a sweeping motion with her arm to implicate the town.

They eat supper at a fancy place called Sam's, sitting outside on a little porch the owners set up for warm months, swatting at gnats and no-see-ums in between bites of food. William scarfs down meatloaf and mashed potatoes. Honey has some angel hair pasta dish. After the meal they hold hands and go for a drive, sticking to the back roads and getting a little silly with the bottle of Knob Creek that William's daddy keeps stashed under the seat.

What you want to do now, she says. But it's not really a question.

They could fuck in the truck like usual, but she wants special so William finds a motel in Bucktown called Pine Tree Inn. The room isn't half bad, small but clean, and it only costs him twenty dollars. He turns on the television and mutes it, lets that blue light fill the room and they kiss standing up, her hands on the back of his neck. And then Honey undresses William and she gets naked too, and they hit the shower together. William uses his mouth on her mouth, her neck, her tits. Goddamn if you don't look good with your black hair wet like that, he says. So she turns around and puts her ass against him and tells him go ahead and grab it like a rope and pull on me. He does it and she lets out a quick breath and says, oh my God. He picks her up and carries her dripping to the bed that smells like somebody else's cigarettes. With the shower still running and Jimi Hendrix guitar licks coming from another room, William and Honey thrash around until they're sweaty and sticking to each other with whatever doesn't end up inside her.

Afterward there's some cuddling. Honey cries and that unsettles William a little. Eventually he asks her what the problem is and she quick says, just 'cause it was so beautiful. But the truth is she's thinking about William's daddy's touch. Despite her mind wandering, Honey is exhausted and she sleeps through the rest of the night and wakes up to a red-throated loon warbling outside their window and a vacuum cleaner banging against the walls in the next room. Her first thoughts are of the woman's head William showed her at the bottom of the gulley, haunted by the image itself but also how somebody could do that to a person, and who it could've been got done in such a way.

CHAPTER SIX

There's a man called Blue sitting at the edge of the stage. It seems to Applejack that all the girls know him but they keep their distance. Suzanne offers him a lap dance and he declines but then he starts putting his paws on her and calling her god-awful names.

I know who you are, he says. You crazy fucking bitch. Show me where them extraterrestrials slipped their dicks in you. I bet you like a big green Martian cock now.

She twists out of his grip and steps away from him, tells him to fuck off and goes out back to see if there are any real takers. Applejack crosses the room and sits in the empty chair next to Blue. He times it so that the man is just putting his drink to his mouth and he punches the bottom of the glass so hard and fast it explodes into Blue's face, cutting him bad, and despite the crowd not a single person will step forward when the state cops come around to investigate. Must be he fell. He'll get twenty stitches over to Cooley Dick and end up with scars that change the way he looks forever.

Applejack has a room just above the Bloody Brook Bar and Suzanne moves in after only a few weeks. It isn't much but having her there helps. They have a fridge and a stove and a bed. They share a toilet and shower in the hall with everybody else. She has brought mostly books and her costumes for work that she keeps on wire hangers. Applejack wants her to quit dancing, but the money is so fucking good, and how else does he expect her to pay her share of the rent. She says Stavros doesn't know about them and they have to keep it that way. That he doesn't like his girls to get involved with local boys. Sitting on the edge of the mattress, she says if he finds out he'll sack her or worse, and Applejack tries not to let her see him smile.

One time, she says. I seen him hit this nigger girl.

He better not hey.

Why, she says. What you gone to do about it.

You'll see.

Suzanne rolls her eyes at him and laughs, sips her drink. He's sitting on the floor with his back against the wall, working on a bottle of beer. He hands it to her and she takes a long pull. Then he gets up and opens the window, jamming a short length of two-by-four scrapwood to hold it in place, and she follows him onto the roof, holding her glass in her hand and the bottle between her lips, biting down on it somewhat with her front teeth to keep it from falling.

That's a good look for you, Applejack says. Then he takes the bottle from her and sits on the angled rooftop and she joins him.

Maybe she was cutting tips, she says once she gets settled. That one he hit.

Still, he says. That's no reason.

Ah, he's okay, baby. She pauses, winks at Applejack, and sips her Jack through a skinny red straw. And maybe that stupid bitch simply had it coming, she says, trying to convince herself or Applejack or both. You know how some bitches are.

Yeah, Applejack says. I sure do know how some bitches are.

A commotion breaks out in the street below. It's the second Friday of the month and that means payday, which means immigrant farmhands cash their checks at Pioneer Bank and get soaked at the local establishments. Matt Skroski is trying to argue with a couple Puerto Ricans who clearly have limited knowledge of English, but eventually one of them tires of his incoherent bellowing and smashes a Bud bottle on the wall and cuts him across the face. An unseen woman screams. Bleeding like that old stuck pig, Matt walks calmly to his pickup and Applejack figures he's going to drive himself to the emergency room. Then Matt guns his engine and jerks his wheel, driving up on the curb, and the woman screams again as he mows down the Puerto Rican before reversing into the street and driving off toward home so his wife can tend to his face.

Shit, Applejack says. You see that.

Well. I guess he had it coming.

Applejack isn't sure if she means Matt Skroski or the Puerto Rican. He gets up and she gets up, too, and they climb back into the apartment so the cops don't spy them and need witness shit when they arrive to sort through the mess down in the street.

Suzanne likes to give Applejack presents. She goes to the flea market in Brattleboro and buys him a wood-framed picture of Elvis Presley—his all-time favorite. It's velvety and on the bottom it says THE KING OF ROCK AND ROLL in ornamental purple script. Applejack hangs it on a rusty nail over the bed they now share and she helps him get it straight the night before she is supposed to be gone just a few days doing what she calls a private party for Stavros, an idea Applejack isn't too keen on.

Applejack used to do more things for Stavros back in the day. Nothing major. Deliver a package here. Pick up so-and-so at Bradley Airport in Hartford. Stand behind him and look tough when he had a meeting with Banana Nose from Springfield. Certain strong-arm stuff from time to time, like holding Goose Bewick's head in the toilet until he admitted to cutting Stavros's supply with baking soda.

The Greek always had a handful of girls he referred to as his go-to pussy posse, down for whatever, and those were the ones who worked the parties. So when Suzanne tells Applejack there is a weekend thing at the new Indian casino in Ledyard and it's no big deal, well, suffice to say he knows better. But he says next to nothing. After all, this thing they're doing is new to both of them. Playing house or whatever the fuck.

And she thinks Applejack is a simple man, a regular fucking guy.

MAY 21, 11:18 p.m.

The parking lot of the Motel Six in Stillwater remained empty but for a few cars. Inside the office, the night manager, Donald Tanner, argued with his wife, Melinda. He stood behind the counter as she leaned against an aluminum cart stacked with once-white bath towels and bed sheets now a deep shade of yellow-gray.

How in the fuck should I know, Donald said. Maybe it's his lucky number.

All I'm saying, it'd be easier if we put him in thirteen.

And all I'm saying is, Stavros didn't ask for thirteen. He asked for three.

Grow some balls for once in your life.

Balls, said the queen.

Yeah I know, Melinda said. If she only had two she'd be king.

Just clean the room, you fucking cow. And don't put nobody next door. You know he likes his privacy.

He tossed her a room key.

They're not coming in until after midnight, he said. Probably around two.

Melinda caught the key, wheeled her cart toward the door. One of its wheels was bum and the thing squealed and listed hard to the right.

I don't know what kind of place you got us running here.

Bullshit, he said. You know exactly.

The telephone rang, startling them both, and Donald picked it up.

———

The crowd at the Castaway Lounge died down a bit. Jill and Peanut made the rounds together, offering two-for-one lap dances. The DJ was playing "Hell's Bells" and Peanut was still in her cheerleader outfit and Jill stayed in character as the naughty librarian. This was a cheap crowd, though, and there weren't any takers. The girls stopped at the table where Applejack, Hoyt, and Nick sat, and the boys made room. Peanut looked messed up and sleepy slow, but Jill was amped on cocaine and pills.

Applejack regarded Peanut, shook his head, and then looked at Jill.

Is she all right, he said. That ain't just booze now.

I don't know.

Well what'd you give her, then.

I didn't give her shit, Jill said. She's a big girl.

Maybe she's just tired, Nick said.

Applejack held Peanut's face up by her chin and looked into her eyes. You all right, girl. Then he looked at Jill. You know she's just a kid, right, he said.

She's only a couple years younger than me.

Jesus.

Stavros came up behind the girls and clapped his hands together. Break time's over. Get this one freshened up, he said to Jill. I got that job for you. He clapped his hands again. And Hoyt, he said, bring that fucking limousine around.

Yeah, Hoyt said. All right.

We got a special guest tonight, Stavros said. Chop motherfucking chop.

Jill helped Peanut stand and they walked slowly to the dressing room. Camilla was just coming out and held the door for them, and Jill grabbed her arm and pulled her back inside. Stavros headed toward his office and the Selectman emerged from the shadows to follow him. Applejack leaned toward Hoyt.

Let me drive this one, he said.

Fuck, Hoyt said. I could really use the bread.

That's not it. You can have the money.

So this one's your little project now, hey, Nick said.

Applejack ignored him, grabbed Hoyt's arm. She's just a fucking kid, he said. I'm asking you, pal.

What is this.

Just want to keep half an eye on her. Make sure she's all right.

Yeah, and what.

I don't know. I got a bad feeling is all.

And what kind of feeling has she got.

Looking at you like you hung the moon, Nick jumped in.

Hoyt dug in his pants pocket and tossed the limousine keys to Applejack. The Selectman and Stavros came out of the office laughing like old friends. Applejack got up and went out the front door. Nick and Hoyt looked at each other, shrugged, and signaled for another round.

CHAPTER SEVEN

The smell of ammonia and almond croissants, smoked meats cooking on the pharmacy grill. The Boston and Maine rumbles by outside. A teenage boy drives donuts in a red rusted pickup truck on the uneven and sun-broken concrete. Watching with some amusement from atop a stool at the breakfast counter, half shutting her eyes against the day, Suzanne holds a cup of coffee in one hand and a Marlboro in the other. She eavesdrops on a conversation between two men in the booth.

He fought heavy, the old man says.

You mean that Jackson Woods.

They call him Applejack.

At the quarry.

I guess they call him that wherever he is.

The old man snorts at his own wit and spits food as he chews.

I mean where he fought, the young man says. Did he fight at the quarry.

That's right. That boy, he might be crazy.

Skinny as a snake and twice as mean.

The old man nods in agreement.

Did it with rib shots that'd make you double over, he says.

I can almost feel it.

Sucking for air. Think you were dead. Then the old man makes a slurping sound and he's done with the bowl of deer meat and vegetable stew that Mrs. Feeney makes upstairs. One of the Polish girls cleans up around him and he slaps her on the ass. The young man keeps his mouth shut unless he's asked a question.

Suzanne shuts her eyes to the day unfolding before her. Vats of rotted cabbage at the pickle shop fester in the July heat, the stink of them thick even with the pharmacy door closed.

Suzanne knows what Applejack wants her to know. Knows he got into no small amount of trouble growing up doing townie-boy shit. He's vague with the details because he doesn't want to scare her off—not that she's the type to scare easy, that much is already clear enough to him. He tells her all about him and Mary: the quarterback and the cheerleader. It was supposed to be perfect. In all fairness, he stopped holding up his end of the bargain first and she stuck around for as long as she could. Applejack tells Suzanne about the drinking and the fighting and the high-speed car chases. The headaches and the pills. She asks about Boy Country, says she heard they were inseparable. She remembers him from that first night at the diner, how he gave her the fucking creeps.

Oh, he's all right, Applejack says.

Retarded or something.

Not like that. A little slow. There was an accident.

What.

It was a television, he says. His daddy dropped a television on his head when he was little. Like three or four I think.

Shit. That's what did it.

It was brand new. Magnavox.

Damn.

Applejack wants to tell her about him and Stavros, too, about the fucking nightmare from a few months ago, but it would complicate things even further if she knew. It is inevitable that she'll find out; somebody'll run his fat mouth. Maybe even Stavros will tell her. That is exactly the kind of bomb he likes to hold over his people. So he'll stop going to the club so much, even on the sly like he's been doing. It's getting harder for him to watch her perform her dirty little dances anyhow.

CHAPTER EIGHT

A pile of old warehouse pallets and crates burns on the bank of the Swift River. Chunks of black ash swirl and the orange flames lick high, like the tongues of a hundred hungry demons clawing up from the earth's darker core. Applejack stands upwind from the group and drinks a beer. The sunset is brushstrokes of pink and purple and a young girl says his name, snaps him out of it. Her name is Cassiopia LeFavre but most folks just call her Cass. Applejack has her under his wing and considers her off-limits—to himself and to every-fucking-body. Coming up fast like town girls will, she reminds him of Peanut.

She puts her hands in the back pockets of his jeans. He shuts his eyes and breathes her in, the scent like a pint of blackberry brandy. Bored cops will bust them down for partying but it's commonly felt to be worth the risk. A bunch of young townies are smoking dope and Applejack takes a hit, holds it in his lungs for a while. When he lets it out, he does so slowly over his shoulder and closes his eyes. He listens to the water slapping against the mud and rocks and the moss-covered concrete posts.

Then he puts his arm around Cass's shoulders and they go for a walk past the rope swing and the train tracks. A fat, puffy-faced cop on horseback looks across the river at them, probably waiting for Mercier to give him the go-ahead so he can kill the bonfire, make a stink, throw some fuckups in the drunk tank.

Cass tells Applejack about the classes she's taking at the community college. She wants to be a nurse. She talks about her job

at the pharmacy. Applejack pretends to listen but mostly he doesn't.
She's a nice enough girl but Jesus Christ this isn't what he signed up
for. At the foot of a cliff they sit on a smooth rock in a dark cave
that smells like rotting fish. Applejack barely notices the stink but
Cass makes a face and complains. She gags a little, pulls the neck of
her sweatshirt over her mouth and nose. They don't feel the wind so
much in here, though. Cass drinks sweet brandy from a thermos and
shares it with him. A late-model Harley Davidson barks, rolling down
Stillwater Road. Coyotes bark fifty feet from the covered bridge. The
wind just outside the gray stone-granite walls is a low-moaning spirit
and Applejack pictures it reshaping the riverbank and the course of
the river itself and bending the longer blades of yellow cunt grass that
survive this climate.

I dream about this place sometimes, Cass says.

Always with the dreams hey.

Yeah, she says. I get stuck in here and they let the reservoir out. I
fall asleep or something and when I wake up there's water everywhere.
There's like an air pocket, and my face is pushed against the ceiling—
the inside of the roof or whatever you call it in a cave. That's when I
wake up all covered in sweat. Scares shit out of me every time, and I
can't get back to sleep.

Applejack looks down at his feet and spits.

What you think it means, Cass says.

Shit, Cass, he says. I don't know nothing about dreams.

They both stay quiet for a few minutes. Then Cass speaks up again.

Well, what you dream about.

Applejack laughs. Shit, I don't know.

But he thinks about it for a while. Cass drinks and puts her head
on his shoulder.

I dreamt I could fly one time, he says.

Like a bird.

Nah, he says. More like a bat 'cause it was night and I could see in the dark.

I think they're blind.

Bats.

They fly by what they hear.

Well that's funny 'cause guess I hear shit sometimes too.

Cass sips the brandy, tries to decipher the meaning, what he thinks he's heard.

Like what, she says.

Applejack ignores her question, but wouldn't she like to know.

Cass looks at him, wonders if he heard about her coworker that has gone missing. People are saying maybe Peanut got abducted by one of those flying saucers everybody's talking about, snatched up into outer space or some such shit. Either that or she's a runaway again. Before she can complete her thought, Applejack breaks the silence.

I dreamt I was a shark one time too, he says.

Oh shit, she says. That's just perfect.

What.

You're so strong and beautiful, she says. Just like a fucking shark.

Applejack spits on the hardpack in between his feet. He doesn't like when she talks like that. A used condom like a shed snakeskin is coiled flesh-color in a crannied nook as a midsummer night fog storms the cave, an army of cold ghosts. Cass shivers and Applejack gets up and she follows him with one of her fingers hooked in the belt loop of his dungarees. They step around fish bones and perfect skipping stones and the rusted carcass of an old delivery truck, and they cross the skinny beach part of the bank and climb the stone steps and follow the dirt path back toward the bonfire. Cass sees a girl she knows and starts to run toward her, but then stops and comes back, kisses Applejack on the cheek, then scampers away again, disappearing into the crowd, the darkness, beneath a scattering of random sparks and flakes of black ash falling down.

Hawk Wilson is in the middle of Sugarloaf Street walking backward, pulling a wood wagon loaded down with trash and treasures. Applejack gives him a handful of coins from his pocket, mostly nickels and dimes, one penny. Two Beer Dick and Walter are drinking in the common among wild ferns and orange-flowered weeds, their usual spot. They're sitting on white five-gallon pails flipped upside down, a couple BMX bicycles leaning against a tree. It's not unusual to see these grown-up men riding around on stolen kids' bikes with their caps backward and knees up by their ears—the result of multiple drunk-driving offenses. They call out to Applejack and he crosses the street.

What the fuck are you boys doing.

A meeting of the minds, Two Beer Dick says, laughing then coughing.

Walter's three-legged English Bulldog, Snapper, is on a heavy chain. He growls and slobbers at Applejack but he's mostly harmless now that he's a cripple. His leg got amputated after being mangled either by a bear trap or buckshot, they were never sure which as it was so far gone by the time they got him to the vet. But Walter is always quick to remind folks that the farmer who did either one or the other, mad about his chickens, eventually took a walk down to the river and was never seen again. Walter fights dogs in the gulley as part of his latest moneymaking scheme. Always something with that guy.

Two Beer Dick gives Applejack a can of warm beer and he takes a long pull straight away. Walter is wearing a short-sleeve button-up work shirt left open to display the homemade tattoo of a woman's face that covers his flat stomach, the words TARA LYNN RIP in prison script. His life has spiraled since his wife overdosed more than a decade ago. Two Beer Dick complains about getting sacked from the pickle shop.

Everybody's cutting back, Walter says.

Two Beer Dick nods his head.

This place is the shits, Walter says.

Two Beer Dick whines for a while longer and when he runs out of steam they all three smoke a blunt together. Walter gets the best green from his cousin's farm in the hills of Ashfield. It smells like skunkweed from a swamp. The moon is high and full and flashing orange bits. Applejack scratches Snapper's ears and chin. Walter tells Two Beer Dick to apply for a job with the motherfucking Water Department.

Those motherfuckers, he says. My brother got in with them and he's half stupid.

Only half now.

Walter laughs and beer comes out his nose.

Fuck they do, Two Beer Dick says.

Just drive around in that green truck you see, Walter says.

Applejack knows the truck, the words WATER SHARK stenciled on the door.

Not with my record, Dick says.

Walter nods his head.

Check the pipes and shit, I guess, Applejack says. The fire hydrants and whatever.

Better than working like a nigger for Skip Price, Dick says. Turning vats of relish.

Yeah, shit. What you gone to drown.

Two Beer Dick laughs and then he stops and asks Applejack about the headaches.

Applejack stares at Two Beer Dick for a few moments. Then he looks away and stops listening. He shuts his eyes because he can feel it coming on now like a stampede.

Two Beer Dick and Walter go back and forth for a while.

Applejack finishes his beer and crushes the can and drops it on the ground at his feet. Walter offers him another one but he refuses. He's tired. So fucking tired nowadays.

Up at the apartment, Suzanne had tried to cook a meatloaf but ended up passing out drunk on the couch. The kitchenette smells like something burning and the place is filled with smoke. Jesus, Applejack says. He shuts down the oven, opens the windows, and tries to wake Suzanne, but it's no use so he covers her dancer's legs with a sheet.

Applejack meets Hoyt at the Hot L. There's a fucking loudmouth in there trying to impress a table of fat girls. He's got an accent from the eastern part of the state and brags that he's a Taekwondo black belt or some such shit. They meet him and a third guy who holds the money in the empty lot behind Habitat, caged in by a rusted chain-link fence that sags in places. Glow-in-the-dark cat eyes watching from the shadowy perimeter, pebbles and pieces of broken glass and sharp bottle caps under the thick pads of Applejack's bare feet, drooping black power lines like buzzing serpents overhead. Then there is the sound of a Max Antes eighteen-wheeler roaring north toward Route 91.

The martial arts expert submits after seven minutes. Applejack catches him with a knee and now the dude's jaw is broken in two or three places—he won't be bragging from that unhinged maw for a while. Hoyt collects a hundred bucks or so and they go to the BP Diner for tough steaks and runny eggs that he'll complain about for weeks. Nobody asks her to, but the waitress brings Applejack a plastic bag with crushed ice cubes for his eye.

CHAPTER NINE

Mercier opens the door slowly and the hinges shrill. The woman sits alone on the couch, rhubarb-like chunks of puke tangled in her hair. She doesn't seem to notice or mind the vomit, nor Mercier's gun. The television is on but the channel is off air and there is a glass with melting ice in her lap and a half-empty bottle of Old Crow on the table. A lit cigarette hangs from her bottom lip. Her natural eyebrows have been permanently removed and replaced by painted lines that arch upward, creating a look of surprise even though Mercier doesn't believe there's anything left in the world that could surprise her. She had a tough time with her lipstick and made a complete fucking mess of it. Waxy red smudges on one front tooth.

Beverly Hills was the first girl in the county to get fake tits and that's when she started calling herself that. Used to dance for Stavros until he told her she was too old to take off her clothes in public. She cried in bed for two weeks straight.

But that was a long time ago. Now she cuts hair in a little shop in Bucktown where she rents a chair by the month, slings beers at the Veterans of Foreign Wars from time to time. She has a history of substance abuse and frequently boards in a halfway house in Ashfield called Fresh Start, but she also owns this trailer in the Whitebirch Campgrounds. A nice enough broad when her mind is right. And not a bad looker either. When she gets cleaned up, that is. Not covered in her own retch.

Bev, Mercier says. Is everything all right.

The woman looks up and runs the back of her hand against her mouth in a circular motion as though she's turning an invisible handle, winding up a motor that will enable speech. Then her hand drops back down to the glass in her lap.

What the fuck you want, she slurs.

Mercier holsters his sidearm and checks the rest of the trailer. I just want to know you're all right. Are you all alone, he says. By yourself, I mean.

Beverly Hills laughs herself into a coughing fit and spits into a wad of tissue rolled up in her shirtsleeve. She looks at her glass. Mercier gets the bottle from the table and tops it off for her.

All by myself, she tries to sing. Then she takes a long pull.

Well, I got a call, Mercier says. About a disturbance.

Beverly Hills looks at him. Oh there was a man, she says. Tried to shove me in his car.

What man is that now.

You don't believe me, she says. That a man could still want me in that way.

Sure I believe you. I didn't say that.

Because I still got it, you know. Beverly exposes one of her breasts to him, which Mercier would admit has held up better than the rest of her. See, she says. I still got it.

Mercier looks away. Embarrassed now, he turns his back to her. Please put that thing in its place, he says over his shoulder.

Okay, she says. I'll do it now.

She snaps her blouse and Mercier counts to ten and turns back around to face her.

Did you recognize the man, he says.

I seen him around.

What's his name.

I don't know his name, she says. But I think he been inside a while.

You mean inside like a prison.

He had that demeanor. Like a mad dog just sprung from a cage.

She describes for Mercier how they had been sitting at the bar and the stranger purchased her a couple three Tom Collins, and after a bit she goes outside for a smoke and he pulls his car around and tries to convince her to go for a ride with him.

What kind of car.

Shit, Beverly says. I don't know about cars.

Can you tell me what color or how many doors.

Beverly Hills belches deep from her belly and looks at the cop.

Fucking heartburn, she says. Please excuse me.

Take your time.

Beverly Hills holds onto her stomach and lets one rip. Are you gone to write this shit down, she says, or what.

Mercier retrieves a small notepad and a pen from his shirt pocket. All right, he says. So you were saying the car.

I don't remember what color, she says. On account of it was dark.

Mercier doesn't bother to write anything down and he looks at Beverly.

And, she says, I was drunk.

He puts the pad and pen away. All right, he says. But he wanted you to go for a ride.

And I told him to fuck off.

And he didn't like that.

I don't know if he liked it or not but he got out and popped his trunk.

And what.

And like I said, he tried to shove me in there.

In his trunk.

In his goddamn trunk that had a chainsaw in it.

A chainsaw.

That's right. I saw that much.

So he grabbed you.

Yeah hey he did.

Like how.

By the shoulder, she says. He put his arm around me like this. She tries to show him.

Did he say anything, Mercier says.

Of course he did. Beverly Hills holds up the bottle of whiskey to her face.

Well, Mercier says. What did he say.

Distracted again, she can see Mercier through the glass. His image is distorted and funny and she laughs. What you think he said. He said get in the trunk you fucking cunt.

Well, Mercier says. Did you get in that trunk, then.

Beverly puts the bottle and the empty glass in between her legs. Did I get in the fucking trunk, she says.

Mercier smiles and looks at his shoes and then back at Beverly Hills.

Well, he says.

Boy, he was gone to kill me, she says. If I got in that trunk, I'd be dead right now.

Right.

Dead as a doornail.

Well so, Mercier says. And then what.

Then I stuck him and run home, Beverly says. Without looking back hey.

She shows him the little knife she used, which she has kept in her change purse since her dancing days. Not much more than a letter opener, but the right tool in the right hands.

The bartender at the Bloody Brook remembers the man who bought Beverly Hills a round or two. Sure she does. Jack and Coke, extra ice. Not a regular but somebody shows up from time to time, over the years. Been away a while. Not sure where, but he certainly is a big fellow. He didn't used to be that big when he first started coming around. Like he went and got all swoll up on fucking steroids or something.

MAY 22, 1:41 a.m.

Applejack sat in the driver's seat of the black limousine parked just outside the front door of the Castaway Lounge. Back doors open, engine running, air conditioning on full blast. Then the front door of the club flew open and Stavros, the Selectman, Jill, and Peanut stepped out. The Selectman had Peanut by the arm, and when they got to the limo he shoved her into the back. Jill followed. The girls were wearing street clothes. Stavros carried a twelve-pack of Bud and a couple bottles of brown booze, and he leaned into the driver's window.

What the fuck hey, Stavros said when he saw Applejack behind the wheel.

Hoyt drank a little too much, Applejack said. I got this one.

Well pop the fucking trunk, then, Stavros said. Before I get a hernia.

Stavros made his way to the back of the car. Applejack reached down and popped the trunk from a latch under the dashboard. Then Stavros slammed the trunk closed and joined the group that had already piled in. The tinted glass divider was up between the front and the back seats. Jill sat right against Stavros like a girlfriend, sipping from his bottle of Old Crow. Peanut was practically sprawled across the Selectman's lap.

Take us to the Motel Sex, Stavros said. I mean Six.

Jill giggled. Peanut was awake but barely. It was taking all of her effort to keep her eyes open. The Selectman had his arm around her neck when the car started to move.

Motel Sex sounds like just the thing, the Selectman said. He looked at Peanut, pushed some stray hair from her face, licked his lips. And hurry, he said. This one's got an expiration date.

Applejack could hear voices through the intercom, but couldn't really see what was going on in back. It was just noise and shadows. He gripped the steering wheel tightly and gunned the engine. The car lurched forward, fishtailed somewhat. The passengers bounced around a bit.

Shit, Stavros said, banging on the divider with the flat of his hand. Take her easy.

Applejack cursed him under his breath.

I propose a group shower once we touch down, Stavros said. Then he looked at Jill, motioning toward Peanut. Maybe that'll wake up your friend, he said.

Jill was drunk and stoned but still raring to go, a real party girl, up for whatever. She looked at Peanut and giggled. The excitement, Jill said. It's catching up with her.

Long as she's good to go, Stavros said.

That's okay, the Selectman said. I don't need her good. Just to go.

He was smiling when he said it, but it was not a nice smile and Jill detected something unsettling in his voice. This fucking dude is creepy as hell, she thought.

Applejack also heard the Selectman's last remark. He clenched his jaw, white-knuckled the steering wheel, and cranked it to the right. Through the rearview he regarded the shadows behind the tinted glass, put on the blinker, cut sharp into the Motel Six parking lot.

CHAPTER TEN

Suzanne is working another party with Stavros even though it's a Monday, so Applejack gets good and shitty. He hasn't been able to reach her by phone. He's beginning to worry and that isn't really his bag; he has earned a reputation for being a carefree sort. Mercier pulls him over on Route 116, says he was swerving all over to hell and back.

Jackson Woods, Mercier says. Have you imbibed this evening.

Not yet I ain't, sir, Applejack says, laughing.

He runs the back of his hand across his nose and sniffs, explains that he's just now going to the bar for a couple three pops after a long day in the fields. Mercier nods because he understands the working man's plight. He's one of the good ones. He asks about Hoyt's tobacco crops, if it's been a decent season.

Oh it's been all right, Applejack says. But not like before.

Mercier nods his head up and down and spits at the ground. No, he says. Nothing ever is, I guess.

There's a bottle of Southern Comfort stuck up under Applejack's seat that he hopes won't roll out and give Mercier any kind of just cause. The cop shines his big flashlight in Applejack's face and all around like they do. Mercier can smell something on him, sure, because drinking and driving is a way of life in Franklin County.

All right, so long as you don't cause a damn wreck, he says and lets Applejack go with just the verbal warning.

Applejack parks in front of Leo's TV. Donna is working behind the bar—they used to have a thing, him and her—and she can tell he's in a bad way so she invites him to the ladies' room for a quick bump during her next cigarette break, but he declines. It's the usual crowd at the Brook. The Red Sox are losing, which seems about right for the time of year. Applejack eats a free bowl of stale popcorn. Somebody orders a pie from Holiday Pizza across the street and he has a couple slices with pepperoni and mushrooms. Then Boy Country shows up and buys a round and they do shots of Wild Turkey. He's acting more funny than usual so eventually Applejack asks him what's up and he says he wants Applejack to check out Pump Road Pond with him.

That fucking pond, Applejack says. At this fucking hour.

Balls of sweat congregate on Boy Country's massive forehead. He wipes at them with the back of his hand and then runs his fingers through his grease-slicked hair. I saw something down there, he says.

Oh yeah, Applejack says. What kind of something.

Boy Country stops looking at Applejack and gets lost in the mirror behind the bar.

Applejack coughs to get his attention. Snap out of it, Boy, he says.

Something bad, he says, rubbing his eyes.

Boy, Applejack says. What in the hell.

I think you just best come and have a peek.

They park over by Buchman's pumpkin patch and walk along the railroad tracks. Applejack brings his bottle. There are crickets and bullfrogs, and they slap at blood-hungry mosquitoes. A couple skinny-dippers are laughing and splashing each other near where the high water settles around a large stone. Boy Country tells Applejack to hush, so they sit quiet by a mulberry tree and drink and wait for the skinny-dippers to leave. It's a guy Applejack recognizes—he plays his guitar at the Castaway Lounge—with some pretty young girl who looks vaguely familiar. Good for fucking him, Applejack thinks. Then the guy and his cherry climb back up the gulley and drive off in a Silverado.

Boy Country lights up a jay and they smoke the shit out of it, some more of that skunkweed from the high timber. Applejack coughs and Boy Country laughs at him. He tells Applejack he was fishing in the afternoon and that's when he first saw it. There isn't anything good to catch in there, but he doesn't know any better. Then Applejack sees what Boy Country saw.

See, Boy Country says. Right there.

I see it.

I think it's a woman's leg, Boy Country says. And it's clear from the tone of his voice that he knows for a fact that it is.

Boy, Applejack says. What kind of game you playing here.

Boy Country stays quiet and he won't meet Applejack's eyes again. Then Applejack smells it and the stench of rotting human flesh is worse than any swamp in August. Jesus Christ, he says.

How does a person's leg end up here like this.

Applejack knows exactly how, thinks of Rodney and his fucking chainsaw.

Peanut's leg is in tatters because critters have been messing with it, Applejack figures. Coy dogs and big cats and such. Boy makes a face as Applejack fetches it, gets it up on the bank, and rests it gently on a dark carpet of leaves. Boy gets sick on his own two feet and then apologizes to Applejack. I'm sorry, he says. But what kind of monster.

As though by discovering the leg, Applejack thinks, Boy Country figures that he is somehow responsible. Don't be sorry, he says. You didn't do nothing wrong.

I swear it on a stack of Bibles.

Applejack looks at him for a long while and shakes his head, and then he coughs some more and spits over his shoulder. Suppose I best let him in on it now, he thinks. He takes a long breath and scratches himself. He looks his oldest friend in the eye.

Body parts'll be popping up everywhere now, he says by way of an opener.

Boy Country listens to the story Applejack tells about Peanut and the Selectman and then Rodney and the chainsaw. At first Boy Country can't believe his ears. He remembers the girl waiting on him at the pharmacy, sure he does, bringing his coffee and biscuit. Then he wants to know are they going to bury this little piece of Peanut, hide it somehow. He's scared the town cops or state police might come after them for it, which is a legitimate concern. Boy Country and Applejack can't be within a mile of a crime without becoming prime suspects. They aren't exactly known around town as upstanding citizens. Applejack sits on a buttonball stump to think, wonders if telling Boy Country was the right idea after all. Damn it, he thinks. Goddamn it straight to hell.

CHAPTER ELEVEN

Their mutual love for the music of Elvis Presley brought them together, but it was her brush with the supernatural that really sealed the deal. The second time Suzanne allegedly got abducted was in Hatfield, about a year after she saw the first flying saucer. She was coming back from shopping for some thigh-high boots, that fake leather shit at Brannigan's Half Off, when she noticed what looked like a bonfire a little ways back from the road. She pulled over, felt drawn to it. She got out of her car. Nobody was around. She couldn't speak to the details, but when she woke up there were crop circles like you see on the television news and she was in the middle of one.

I never even got scared, she says.

Well, Applejack says, that's really something.

On my way back in that cornfield, it was like I was melting into the earth.

No shit.

I felt relaxed, and it made my asthma better.

Then what, he says. After that.

Well after that it gets foggy.

You don't remember an alien. What he was wearing or nothing like that.

No, smartass, she says. I don't remember nothing like that.

She goes to see a psychic named Barbara Cooper in Northampton, who asks a crystal owl statue whether or not the crop circles are for real. The owl says yes, of course. Then they all three go down to the site together and Barbara walks around holding the owl in one hand and an amethyst pendant in the other. Barbara asks the owl if the aliens will be returning soon—she pronounces it *the Eileens* and Applejack pictures a gaggle of blue-haired ladies on the way to St. Stanislaus Church. Then the pendant begins to swing in a clockwise circle, which she says means the owl is sure of it. The Eileens will be returning soon. And they're very interested in visiting Suzanne again.

The owl knows this to be true, Barbara says.

But what does it mean, Suzanne says.

Well, the owl doesn't know everything.

Applejack laughs and Suzanne gives him a look.

The connection gets real fuzzy as soon as the prepaid hour is finished.

We can discuss additional services, Barbara suggests.

Everybody's working an angle, trying to make money off this thing. Television crews from Springfield and Hartford nosing around, documenting the activity. Charlie Smiaroski sure doesn't mind all the attention his cornfields are getting, even sets up a small gate and charges two dollars per. People wearing hats made out of aluminum foil pay to take naps, stroll around, and acquire measurements with all manner of gizmos and gadgets. The old farmer sells commemorative crop circle T-shirts, caps, and mugs from his vegetable stand on Route 47. He claims it's a public service, that his customers insist.

Suzanne's about the only one not trying to profit, and Applejack wonders then what's in it for her, all the shit she takes from fuckups at the club and whatnot. Folks with opinions.

CHAPTER TWELVE

The Castaway Lounge is closed, and on the inside it looks like a construction zone with foldout ladders, power tools, and orange extension cords strewn everywhere. The actual bar is under a sheet of plastic covered in a fine coat of drywall dust on it. Several empty and upended tables surround the small stage and its brass pole. The odor of fresh paint mixed with cigarettes. Stavros is behind the bar, under the plastic, pouring himself a drink. Applejack, Hoyt, and Nick sit around a square table near the back of the room. Boy Country is pushing a broom in the corner. An oscillating fan on the floor blows smoke all around and keeps messing up his pile of debris. Nickels and dimes are scattered about the table. Stavros joins the group, fresh drink in hand.

Like old times, he says.

Applejack is having second thoughts, wonders what the fuck he's doing back at the club. But Stavros called and he figured maybe a face-to-face could be just the thing. And now it's looking like same old, same old. Fuck this, Applejack thinks.

Stavros checks his watch before picking up his cards, fanning them. Where's Scotch, he says. He gave me his fucking word.

He'll be here, Hoyt says. He's conflicted is all.

Stavros regards his hand, not pleased with what he's been dealt. Conflicted, he says as he looks over his shoulder.

You know, now that he found God and everything, Hoyt says.

But he was out there before, Applejack says. Sleeping in his van.

Shit, Stavros says, looking toward the door. Where'd he go off to, then.

I woke him up, Applejack says. And he said he had to get supplies.

Stavros shakes his head like a river dog trying to dry itself.

Supplies my ass, he says, his loose jowls flapping now basset-hound style. Stavros throws his cards face up on the table and grabs his nuts. I've got his conflict right here, he says through a face full of smoke.

Everybody laughs but for Stavros.

This is a big fucking deal, he says.

Yeah, we know, Hoyt says. It's a big fucking deal.

It's make or break for me, Stavros says. What I got going here.

Stavros explains again about Banana Nose in Springfield and the fact that the ball-busting prick has a new crew all ready to step in if he doesn't turn things around.

And I mean on a fucking dime, he says. That fucking Rodney, for example.

What about him.

Don't be stupid, Stavros says. Why you think he's here.

Well, why is he here.

Stavros pushes his chair away from the table, downs his drink. Just thinking about it gives me the shits, he says.

He gets up to head to the toilet but what sounds like gunplay outside startles him and the rest of group. All the talk about western New England mobsters has made them jumpy. The front door of the club flies open. Parked just outside is the old Econoline with the backfiring exhaust. Scotch staggers in. He's in his fifties but looks much older, his face weathered and wrinkled, his alcoholic nose like a pincushion. Behind him the lights from his van are bright, and on the other side of the windshield his small dogs are barking and jumping up and down. The front door closes slowly on the van and the noise.

You fucking cocksucking drunk, Stavros says. About to give me a coronary.

The room is silent but for a low hum and Loretta Lynn emanating from a transistor radio. Scotch carries a bucket of black paint, brushes, and a tattered Bible. He's obviously in no condition to paint. He stumbles around until he sees the group at the card table. Then he tries to stand still and shoot them a pious glare, but he's having difficulty maintaining his balance—pious is simply out of the question. He puts down his gear and flips through the Bible, as though searching for a specific passage.

Thirst of desire, he says with a heavy tongue, is never filled.

Fuck you on about, Stavros says. Misquoting scripture again.

Scotch holds the Bible over his head with two hands.

I had a vision, he says. Got to kill the bird. Scotch places the Bible carefully on the floor. Then he uses a large screwdriver to pry the lid off the bucket of paint, or tries to. Stavros and the others are watching him closely, laughing a little, nervous, giving each other curious looks across the table. Scotch finally gets the lid off and he picks up the bucket and makes his way toward what is intended to be the new VIP corner, where a beach scene and six-foot parrot has been painted on the floor—a strikingly beautiful mural. The guy is talented when he's sober. He holds the bucket of paint with two hands, ready to pour it onto the floor. But first he looks at Applejack and each of the other men in the room, and it almost seems as though he wants somebody to stop him, to tell him *not* to kill the bird, to tell him that his parrot is fucking magnificent.

A small part of Applejack does want to tell the old drunk his parrot is beautiful, because it is, but he remains silent. In fact, nobody says anything until Hoyt speaks up.

Go ahead, numb nuts, he says with a raised voice. I fucking double dare you.

The blustery challenge snaps Scotch out of his trance. Barefoot with his pants rolled up like some kind of beachcomber in search of a beach, he glances at Hoyt and then spills a little paint on the short, hooked bill. Then he looks down at the parrot, which now seems to be crying fresh black tears. Scotch loses his balance and slips and the bucket overturns completely and he is covered in black paint. His parrot appears ruined. He tries to get up but he slips and falls again, flopping around, only making it worse. Eventually he lies there and sobs.

Motherfucker, Stavros says. Then he claps his hands together and the boys spring into action, except for Applejack, who hesitates before getting up. He stubs his Swisher Sweet into an old coffee cup and blows half a smoke ring.

Shouldn't do this no more, he says to the Greek. Low profile and whatnot.

Stavros shrugs his shoulders.

Fuck, he says. The fucker asked for it.

Did he now.

Just do what you do.

Fuck, Stavros.

One for the road, he says. You owe me that at least. He's not happy that Applejack's conscience seems to be taking him away from the club. Or maybe it's not his conscience at all and the bastard has something else up his sleeve. Either way, it's good to have a hard man around in this business. A hard man with a cold heart. It's also smart to keep close the people who know shit, who have some amount of dirt on you. *Who know where the bodies are buried* is a phrase he's heard before. *Birds who stray furthest from the flock sing the loudest* is another one he likes.

Applejack shrugs his shoulders too and sighs heavily and rises. He seizes Scotch by the belt and drags him to the front door, leaving a black trail of paint across the main floor. Flailing, Scotch manages to get hold of his Bible. With his other hand he grabs a leg of the unplugged jukebox, which slows Applejack down somewhat, but the younger man eventually jiggles him loose. Nick and Hoyt follow.

Stavros, relieved, heads for the shitter.

CHAPTER THIRTEEN

It's dark outside but for a smattering of fireflies at the edge of the tree line. Loose branches of a hundred weeping willows undulate in a late summer breeze. A cacophony of crickets and small critters, the telltale rhythms of New England nighttime. The stone and dirt parking lot is not well lit; a single lamp high on a pole flickers on and off. Soft, chalky moths bounce around it, looking for a warm place to die.

Scotch lies on his back, sobbing. He knows what's coming and seems for the most part resigned to his fate.

All you had to do was paint, Applejack says.

Scotch finds a passage in the Bible and first he reads it with his finger. Lead me, he eventually says, with a block of wood in my mouth.

Forget wood, Nick says. You're about to have no teeth in your mouth.

No more Bible bullshit, Applejack says. Boy, you need to stop with that.

Scotch looks up at Applejack pleadingly, wipes snot from his face, garbles something about the wrath of the King, the Almighty, and he points to his rusty van still running and parked near the woodlot, puffing gray smoke from its tailpipe, the dogs barking inside. He appears to be having second thoughts about taking a beating. He's begging for mercy now, hands in praying shape, trying to make a case for himself. Applejack takes a deep breath and looks at the van, which is a real piece of shit. Rusted quarter panels, sloppy Bondo patches.

The windows are fogged and smeared with dog saliva. The dogs are going nuts. The Jesus figurine is swinging from all the commotion.

Just don't break nothing, Scotch says. Please, I don't got insurance.

All right hey.

Applejack closes his eyes against a headache. Then he opens them and looks resolute, like he's made up his mind about something and without warning he turns and drills Scotch with a hard kick in the face. Scotch tries to crawl away but Applejack kicks him twice more in the ribs. Hoyt stands him up, and after looking to Applejack for approval, he holds Scotch while Nick goes to work on him like he's a heavy bag.

Nick is small but he has boxing chops. He's focused and efficient and appears to be treating this like a routine workout. Scotch spits blood and vomits, splattering Nick in the process. In the end Scotch is barely conscious, and with his mouth all tore up it looks as though he just won a blackberry pie-eating contest. Hoyt carries him over his shoulder like a large sack of potatoes. Nick opens the back door of the van and helps Hoyt put him almost gently inside. The dogs are still going crazy. They lick Scotch's bloodied face between barks. Scotch clutches his Bible like a fucking lifeline.

The house of sin, he bubbles through swelled-up lips, burns for three days and nights.

What house, Nick says. What sin.

Hoyt slams the back door of the van.

MAY 22, 2:09 a.m.

In the room at Motel Six, Stavros poured Old Crow into clear plastic cups and Jill nursed a beer, fussing with the clock radio, trying to find a station worth a damn. The Selectman was sitting on the edge of the bed with Peanut, holding her up and talking softly into her ear. Whatever horrible shit he was saying made her cry.

Well, Stavros said. Let's get this party started.

He handed a cup to each of the revelers. The Selectman took Peanut's. Jill settled on Rock 102 out of Springfield, cranked it up some, put her bottle of beer on the dresser, and went to work on her shot while Stavros started to rub her shoulders. The Selectman downed his drink. He held Peanut's hair back and helped her address her own whiskey in small sips.

Come on, sugar, he said. Take your medicine now.

Peanut spit up a bit and mumbled something. The Selectman pushed her back on the bed with one hand and finished her drink with the other, threw the empty red cup at her. It bounced off her chest and onto the floor.

Stavros, he said. What the fuck.

For fuck's sake, Stavros said. Jaws of Life just to get her legs open. No wonder she's a virgin.

Stavros put his hands around Jill's neck and spoke into her ear. Here's what we're gone to do, he said. Me and my old buddy here.

That hurts, Stavros.

We're gone to have a couple drinks and talk about old times.

Jill struggled to get Stavros's hands off her neck but he was too strong.

While you fix your friend there, Stavros said. Then he let go of Jill and shoved her toward Peanut. Fix it so she's good to go, he said. And you know what I mean.

Jill rubbed her neck where he'd had her, where he left big red handprints. She had never seen him like this before, this fucking rough. Fuck, she said. That really hurt.

Then she turned her attention to Peanut, helped her stand up. They stumbled toward the bathroom, stopped in the doorway when Jill remembered something.

Throw me my purse, she said. I might got just the thing.

Stavros looked around and saw her purse on the nightstand near the clock radio, tossed it to her underhand.

The Selectman laughed. Better be some lube in there.

Hurry the fuck up, Stavros said.

The girls went into the bathroom together and closed the door.

Stavros made another drink for the Selectman as he absently flipped through the pay channels on the television, stopping on the porn menu.

You seen this one, the Selectman said.

Stavros regarded the screen: Emanuelle Around the World.

Nah hey.

I caught it at the drive-in. She fucks a dog.

No shit.

Or maybe that was another one. It was a double feature anyhow.

Stavros reached into his shirt pocket and produced a baggie of coke, wagged it in front of the Selectman's face.

I got party favors too, he said.

Just what the doctor ordered.

Thunder rumbled in the background and the Selectman put his hand in his pants and looked toward the window. Think the rain'll hurt the rhubarb, he said.

———

Drops of rain hit the limousine windshield hard. Applejack had parked in getaway mode and so that he could see the door to room three. The engine was off but he had the radio on Rock 102. He checked his watch. In his peripheral vision he noticed a dark figure just outside the door to the room. Applejack squinted at the shape and then flicked the wipers on to get a better look, but when he did, there was nobody there. He tapped on the headlight switch and there was a magnificent ten-point buck directly in front of the limousine, frozen in the glare of the halogen lamps. Applejack turned off the lights, and for another couple beats the North American Whitetail stared at him as if in judgment, then looked away and bounded off. Fuck you too, Applejack said.

CHAPTER FOURTEEN

Honey dropped out of high school at sixteen to follow her boyfriend's band as they played backwoods honky-tonks around New England, but two years later the now ex-boyfriend is in rehab, his former rock-and-roll mates are washing dishes in a greasy spoon at Hampton Beach, and Honey has completed a graduation equivalency program through the local community college. It didn't surprise anybody when she became a dropout, least of all her, and her seamless transition into the life of a pole dancer was also fairly predictable. But not a single person expected she would one day enroll in the University of Massachusetts. She'd been regarded as the worst kind of town girl, after all, and the bar had been set pretty low from the jump. But patterns and rules suck to a girl like her, and she dodges like a pro, no matter how divinely conceived some plans are believed to be.

Closely cropped landscaping and flat and ugly concrete buildings make up the campus in Amherst. The student union this morning is packed with incoming students and their parents who have arrived for freshman orientation. On break from leading tours, Honey and Jill sit on the front steps drinking coffee and sharing a blueberry muffin. Jill is a few months older than Honey—another town girl trying to better her situation through the rigors of higher learning, is how Honey sees her new friend. And, okay, she too picks up cash by stripping for desperate men and recruiting young girls for Stavros. Apparently the old fucker pays her fees for a couple classes every semester even though Jill jokes that she's studying to be an astronaut, just taking up space. Honey wouldn't mind scoring a deal like that someday.

Jill is holding a piece of paper that Honey just handed her, the university seal in the top left corner; the younger girl's financial aid application has been denied.

This is bullshit hey, Jill says. They can't do this.

They already did it.

Did you go to the office.

Stood in line for like three hours.

Jesus, Jill says. I hate this fucking place sometimes.

Maybe like a computer glitch or something.

A glitch.

Could take weeks or even months to figure out.

Months, Jill says. Fuck that.

I know.

Can you call your parents for a loan.

They don't have shit, Honey says. And besides, I burned that bridge already.

Oh right, Jill says. Well, what about your new man.

Honey wonders if she means William or his daddy, if rumors have started flying yet.

Well, she says. I don't want to be beholden.

Not to him.

Not to anybody, she says, figuring that might cover her bases. Honey looks away from her friend. Whatever, she says. Maybe I'll get back out there hey.

You mean at the clubs.

Yeah.

But I heard about the fire at Anthony's hey.

Maybe you can talk to Stavros, Honey says. I done pretty good down there too.

Where she met William's daddy, she's thinking.

Jill really perks up at this development, genuinely excited, claps her hands. Shit yeah hey, she says. This is gone to be fun.

Just a few shifts, Honey says.

Right, Jill says. But you know the money is wicked fucking good.

Honey checks her watch. Oh shit, she says.

The girls stand and hug and head for their next tour.

Stavros punches numbers into an adding machine with a long ribbon of tape coming out the back. His desk is a mess of receipts and invoices, and there are tidy piles of bills in various denominations. His false teeth are in a glass of water. He takes off his glasses and rubs his eyes with his thumbs, yawns, curses under his breath. Over his shoulder is a door marked EMERGENCY EXIT that leads to the parking lot.

A soft knock on the other door, to the bar area. Stavros grabs the cash and puts it in a top drawer alongside an old Smith & Wesson, the butt end sticking out beneath some paperwork. He looks at what he refers to as his favorite peashooter for a couple beats as though considering taking it out, but then elbows shut the drawer and leans back in his noisy old chair. He puts his teeth in his mouth, gums them into place, and gets them settled after a little bit of time. He puts on his eyeglasses and stares at that damn door.

Yeah, he says. Who in fuck is it hey.

The door opens and Jill enters, smiling and chewing gum. She's wearing impossibly tight Daisy Dukes and her tits are spilling out of a pink cotton tube top.

Jill closes the door.

Hey, handsome, she says.

He knows it's a bullshit line but he still feels handsome when she says it. Look what the cat dragged in, he says.

The place looks wicked good, Stavros. I like what you done.

She wiggles her ass over to the chair on the other side of his desk and sits down, makes a production out of crossing her legs, uncrossing them and crossing them again.

Oh yeah, Stavros says. It's an island theme, see.

Fucking sweet.

To go along with the castaway thing, he says. Tropical and bamboo and shit.

Jill snaps her gum and nods her head enthusiastically. Clever as shit, she says. You always got such good ideas.

We were even gone to have a parrot, Stavros says.

Oh I fucking love parrots.

Stavros coughs and thinks of Scotch in the hospital now after the latest beatdown the boys put on him. He even stopped by during visiting hours with a box of chocolates from the gift shop, but the old drunk was still eating through a tube.

Yeah well, he says. The whole parrot thing didn't work out.

Jill uncrosses her legs again. The sound of the vinyl seat sticking to her skin. Whatever, she says. It's like paradise to me hey.

Now you're talking. Stavros leans back in his chair and yawns. Where's my manners, he says when he's done. You want a bump. He sits forward and takes a sandwich bag from his shirt pocket and pours a generous portion of white powder onto a clear area of the glass top of his desk, chops it up with a gold credit card, forms a single line about three inches long. How's school, Stavros says. You look fried anyhow.

It's all right, Jill says.

She leans over and takes a couple snorts, and he does the same.

One class is kicking my ass, she says. Statistics.

How hard can that be, he says. We're all just statistics.

Jill laughs and leans over the desk again and Stavros gets up and walks to the door, jiggles the handle, locks it. Jill sits back and wipes her nose with the back of her wrist. Stavros comes up behind her, puts his hands on her shoulders. She tenses up for a second and then relaxes, resigned. What the fuck. She has been here before.

So, Stavros says, you just come by for a little pick-me-up.

Actually, she says, I want to ask if you're all set for girls.

Go ahead and ask then. Don't be shy.

Well, she says, I have another friend.

Oh Jesus. Stavros tries to laugh it off. Not another virgin, please, Jesus.

Nah, she says. Not like that.

Well I might could use some new talent around here, Stavros says.

She's real fucking cute, Stavros.

I just fired that spic with the tits, he says. Does she have any tits.

You mean Camilla, Jill says. What'd she do.

Turns out she's the worst kind of thief, Stavros says.

What's the worst kind.

The kind doesn't think she's doing nothing wrong.

Jill laughs.

The good ones know it's wrong and say fuck it, Stavros says. I can live with that.

Right.

Well I can almost live with that. It's a matter of ethics.

Even with her questionable moral compass, Jill recognizes the irony of Stavros lecturing about ethics. Stavros's hands are thick and strong as he kneads her shoulders like a baker leavening bread. His father ran a pastry shop back in the motherland and that was what his parents expected of him, to take over the family business, preparing baklava and finikia and diplahs—recipes dominated by nuts and honey. But he left that dream for his brother so he could chase his American version of it. He wonders now and then if he made the right choice, if a simpler life could have suited him. A life without all the bullshit.

Jill coughs quietly when he presses her traps too hard and he backs off somewhat. She closes her eyes and rolls her head, tries to get what she can out of the transaction because soon enough he will expect recompense. She understands men, exactly how this is going to work.

So what kind of girl is she, he says. Your friend.

She's good. You know—a local girl.

I mean looks-wise, he says. I need a real moneymaker hey.

Honey danced here before, you might recall.

Oh right, Stavros lies, looking at the ceiling. Sure I do, he says. But she's not like that other one from a couple months ago.

Jill knows he's talking about Peanut. That whole shitstorm'll keep coming up, but for the most part it seems to have blown over. The cops haven't knocked on her door at least, so dipshit Rodney's plan must be working. Peanut was a sweet kid and this isn't the sort of business for a sweet kid to get into. No, Jill says. This girl's nothing like that one.

Because that's the last fucking thing I need.

No, Stavros. This one's got more experience and it won't be like that.

All right.

I promise. She danced at Anthony's too.

That fucking place.

I said I'd talk to you, Jill says. Put in a good word.

Stavros removes his hands from her shoulders and as he does so she opens her eyes, girds herself. He unzips his fly, reaches a hand into his pants, smiles down at her.

Would it be the usual finder's fee, Jill says.

Stavros laughs. Well, but you owe me from the last one, he says. That's still giving me headaches.

Aw, Stavros.

Plus, he says, it all depends how *good* a friend this one is.

Jill shrugs and takes the gum out of her mouth, sticks it under the arm of the chair, pops her loose jaw into place with her two hands in the shape of a V under her chin, then tucks loose strands of hair behind her ears and turns toward him with her strawberry-glossed lips parted, eyes closing again. She hums the "Star Spangled Banner," because that's what he likes.

CHAPTER FIFTEEN

Hoyt Bowers has been collecting Ford Mustangs since he was old enough to legally drive one. His obsession started when he was fifteen and Dutch Sanders taught him how to navigate the back roads of Bucktown and Hatfield behind the wheel of a mint-condition 1964 ½ original with a four-barrel Holley carburetor and a V8 engine. A former U.S. Marine, retired groundskeeper for the state police, and lifelong pony car aficionado, Dutch suffered from a debilitating case of arthritis that combined with unmonitored diabetes to leave his fingers and toes as twisted and gnarled as old hazelnut branches. When it got to the point where he could hardly even hold a steering wheel anymore, he told young Hoyt, in so many words, chauffer me around town and I'll teach you how to drive. Hoyt jumped on the deal and kept to it long after he received his license, until Dutch lost his limbs, one by one, to the disease he refused to treat and finally let kill him.

Upon Dutch's passing, his pothead son came out of the woodwork to claim what he could. But Dutch's wife, who was also the pothead's mother, had grown fond of Hoyt over the years and recognized the bond he had formed with her old man, and as she was burnt out on the pothead's dogshit attitude, she made sure Hoyt got the pink slip for the Mustang. Over the next decade he cherished his inherited vehicle, washing it every Saturday morning during the warm months and putting it up on cement blocks for the cold ones. In addition, he purchased a 1967 fastback that he restored in his father's barn and a 1965 coupe with a rebuilt 302 that he uses as a winter beater, and along the Mustang way he established a reputation among local cops as a lead foot and a true dickhead. Hoyt outruns them on a weekly basis, challenging them on Connecticut River Road and along Route 116 and once even around the hairpin turn in North Adams. Although he recognizes the ridiculousness of attempting to elude policemen who know him on a first-name basis, competed against him in Little League and cavorted with him on the shores of Ashfield Lake, he's not one to resist the temptation to offer any authority figure his middle finger. It has gotten to the point where the cops simply wait in Hoyt's driveway to cite him or arrest him for his latest bullshit driving stunts.

Hoyt bides his time in his fastback out in front of the Bloody Brook Bar, nursing a cup of coffee, elbow out the window. He coughs and then he spits on the sidewalk and looks at his wrist to check the time, but there's no watch there, just the sunburned outline of the cheap plastic one he stomped when its battery died. He taps the horn lightly with his free hand and it plays the "Look Away Dixieland" tune just like General Lee from *The Dukes of Hazzard*. He always gets a fucking kick out of that silly noisemaker.

Inside his room, Applejack is flat on his back in bed but already dressed for the day. When "Dixieland" starts to play for the third time he opens his eyes and stares at the ceiling for a couple heartbeats. The horn sounds again and Applejack rises, checks his pants pockets out of habit, and locks the small room behind him.

He makes his way down the cigarette-scarred carpet to the exit. The sun hits him hard in the face and he puts one hand up against the day as the other opens the car door. Where'd you get that fucking horn hey, he says.

Lenny Grybko had it in his garage, Hoyt says. I don't know where he got it from.

That's some funny shit. Applejack slides in, takes a fresh pack of Swisher Sweets off the dashboard, and fumbles with the plastic wrapper. Takes one out and puts it on his lip, checks his pockets. You got a match, he says.

Sure I do, Hoyt says. Your face and my ass.

Applejack shakes his head. That's no match, he says. That's a beauty contest.

Both men laugh at the old joke and Applejack looks out the window.

Here, Hoyt says, producing a lighter decorated with the likeness of a naked woman.

Applejack cups his hands around his cigarillo, wards off the warm pine breeze coming off the road, and on the second or third try it fires and he sets the Zippo on his thigh, regards the image there. The rose-red lipstick, penny-colored nipples—just another addiction he feels powerless against. He inhales and holds the smoke in his lungs and closes his eyes, listens to the four-barrel carburetor hissing under the hood, soft music on the radio, Hoyt's sixteen-inch white-walled Michelin Eagle GTs humming fat along the blacktop, and farther off an old band saw ripping boards at Erkel's Christmas Tree farm.

CHAPTER SIXTEEN

The twenty-four-hour BP Diner is packed and noisy even at three in the morning. Smoke rising from the grills and ashtrays mingles under the fluorescent lights and hangs in the thick, greasy air. Drunks young and old claim the booths while the counter stools are manned by road-weary truckers, farmers, and hunters waiting for sunrise. In the middle of the after-hours carnival, Mercier and Letorneau, working the midnight shift, tank up on coffee, eggs, and smoked meats.

Letorneau waves his fork over his plate. My asshole's funeral's in a half hour, he says.

Mercier laughs at the line he's heard a thousand times, thinks it's from some movie he can't remember. Letorneau shoves a forkful of eggs and sausage into his mouth. The waitress stops by and warms his coffee, and he whacks Mercier on the arm while leaning into the counter and watching her as she walks away.

Jesus Christ, he says. That's a nice pooper. He sits back and enjoys the view.

She can't be but eighteen, Mercier says.

If there's grass on the field, you play some ball.

Mercier chuckles between bites.

That's my personal motto, Letorneau says.

You're a bad man.

Ah, she'll be dancing for Stavros soon as she graduates.

I hear he might not be around that much longer.

Letorneau nods in agreement. He's heard whispers about the state police digging into some trouble from a while back, the case about that girl gone missing and its possible connection to the club and Stavros's extracurricular activities. In his opinion, the Greek's association with organized crime has always been dubious at best. And truth be told, Letorneau has mixed feelings about any kind of collaboration with the state police. He has taken the written exam three times in six years and scored pretty high each session, but never even made the callback list for physicals, not once. And everybody knows he's been passed over. He feels like some kind of fucking laughingstock. Plus Stavros lets him in the back door for a free taste every now and again when he happens by the neighborhood. So, he's thinking, how can I monkey wrench the troopers' efforts in the investigation, let it be known they aren't so damn perfect after all.

He and Mercier resume their attack on the food in front of them as though they haven't eaten in days, until their radios cackle about some kind of domestic dispute over on Long Plain Road, Letorneau motions the waitress for a to-go cup and Mercier wipes the last bit of runny yolk off his mouth with a thin paper napkin.

CHAPTER SEVENTEEN

Later that same night, back at Grandma's, Applejack waits for a woman who wants to remain anonymous. She heard about him from a friend of a friend who will also remain anonymous, she said on the phone. He doesn't give a shit about all that; her money is green just like everybody else's. He turns on his stool when she walks in and Grandma snubs out his Pall Mall. The door closes on the sun setting over the roof of the busted sawmill.

The woman approaches him. Up close she looks like a Hollywood actress whose name he can't think of just yet. He might ask her if she gets that a lot. Maybe that's a good opening line.

Are you Applejack, she says.

The one and only.

But that's a kids' cereal, she says. I was expecting a younger man.

Applejack laughs. All right. He takes a tug from his half-full bottle.

Well, how old are you anyhow, she says.

Old enough.

Is it meant to be funny or something.

Ah, it's just something that stuck.

The woman orders a glass of wine even though Grandma warns her against it. It's like donkey piss, he tells her. But she orders it anyhow and pulls a stool closer to Applejack. Applejack looks her in the eye.

I hear you need help with something, he says.

There's a fucking guy, she says. Needs his attitude adjusted.

Applejack laughs into the last swallow in his glass. She talks about adjusting the guy's attitude like they're simply going to turn a screw to the left or right, tweaking the idle on a carburetor. He likes her already, no beating around the bush with this one. The top three buttons of her work shirt are undone and he can see a lot of her chest and her black bra and the small gold cross she wears on a thin silver chain around her neck.

The nametag on her work shirt bears a man's name. Must be her new fella, he thinks to himself. He decides she's sexy as hell. Maybe she's Australian or something, the movie actress he's trying to think of. What would he know from Australia. Fuck me, he thinks. It'll come to me. Memory loss is becoming a real issue of late. The doctor has warned him about migraines, memory loss, and irritability.

You work at the paper mill, he says finally.

What.

Your shirt.

She looks down at her shirt as though she forgot she even had one on. Oh right, she says. Been doing third shift coming on ten years now.

That place smells like rotten eggs, he says, meaning not just the mill but the town that holds it. He knows it's a sensitive issue with the locals and loyal millworkers alike, and he says it to try to get a rise out of her. He wants to see what she's made of.

Well, she says. We like to say it smells like money.

He attempts to smile at her but she looks away. Is this Lou, he says, that we're talking about here.

She regards the nametag on her shirt. No, she says. Sadly, Lou's not around anymore.

And if he was.

Well, I wouldn't be here right now. Let's just say that.

Applejack waits for her to continue until it's clear that she's not going to. All right then, he says. Where can I find this other guy with the attitude.

She turns back to him. That easy, huh, she says.

Why make it hard.

Want me to write it down, she says. Where he's likely at and when. She puts her wine on the bar and starts to fumble in her purse.

No, he says. Just tell me in my ear.

The woman looks at him. This guy is flirting, she thinks.

In your ear, she says.

Applejack laughs and pinches his ear between his thumb and bent index finger.

And what's this scar, she says. I bet there's a story there.

He puts his hand over the white line that drops from his ear, intersects his jawline. Yeah hey.

Well, she says, is there a story behind it.

Sure there is.

She waits for him to tell his tale but he stays quiet, figures it's his turn to clam up.

Did it hurt, she says.

No, it wasn't bad.

All right, she says. Still want me to tell you in your ear.

Yeah hey, he says, smiling again. Just in case.

In case what exactly.

He just wants her to lean in on him so he can get a whiff and she knows this to be true. So she leans toward him with the address and he closes his eyes, breathes her in. Then she sits back and he opens his eyes.

Hey, he says. What you wearing.

What am I what now.

You smell real nice, like something.

Oh that's just fresh lemons, she says. For the egg smell, like you said.

She stays close to him, much closer than she needs to. Applejack always knows when his shit is working and he has this one in the bag for sure. He doesn't usually mix business with pleasure, but rules are made to be broken, and that's his one fucking rule anyhow. The side of his hand is against her outer thigh now. He's getting warmer.

He thinks of Suzanne but just for a moment. She's been creeping into his thoughts at times like this. He has always pictured his mind like a collection of separate rooms where he keeps the different people and dealings in his life from congregating and conspiring, rooms with locked doors that he only opens when he needs to, but this Suzanne somehow roams around like she's got free run of the place.

Fucking woman has already got some kind of hold on me, he thinks. He shakes the distractions from his head, gets back on track with the job at hand. All right, so tell me what he looks like, he says.

She pauses for a couple heartbeats, sticks her finger in her wine. Dark and handsome, she says as she licks her finger. And he's a rather tall fucker.

Rather tall, he says. Is that how you like them.

She looks at him. Not anymore I don't.

Grandma comes by with a refill, the Pall Mall hanging off his lip. The woman uses her hands to fan away the smoke and she coughs a bit dramatically to make a point. Grandma goes away, sheepish.

I wish people wouldn't do that, she says to Applejack.

What's that now.

Smoke in bars, she says. Public spaces.

Well, he says. If wishes were horses then beggars would ride.

I'll drink to that.

They clink their glasses.

She sips at her wine, nods her head, and moves away from him just a tiny bit so they are no longer touching, but it doesn't matter. Applejack is getting the same kind of butterflies he used to get before a big fight in the scrapyard or down at the rock quarry. When he was a young man. When it was exciting. That feeling he's always chasing.

All right, he says. I can do him tonight or tomorrow.

That'll be fine.

Now let's have us another drink.

She looks away from Applejack for a minute. She knows what is happening here, what is about to happen. It adds another element of excitement to this already bad thing she is facilitating. She finishes her wine. Applejack finishes his drink, too. Grandma comes back around with another pour. He leans over the bar with his hairless, buggywhip-skinny arms outstretched and his hands flat. Now he has something to say.

Listen, he says to the woman. Bothered, and he's trying to avoid Applejack's eyes. Last time I checked this was America, he says.

The woman doesn't say a thing, biting her tongue. She knows a lecture is coming.

It's my constitutional right to smoke in my own Gotdamn place, Grandma says.

A real mouthful for him, the woman thinks. There are several seconds of silence as the woman tries to hold back but she can't. I don't think it's actually in the constitution, she says.

Well then it's my Gotgiven right.

I don't think God gives a shit about that, she says, to be honest.

Grandma twists his face.

I suspect he's got bigger fish to fry, she says. Famine and shit. Diseases.

Grandma turns red now. Applejack laughs. This one is a pistol, he thinks.

But this is my fucking bar, Grandma says.

So then you're Grandma, she laughs. With your name on the front.

That's right.

Surely that's meant to be funny, she says, looking at Applejack. You guys and your funny names.

Funny nothing, Grandma says. This is my place.

Well you got me there then, she says.

Grandma seems pleased.

Can't argue that with you then, she says. Mister Grandma.

Grandma thinks he's won the argument and he settles down for now. The woman finishes her wine, makes a face, and shakes her head like she's going to puke up that donkey piss now, thinking she should've taken Mister Grandma's original advice on it.

But listen, she says. I got allergies, so please put that out now.

The fuck you say.

The smoke, she says. I'm allergic.

Applejack can tell she's the type who needs to have the last word. Most gals are like that, can't just let shit go. Grandma looks as though he's going to fucking explode. Time for me to put an end to this, Applejack figures. He shushes the woman and reaches out, puts his hand on Grandma's forearm. Grandma, he says. Come on, man.

Grandma doesn't look up right away. He's known Applejack a while.

Grandma.

Grandma finally meets his eyes.

Applejack removes his hand and swallows the rest of his drink. We're leaving, Applejack says. You can fucking smoke all you want.

That calms the barman down. His shoulders relax. His face takes on a normal color.

Yeah, Mister Grandma, the woman says. I didn't mean nothing by it. She almost feels bad, didn't mean to get him so riled up. Just busting your balls, she says.

Applejack leaves some tip money on the bar and follows her out the door.

Applejack truly doesn't consider it cheating, although he knows Suzanne would certainly have another opinion on the matter. But that would be the pot calling the kettle black as far as he is concerned. Her and her customers and whatnot. The fucking after-hours parties she does, the private sessions. And the truth is that he has been trying to cut back on hunting strange pussy of late, but old habits die hard. He can't quit it like that—not cold turkey, anyhow.

The woman gets undressed slowly after they smoke a little dope. She folds each article of clothing neatly and places them on the back of a chair. What's that yelling down there, she says.

Grandma.

What's he yelling about.

You and your smoking allergy probably.

Are you serious.

Nah, he just yells sometimes, Applejack says. That's what he does.

Should we go see about him.

Nah, he's all right. He's known for that.

Grandma has a mild form of Tourette's syndrome that manifests itself in verbal outbursts and occasional and uncontrollable spasms. It's one of Applejack's favorite things about him. Sometimes one of his arms will jerk sky high like he's a puppet on strings. Eventually it'll flap back down to his side like a cruel kid cut those damn strings.

The room above Grandma's is convenient, but it's a mess. The window is open a crack and they can hear and smell the river rushing by. The woman tells him to go ahead and get naked also. He doesn't want to know her name and she isn't about to offer it. She asks him about his scars and he explains the ones that aren't too personal. She uses her hand on him for a while until he starts to scuff and then she gets some lotion from her purse. They get into the small bed together and kiss for a few minutes. Her tongue makes him think of a hummingbird the way it darts in and out of his mouth, small and quick. Then she sits on him and rocks back and forth while he touches her. His hands are surprisingly soft and gentle.

Are you clean, she says.

For the most part.

I'm not gone to regret this then.

Oh, I didn't say that.

Jesus Christ, she thinks. The fuck am I doing with this rotten apple.

So, she says. What do you like.

He closes his eyes and moves beneath her to a familiar rhythm, as though they're together on a small boat in the reservoir. Then he opens his eyes and looks straight at her.

This is fine, he says. I like this just fine.

What else.

Oh, he says. Everything else too.

He finds her spot and she closes her eyes and an electric current runs through her. She peels herself off of him and stretches on her back on the old mattress.

Where did you come from, she says after a few minutes of listening to the hush-hush of the river.

They rest for a little while. Catch their breath.

You know what else I like, she says as she suddenly rises and straddles him again.

What, he says, caught off guard but just a little bit.

This, she says.

She puts her small hands around Applejack's neck and with her thumbs presses against his windpipe, gradually increasing the pressure, effectively closing his airway, and he lets her do it. He's curious what this is all about to her. She stares into his eyes, convinced that she will see them flicker like candles as his spirit begins to slip away from its earthly vessel. Instead his eyes narrow like he's ready to swing on some bad dude and he knocks her hands away from his neck when he's had just about enough.

No wonder she can't keep a man, he thinks.

Then she wants it rough so that's how he gives it to her. It's a sweaty and athletic and sometimes violent romp. Afterward they drink warm, rusty water directly from the faucet near the washer and dryer and they rest and the wind outside is an unholy ghost. The woman kneels beside the mattress and says a soft prayer and it unsettles him. He moves to sit on a pepper crate by the window. Outside, a pack of coyotes knocks over the trashcans behind the bar and bark at the fat raccoons waiting in the wings. Pressure builds underground and a manhole cover pops like a champagne cork and falls through the air, slow in Applejack's mind like a penny dropped into a glass of water, and then it clangs real-time back to the blacktop. Fog shrouds the boot-shaped moon and farther stars. Applejack looks over his shoulder, she's still on her knees but quiet now and so he returns to the mattress alone and falls asleep, and when he wakes up the woman is gone. There's no sign she had been there at all but for the damp, sticky mess and the animal stink of all the things they did to each other. He breathes it all in and closes his eyes for a lonely moment and the memory is set. It'll surprise him someday—hopefully not when he's with Suzanne.

MAY 22, 2:27 a.m.

Jill and Peanut came out of the bathroom together talking in hushed tones. Peanut appeared livelier now but still not quite normal. Stavros and the Selectman looked up from the table where they'd just finished doing several lines of snow-white coke.

Right on fucking cue, Stavros said. What'd I tell you. My girls are professionals.

Bring that sweet meat over here, the Selectman said.

Jill walked Peanut over to the Selectman and he pushed his chair back and adjusted himself so she could sit on his lap, chalk dust on the tip of his nose. He started to feel up Peanut, grabbing at her tits while Jill bent over and took a quick snort from the scraps on the table. Stavros slapped Jill on the ass playfully as she did so and she turned to him, took a half step forward and pushed his legs open with her knee, then she started to grind and the Selectman watched her pale figure swaying to and fro as the radio played "Lonely Ol' Night" by John Cougar Mellencamp.

That right there, the Selectman said, is a world-class ass.

Jill fake smiled at him over her shoulder and then turned back to Stavros.

By the time the song ended she was completely naked and on her knees, tugging at Stavros's rhinestone-covered belt buckle. The Selectman focused on the small of her back: a green cross cracked down the middle with the word FAITH *beneath it. This girl has been around the block and then some, the Selectman thought. Turned on by the show and still all over Peanut, he stood up with her in his arms. She went limp as he started dragging her toward the bathroom.*

Maybe that shower idea was a good one, he said.

Stavros was pulling his shirt over his head, not terribly concerned about the Selectman's problems at that point in time.

Yeah hey, he said. A fucking shower might could do the trick.

He stood up and Jill, still on her knees, started to bob on him. Stavros put his head back and closed his eyes.

The Selectman carried Peanut into the bathroom and kicked shut the door with his foot. He sat her on the toilet while he got undressed. He was in a big rush and he stood her up and took off her clothes too, leaving them all in a pile on the floor. She tried to push his hands away at first but she was too weak and he was persistent if nothing else.

Come on, he said, you fucking cock tease.

He got the shower going and after half a minute he guided her inside. The cold water shocked her at first and jolted her awake, which had been his intent all along. She mumbled something about bee stings and seemed to smile at him. He laughed and then checked the temperature, warmed it up, jumped in with her. He stood behind her and started to rough run his hands over her body. She leaned back against him and moaned.

That's more like it, the Selectman said.

Then her eyes rolled back in her head and her body sagged and she slumped forward and he barely managed to catch her around the waist.

What the fuck, he said. You dumb fucking cunt.

He shoved her forward and her legs gave out beneath her, like those of a newborn foal, and going down she hit her head hard on the spigot. She was out cold and right away blood came out of a small but deep gash on her scalp, swirling red-brown down the drain.

Fuck, fuck, fuck, the Selectman said.

He shut off the water. The blood didn't stop.

Fuck, he said.

He scooped her up and arranged her on her side on the floor on some once-white towels. She moaned again. He sat on the toilet and inspected the wound in her scalp, tried halfheartedly to stop the bleeding with the heel of his hand. Peanut seized, jerked out of his grip, and rolled over onto her back, her skinny legs bent and slightly open. The Selectman used his foot to push one of them farther to the side. He stared. A perfect little peach, ripe for the picking. What the fuck. He let out a deep breath. I paid for this shit.

CHAPTER EIGHTEEN

Honey is sitting in the back of a nearly full classroom next to an empty chair she's reserving with her book bag. She's taking notes. A young assistant professor is giving instructions for a term paper on the Tennessee works of Cormac McCarthy that he wants at the end of the semester, advising the students their papers will count big time toward final grades. A bustle of activity catches Honey's attention and she looks up and laughs into her hand. Jill has entered the classroom through a rear door, all eyes on her and she's enjoying the fuss. She makes her way over and takes the empty seat next to her friend. She's wearing dark sunglasses and baggy sweats, a faded Minutemen cap pulled low, and looks thrashed, hungover.

What happened to you, Honey says.

Worked late for the Greek, Jill says. Holy shit.

You all right.

I got the biggest fucking headache right now. She coughs into her hand. Ouch, she says.

Honey laughs.

Oh hey, Jill says. And I talked to Stavros again.

And.

You can start tonight.

Oh shit, Honey says. Tonight already.

The shift starts at eight, but come in like an hour early so he can see you.

Sure, I guess.

So he can make sure you're all right, Jill says. You know.

Jesus, Honey says. But he seen me before.

I know, but it's been a while. He don't always remember so good.

Honey puts the end of her pen on her bottom lip and shakes her head. William's daddy made it clear he doesn't want her dancing anymore. Not for anyone else, at least.

What's a matter, Jill says, thinking about her commission, her promise to Stavros.

Nothing, Honey says. I mean—it just seems so soon.

You need the money, right.

Shit yeah.

We'll do a little happy hour first.

All right.

The assistant professor clears his throat and his voice rises. Honey shushes Jill, turns back to her notes, tries to focus. Jill puts her head down on the desk and closes her eyes.

CHAPTER NINETEEN

Hoyt's father has more than a hundred acres of land where he grows everything from shade tobacco to cucumbers to strawberries. Ten years ago he would pay top dollar to have local boys work the harvests for him, but nobody wants to put in an honest day anymore and so now he mostly hires Puerto Ricans on the cheap. He has long since given up trying to groom Hoyt for a future in farming, but he lets his son live rent free in a small ranch-style near Willow Creek Crossing so long as he tends the tobacco there.

Franklin County was once noted for its tobacco output and spawned the likes of the Consolidated Cigar Company. But, as Hoyt's father says, cigars have gone the way of ladies' hats. Shade-grown can still fetch a profit, however, as wrappers for the good shit from Honduras and the Dominican Republic. And so in order to eke out what money he can from his modest crop, Hoyt's father runs the farm with a combination of Yankee frugality and petty tyranny.

Hoyt's nature is more forgiving and he's more laid back in his approach to running a crew. Today he's straw boss to a vanload of Puerto Ricans come up from Holyoke or thereabouts. Lucky for them, he tells Applejack.

Venga, he says to the oldest boy in the group. Come here.

The boy saunters over.

Mucho trabajo hoy, Hoyt says. No fucking around today.

The boy smiles and shakes his head.

Tell them, Hoyt says, indicating the rest of the group with his hand. No mas juevon, Hoyt says, this time grabbing his balls to make the point.

The boy laughs through white teeth and returns to his group.

You start aqui, Hoyt calls after him, pointing to the section he wants them to pick.

It's not yet eight o'clock in the morning. Applejack and Hoyt are already sweating like red-mottled madmen among the seven-foot-tall tobacco plants beneath a vast expanse of cheesecloth netting that alternately heaves and subsides like the waves on some white and otherworldly ocean. They are working in parallel furrows, each man carefully removing three leaves at a time, snapping them together from the stalks in a downward motion. It's more than a hundred degrees under the netting in deep August, and the sweat mixing with raw tobacco juice stings their eyes like hot peppers. The distance from one net pole to the next, referred to as a bent, is approximately twenty feet. In their prime Applejack and Hoyt could pick more than three hundred bents a day, but they'll be fortunate to clear two hundred on this one, which is still better than what any other pair of men could deliver in the oppressive heat.

At high noon, Applejack and Hoyt sit in the shade of a gray-sided barn on the tailgate of an old F-250 eating lunch and drinking cold water from a garden hose. Nearby, the Puerto Ricans break, too. The boy approaches Hoyt and Applejack. The white men look up at him and he gestures toward the coiled hose.

Agua por favor, he says. Water for us too, please.

Hoyt nods his head. Si, hermanito, he says. Go ahead there, little brother.

Gracias. The boy uncoils the hose and stretches it until it reaches his group. They take turns drinking and soaking their heads and the T-shirts that are in their back pockets.

Applejack has a turkey sandwich and potato chips, and Hoyt swallows down big bites of cold leftover biscuits and gravy from the BP Diner. The immigrants eat day-old bread and cheese and then return to the field. Applejack and Hoyt pass a cigarillo back and forth.

Now let's get them fuckers hung, Hoyt says.

They place the still-wet tobacco leaves onto a three-sided wagon hitched to a Farmall tractor. Their forearms become red and raw and sticky. They unload the leaves into the long barn, then stitch and hang them to dry among shafts of light and clouds of dust. After about two hours of this, Applejack hears some kind of a commotion from the direction of the dirt road that leads to Hoyt's house. He climbs down the rafters and wipes his hands on his dungarees. Hoyt eases himself down, too, and the men exit the barn together, squinting against the day's glare.

What the Christ, Hoyt says.

Hoyt's father is bombing along the dirt road in his Yamaha ATV, steering with one hand and waving a large bottle of something with the other, yowling out one side of his mouth around the flat-faced, unlit stub of an El Producto cigar. Applejack and Hoyt exchange amused looks and wait for the old man alongside a fallow pit. He hits a wide rut and almost ends up ass over teakettle in the ditch but stops just short. A breathless Hoyt Senior kills the engine and dismounts the mud-caked rig, hands the bottle of champagne to his son, and points at the heavens.

Look at that, he says. Then he leans over and puts his hands on his knees, coughs and spits in the dirt. He notices his son and Applejack still watching him. Don't look at me, he says. Look at that up there.

Hoyt and Applejack turn to the eastern sky just in time to see a massive bright yellow hot-air balloon in rapid descent. Inside the basket, a shadowy figure hustles about, getting ready for a safe landing.

Some country folks don't take kindly to intrusions, especially from overhead due to all the talk nowadays of flying saucers; according to local lore, however, if the balloon man touches down on your property, your harvest will be abundant.

Three short bursts of flames slow the speedy decline with throaty roars that spook the Belted Galloways munching cunt grass in the adjacent field. Nobody moves as the balloon swings, stalled out it seems, directly above the property line.

Well shit, Hoyt says. Where's he gone to put her down.

His best bet is over to Stokarski's, Applejack says. With them Oreo cows. He laughs a little when he says it and so does Hoyt Junior.

But not Hoyt Senior. Fuck me, he says. And fuck you for saying such a thing.

The rudimentary flying machine casts a long shadow on the men as it hiccups and stutter-steps toward Ronald Stokarski's pasture. And so here comes Ronald in his shiny new red diesel, more chrome than a Cadillac and his name painted in big letters on both doors. The balloon lands, unable to defy gravity any longer, and Ronald produces his very own bottle of bubbly to share with the pilot. There is a loud pop and the cork goes flying. And then, with a curious ceremonial flair, the gentleman farmer and the balloon man touch glasses and interlock elbows like honeymooning lovers as they down champagne.

Hoyt Senior asks did they see the bastard look at him and wink.

Later that same day, from the window of Hoyt's farmhouse kitchen, it looks and smells like rain outside. At dusk dark clouds form and a palpable humidity rises from the blacktop in translucent waves. Thunder rumbles in the distance like the percussive minions of some archaic drum major that has been vanquished to the hills. Applejack and Hoyt sit at a foldout card table nursing magnum-sized cans of

Bud. Their forearms and the backs of their necks are sunburned a deep crimson. Applejack removes his John Deere cap and tosses it, watches it spin to rest on the linoleum floor. He runs his hand through his hair.

Sure as shit, Hoyt says, there's a summer storm coming.

Just another day in paradise.

Oh. Is that what this is hey.

Shit, what would I know. Purgatory, maybe.

Considering the life he has lived, Applejack is not so sure they'll even let him get a taste of that holding cell when his time comes. Not without some reconciliation.

Ha, Hoyt says. But you'll miss it when you're gone.

Like a hole in the head.

Careful what you wish for.

Applejack laughs and leans forward and they bang their cans of beer together. They each take a long pull and then Applejack speaks.

What you make of that deal out there today, he says. With the balloon and shit.

Well, Hoyt says. I don't put much stock in it.

You mean superstitions or whatever.

Right.

But your old man.

Now that's another story altogether.

They look out the window again. Sunsick Mountain governs the horizon, shrouded in white mist and looming like a phantom tanker cutting through the patchwork fields. Even farther in the distance, a jagged lightning bolt rips through the darkening sky over Ashfield and a tree explodes into splinters.

Shit, Applejack says. She's a real fucking beaut.

Hey, Hoyt says like to change the subject. So how'd Stavros take the news that you're leaving.

About how you'd expect, Applejack says. He laughed it off and said I'll be back. He said everybody always comes back.

Old dogs and new tricks, Hoyt says. But what about his new heavy.

That Rodney, Applejack says. The fucking Marine.

I got my own opinion on him.

All right hey.

His little act with the chainsaw, Hoyt says.

Applejack closes his eyes again and nods. You want to get something off your chest, he says, then go ahead.

It's like he had a taste for it. Cutting a person up.

Applejack opens his eyes.

And then hiding the pieces of her like Easter eggs, Hoyt says.

The kind of shit that'll come back and haunt us.

You think we're fucked.

I think we could be fucked hey.

And so that's why you're fucking off out of here.

But not before I see to a couple things.

And what about the rest of us.

I can't worry about you all now.

Applejack and Hoyt stop talking and keep drinking until they're good and cocked, barking and howling at the moon through the kitchen window like a couple coyotes.

CHAPTER TWENTY

The Selectman owns a soft-serve ice cream stand, a used car lot, a septic tank cleaning service, and Michelle's Cafe. Most people in his district doubt he's got anything but his own interests in mind. But come the end of his term nobody runs against him, and so his reinstatement seems all but inevitable.

Today he's dealing with Robert Moss, also known as Bob the Fag, who acts as his assistant regarding various matters. They stand at the kielbasa cart at the steps of the town hall. Bob takes notes on a yellow legal pad. They're working up a bullshit storyline for a special public meeting to address a dispute over a proposal to initiate right-of-way access for a snowmobile track come winter. The Selectman is all for it, but there are rumors that he accepted illicit payments from the sled shop owner to help push the project through before the cold season.

He doesn't like the word bribery—patronage is more suitable. He likes to think of it as a necessary greasing of the wheels. It's how business has always been conducted. I don't want to address that head on, he says. But I'll fucking deny it if it comes up.

All right.

Some loudmouth is bound to bring it up. Mick Willis or somebody.

They could, the fuckers.

Well, and then something about Ben Franklin.

Ben Franklin.

He had some good quotes, the Selectman says. About being pennywise and shit.

All right.

And you know the rest by heart: My record shows, blah blah blah.

The crippled kid running the cart, one arm way shorter than the other from some kind of birth defect, hands the Selectman two sausages with everything and extra sauerkraut and onions, and the Selectman hands one to Bob, who fumbles around with his pad and miscellaneous loose papers. The Selectman reaches in his pants pockets, front and back, searching for his billfold or at least putting on a good show, then looks at Bob the Fag and shakes his head, maybe feigning embarrassment. He's got more money than God, but this is his modus operandi.

Shit, he says. I left my billfold.

Don't worry, sir, Bob the Fag says. I got it.

He's used to taking care of his boss in this way, and he's happy to do it. He puts his stuff down on the sidewalk and pays the vendor cash. Then he turns his attention back to the Selectman, who is already half finished scarfing down his kielbasa and now checks out a professional young woman making her way down the steps. Sure she's got on a business suit, but he's already got her undressed in his mind. The woman notices his attention, doesn't like it, and throws him a disapproving look, shakes her head at Bob too.

Fucking dyke, the Selectman says almost under his breath. The woman hears him but chooses to ignore it and walks on. The Selectman looks at Bob the Fag.

You believe that shit, he says, spitting food at him.

Oh I know her, Bob says. She's all right.

The Selectman laughs. You know her, he says. And how would you know a woman exactly.

Some kind of special investigator for the state police, Bob says.

What's that now.

That woman there. I just met her the other day ago. Bob points and the Selectman watches the woman in the suit cross Federal Street.

What's she special investigating around here.

Bob shrugs. Beats me, he says, playing the idiot if that's what his boss wants.

The Selectman feels like he's going to be sick. Sniffing around like a damn bloodhound, he says. Bloodhounding me.

What.

Nothing.

All right, Bob says. So there's the thing tonight and the funeral Saturday morning.

Oh right.

Can you give me a little more on that.

What you mean.

You haven't even told me who died.

Just an old friend, don't you worry about it.

He takes the last bite of his sausage, considers spitting it out, and grabs a can of soda from the vendor's ice chest as though he's entitled to everything on God's green earth. Opens the Coke and takes a slug while Bob the Fag hands the kid running the cart another bill. The bubbles from the Coke help settle the Selectman's stomach for the moment.

What's the thing tonight, he says.

Kathy Reed's fundraiser.

The Selectman belches into his hand. Oh shit, he says. You couldn't get me out of that.

Bob gives the Selectman a look, gently chastising him. Your biggest supporter, he says.

My biggest whatever-the-fuck. Headache maybe.

The Selectman's candy-apple-red Ford Ranchero with tinted windows pulls up to the curb. Mint condition, looks like it just came out of the showroom even though it's practically fifteen years old. Just washed and detailed, still dripping water.

I'll see you Monday morning, the Selectman says. Probably around noon.

A large man in a mechanic's shirt gets out of the Ranchero and leaves the door ajar and the Selectman gets in without saying anything to him. The man closes the door and puts his head down and walks away. Bob the Fag knocks on the passenger window, which opens about halfway, and hands the Selectman an envelope. These are the raffle tickets, he says. For tonight.

The Selectman reaches out and takes the envelope.

Thanks, fucknuts, he says.

He sits back in his seat, out of sight, and then abruptly leans forward again.

You've got ketchup on your shirt.

The Selectman pulls away as Bob works at his T-shirt with napkins damp from his tongue.

CHAPTER TWENTY-ONE

Rodney Nartowicz tells Applejack he weighed two hundred and thirty-five pounds when he first got out of Cedar Junction. There's nothing much to do in there but pump iron, he says. And shoot steroids in your ass. The really good shit comes up from Mexico, and that's just about the only good thing to come out of that hellhole.

It was a chance meeting at Jerry's and now the point is for these men to get smashed before noon. They eat pickled eggs that have been floating in pissy brine in a big glass jar on the bar. They drink beer that is dark and thick as motor oil. They order shots of Wild Turkey 151. The bartender has a face like an orange rind.

That's it for you two, he says.

Applejack tells him to fuck off, Rodney wants to kill him. He leaves them be but keeps a close watch from the other end of the bar.

My mother died when I was inside, Rodney says.

Sorry for your loss.

Ah, she was a miserable cunt just like the rest of them.

Applejack raises his glass.

Rodney tells Applejack they wouldn't even let him out so he could attend her funeral. And that his kid brother sold all her shit and went to Vermont with a pile of cash.

That's a raw deal, Applejack says.

Plus he got the Impala, Rodney goes on. And I wanted the fucking Impala.

Applejack shakes his head. Yeah, I remember that car.

Wait till I see that fucker, Rodney says. Brother of mine or no.

Rodney hotwires an old Buick. They ride around, the radio playing Waylon Jennings. Applejack asks Rodney about his crimes but he doesn't actually call them that. He asks about the escalation of his misconducts, how snagging a pack of gum from the pharmacy grew up to be a bullet in some dude's eye socket. Rodney says the weirdest part is the way some unimaginable act gets so imaginable, easier every time. He tells Applejack he's always wanted to test the taboo boundaries and do all the undoable things. He's wanted to see what the big deal is and he has discovered that despite the societal uproar it is not a big deal to him—none of it is. And so mostly now I'm just bored, he says.

The sun is a hot stain in an otherwise perfect sky. They stop at a roadside bar called Horizons. It's never good being near sober in a room full of drunks, Applejack thinks, takes a long-ass pull from a bottle of beer that was in a bucket of ice by the door.

You hear they found her leg, Rodney says with a sly smile. One of them, at least.

Applejack looks at him. Rodney laughs.

But they're blaming every-fucking-thing on flying saucers, he says. Those silly fucks.

Right.

Car won't start—aliens. Wife won't give up the pussy—must be aliens.

Well, people do get caught up in shit hey.

I guess that makes it easier for them, Rodney says. These fucking sheep.

Then he talks about humping gear and asshole drillers and the rifle range. He says the main thing he learned from the Marine Corps was to never run in front of the pack and never stray too far behind. It's best to be in the middle, he says. Unnoticed is good but that's different than sheep. The guys in front are showing off and need to get knocked down a few pegs and the ones in back are laggers. Applejack tells him its sound advice for anybody, not just grunts in boot camp, and Rodney gives him an a-fucking-men.

Applejack goes quiet as he looks out the window, and a breeze moves trees that become black dancing silhouettes against the glaring gray sky.

Now about that leg you said, Applejack says like to change subjects back.

Oh nothing, Rodney says. I shouldn'ta said shit.

I understand about cleaning up, Applejack says. But you're treating it like a joke.

A joke.

That's right. Like it's fucking funny somehow what happened to her.

Rodney can tell Applejack is agitated and it's a real buzzkill.

Cleaning up is one thing, Applejack says. But it becomes a matter of respect.

Let's just drop it then, why don't we, Rodney says.

Applejack wants to drop it but there's some shit just can't be dropped. State cops are looking for her, he says. From that night. They're not dropping anything are they.

The rest of her, you mean.

There you go again. You know what I fucking mean. That's heat on us.

So she was a friend of yours or what the fuck.

No, I just met her.

But you got close or something. I mean why all this hey.

Rodney fingers the still-tender and discolored spot on his head where Applejack walloped him that night. Not a big dude but he sure packs a punch, Rodney thinks.

She was just a kid, Applejack says. That's all. A real waste if you ask me.

I didn't.

And unnecessary. In case I didn't mention.

Rodney flexes his biceps, admires them, and then smiles self-consciously. Yeah she was young hey, he says. There wasn't much to her.

He holds his hands and arms in such a way like to act out ripping a log and he laughs, trying to make the sound of a chainsaw in his throat. Remember that shit, he says. He downs his drink. What a mess that was, he says, as though they were in on it together.

Applejack decides then and there to break bad on Rodney. Maybe not today or tomorrow or even next week, but this motherfucker is going to pay for what he did.

Rodney looks at him and tries to read his mind.

You ain't mad at me, are you, he says. All I done was clean up for Stavros.

Well, Applejack says. I guess I know what you done 'cause I was there.

Rodney smiles. Not for the best part you weren't.

They sit in silence for a while. Somebody plays a Johnny Cash song Applejack knows so he croons along. *Always be a good boy and never play with guns.* At first it's funny and nobody seems to mind, but then people start looking at him and talking behind their hands. Rodney notices too and he laughs. The girl serving drinks won't come near them anymore, even when Applejack shouts for a round. This bartender is another dick and he runs his finger across his neck to indicate that they're cut off. Applejack shows him one of his fingers too and the fucking dipshit about hops over the bar. One of his customers holds onto him before he can get to Applejack and that's his good luck, because he doesn't know. He calls Applejack something and Rodney throws a chair in his direction and the girl goes to phone the cops and that's their cue to leave.

MAY 22, 2:48 a.m.

Stavros and Jill were both naked and sweaty in the bed. Stavros tried to catch his breath, lying on his back with Jill squatting over him. The blankets and sheets all over the place. Pillows on the floor. The television muted on the rolling credits for some triple-X feature while the screen cast an eerie blue light on the room. They listened to the Selectman in the bathroom talking dirty and moaning with pleasure through the thin walls.

Sounds like he's giving it to her now, Stavros said.

I knew she'd come around. She's a good kid.

Jill moved off the Greek like a weary young gymnast dismounting an old piece of equipment barely up to task, reached for her pack of Marlboros on the nightstand.

You fucked me real nice, Stavros.

Stavros smiled and closed his eyes. Jill struck a cardboard match. On the other side of the wall, the Selectman let out a primitive yell that was followed by a loud thud. Stavros opened his eyes and looked at Jill as she broke into nervous laughter. Stavros winked.

I guess he's done.

That guy's a fucking animal. Jill took a long drag from her cigarette and held the smoke in her lungs, the sharp smell of flint in her nostrils. These pigs and their appetites.

Then the bathroom door opened and the Selectman entered the bedroom. He was naked but for a towel wrapped around his waist—a small towel that just about covered him. There was something on his face and hands and chest, but in the blue light Jill couldn't really tell what.

Stavros looked up too and regarded him, turned on the bedside lamp. That's when they saw it was blood. A whole lot of fucking blood.

Jill gagged and covered her mouth.

What the fuck, Stavros said.

I don't know. The Selectman rolled his eyeballs around the room for a drink. You better check on her.

Jill wrapped herself in a sheet and stared at Stavros, her eyes so wide it looked like a fake face. He sat up and snatched the cigarette out of her mouth and took a long drag, exhaled through his nose. Jill looked at the Selectman.

What'd you do, she said.

He sipped from a plastic cup and looked at her, half-lidded.

Jill turned toward the bathroom. Peanut, honey, she said. You okay in there.

Peanut didn't respond.

Jill got up and clutched the sheet to her chest and shoved past the Selectman and into the bathroom and saw Peanut's body on the floor and stopped in her tracks.

Oh my fucking God, she said.

She dropped the sheet and fell to her knees, lunged for the toilet, and emptied her guts. She wiped at her mouth with the back of her hand and surveyed the room. Peanut's eyes were open and the Selectman's big, bloody handprints framed the vanity mirror where the reflection of his pig face would've been.

Stavros tugged on a pair of boxers and came up behind Jill—the cigarette still hanging from the corner of his mouth, ashes building up on the end of it. He studied the mess and he turned back to the Selectman, who was already pouring himself another drink from the nearly empty bottle of Old Crow. At least his hands were shaking as he poured. At least he was feeling something. The Selectman swallowed.

She was hopped up on something, he said.

But all that blood, Stavros said. Jesus Christ.

She must've hit her head. I don't know. The Selectman pointed a finger at Jill. Whatever you gave her is what did it. You did this thing. Then, looking at Stavros, It's her fault.

But you fucking fucked her like that, Stavros said. Ashes dropped off the end of the Marlboro onto the linoleum floor.

Both men watched as Jill crawled over to Peanut and checked for a pulse. Nothing. She tried what she remembered of CPR as the men watched. She looked up at Stavros and shook her head. She held Peanut's head in her hands and brushed some hair out of her face, gently pushed the lids down over her eyes.

With her eyes open like that, Stavros said to the Selectman.

I don't know, the Selectman said. Maybe I blacked out, but this is bad for me.

Jesus Christ.

You got to get me out of here.

Stavros, Jill said. She's fucking dead.

Hold on.

He can't just do that to a person and get away with it.

Is this cunt going to be a problem, the Selectman said.

Jill spun on him. You're a fucking monster.

Pull yourself together.

Jill backed away, the Selectman finished his drink, and Stavros got dressed.

Look, Jill said. She even shit herself.

Put some clothes on, Stavros said.

But look at her.

Stavros yanked Jill up, slapped her hard enough her head snapped against the blow. Put some clothes on and then go tell Applejack I need bleach and plastic bags.

Fucking plastic bags, she said.

He's out there in the car. And those hospital gloves.

Oh my God.

Jill got dressed quickly, wanted to get the fuck out of the room. Out of the shit she was in. She'd gone from shocked to angry to scared for herself. The Selectman stood there in the small towel, casually sipping his drink. He watched her unlock the door and step out into the rain. Stavros closed the door behind her.

CHAPTER TWENTY-TWO

A park ranger in a green work shirt and cutoff dungarees slices an aluminum motorboat across the center of the reservoir. Early morning sun reflects off the surface of the water. Sitting up front is the woman from the state police. She's looking through an expensive pair of binoculars. The ranger doesn't know what she hopes to find.

Boy Country wants to be a singer but he can't carry a tune or sing in key. His daddy has a pig farm in Colrain but they had a parting of ways over what the old man referred to as his general lack of ambition, and so when he's not cleaning up at the club for Stavros he folds clothes for minimum wage at the laundromat in Bucktown. He told Applejack once that you look at people different after you see their shit stains up close and personal. They had come up together in town and in fact Boy Country was the one who introduced Applejack to his ex-wife, Mary Jablonski. That was back when they were kids and the trouble and mischief they got themselves into was considered harmless and at times, to certain people, even charming. Mary was among the charmed for a bit. But nowadays she goes around saying he never grew up, that Applejack is still like some fucked-up kid, doing fucked-up kid shit that'll land him in prison or worse even.

Boy Country waits by the ATVs. Mary comes out on the porch shaking her head, waving a red-and-black-checked dishrag like to signal the final lap around a race course.

Jackson Woods, she says.

Applejack looks at her and keeps approaching.

I'll call the law, she says, in reference to a year-old restraining order.

Applejack stops in the middle of the yard, stands there smoking.

Really, she says. A motherfucking joint, even with the shit you're in. She turns as if to go back inside the house.

Hold on, he says as he exhales over his shoulder. How's the dog.

Mary faces him again, now with her hands on her hips. That damn dog, she says.

And like you give a shit about a dog. That's how she is.

As if on cue, a dog barks twice inside the house.

That's my baby, Applejack says.

Mary has been taking care of Applejack's German Shepherd, Kendall, whose bad hips and various other maladies require near-constant attention. Mary has to carry the poor old girl over the threshold and across the lawn when she needs to pee.

Can you keep her for a little while more, Applejack says.

Mary rolls her eyes at him. Like hell I can, she says. Why, where you off to.

I don't know. Nowhere.

Well that's just perfect.

You look good anyhow, Applejack says. Off the sauce, I hear.

Mary pushes a bit of hair behind her ear and regards him.

Fuck you, she says. I'm calling the law.

Applejack flashes a smile that used to work wonders on her. Aw come on, he says.

Anyhow, she says. I been hearing talk.

Oh yeah. What kind of talk.

The cheap kind, she says.

He laughs.

Is there any other kind, he says. Come on now.

Oh, this and that.

He looks away from her and then back.

But that you got yourself in deep this time, she says. Getting deeper every day.

Applejack laughs again and takes a considerable puff. Yeah, he says. Well.

Yeah well shit.

There's some money in the account. I put it there.

No need for that.

All right. But it's there.

So that's it then.

And keep your damn doors locked, he says.

What now.

All that trouble.

You mean them sightings and whatnot, she says. And that missing girl.

Well.

I just wish a flying saucer would take me up out this shithole.

Flying saucer my ass, he thinks. Maybe some dude with a new car and real money. But what he says is, Careful what you wish for.

None of mine ever come true any-fucking-how.

Shit, he chuckles. Beggars would ride and all that.

If there's one thing Mary knows for sure it's that Applejack loves women, but never for very long. How that one wish of hers got sucked down some drain. It's a thing he learned early, how to get women and then how to get rid of them. Something about his pain and suffering that he numbs with sex. And women can tell. Not all, but most. They recognize his hunger and they want to feed him, something primal at work. Applejack got lots of practice, starting from when he was just a boy and maybe continuing into last night, Mary figures. He fucks everything in sight, plain and simple. But certain women see that he hurts—they see that, too, and want to fix him. He gives a lot and then he gives nothing. Mary ponders on her favorite Stevie Nicks lyrics: *You can take me to paradise, then again you can be cold as ice.* But Applejack does slip up. He can fall hard.

She had known he was cheating before they even got hitched way back when. Sometimes it was just whores. Other times it was girls from this town or that one with big ideas. Maybe she could've handled his sneaky side-dish fucks or his boozing, but not both together. He never understood what she meant by that. To him they were the same thing, the way they evened him out for a period but always ended in a big, sloppy mess.

Mary watches him walk off toward the knoll and disappear into the low-hanging midsummer fog like a haunt. She hears the high whine of the Jap-made motors as he and Boy Country fire up their rigs, turn them around by the barn so they can head up Settright Road and across the fields of alfalfa to Plain Road. She knows well the route, has ridden it with him many times on four-wheelers and winter sleds alike. Son-of-a-bitching bastard, she says aloud, watching their headlamps cut the mist and then, when they arrive at the bend, all she can see is the red pinpricks of their taillights and then nothing. Even sound disappears, absorbed into the impenetrable province of the black valley night.

CHAPTER TWENTY-THREE

William needs a job so he walks the three-mile stretch of 5 and 10 into the center of town and gets hired on by Charlie Smiaroski to help dig up some potatoes. Charlie's is a fifth-generation family enterprise. He and his brothers harvest more than a thousand acres of red, yellow, white, and russet spuds across both Franklin and Hampshire Counties. Charlie buys William a can of orange soda and a bag of chips at the pharmacy, which also serves as the unofficial hiring hall for local farmers and tradesmen, and they get into his red and white pickup truck that is parked in the street out front.

Charlie turns the key in the ignition and the engine catches. He pumps the gas pedal while fiddling with the radio dial, looking for some easy listening. He settles on a station out of Northampton. William cracks open the soda and it sprays on the dusty dashboard. He apologizes softly and wipes at the spurt with the bottom of his T-shirt.

That's all right, Charlie says. You ready to work today, boy.

Yes, sir, William says. I got bills.

Charlie laughs as he checks his rear and side mirrors, mostly out of habit. There are very few other vehicles around for him to be concerned with. William drinks. Charlie retrieves a pouch of Red Man chewing tobacco from the rear pocket of his dungarees, unfolds and opens it, collects a wad between his thumb and pointer finger. He jams it against the inside of his cheek and works it with his tongue, tastes the sweet bitterness. There is an empty beer bottle in the console that he can spit into if he wants. Charlie returns the pouch to his pocket.

Fuck kind of bills you got at your age, he says.

Well, William says. There's this girl.

Oh shit, Charlie says. Isn't there always. Then he spits into the bottle. Say no more, he says, a fleck on his bottom lip.

William is constantly thinking about Honey now. Smelling her, tasting her.

The pickup stalls and Charlie curses under his breath and turns the key again. He pictures in his mind the young girls he used to know and the women they became. Never much with the ladies himself, he married the first one to say yes and hasn't looked back.

The old pickup truck chokes.

Son of a bitch, Charlie says louder now. Throttle cable's loose again.

He toggles the clutch and gas until he manages to get the revolutions high enough for the pickup to cough and stutter-step, lurching onto South Main Street, puffs of gray smoke like rabbits jumping from its rusted tailpipe.

Don't suppose you can mechanic any, Charlie says and spits out the window.

Yeah hey, William says. My daddy taught me some.

Well then, Charlie says. We're gone to keep you plenty busy.

They drive in silence for a while but for the radio playing and the pickup's depleted pistons rhythmically misfiring from time to time. The window is stuck all the way down and air coming into the cab delivers the warm, wet smell of cow shit. When they reach Route 47 Charlie opens up the engine as best he can and William closes his eyes and puts his forearm out and he moves it slow and somewhat serpentine against the airstream. Charlie describes what he calls the commotion around flying saucers landing in his cornfield just due west of the big river.

Yeah, William says. I heard something about that.

What you make of it.

Probably just them balloons, I guess.

You think. Even at night.

Shit, William says. What would I know about that.

You seem like one of those smart fuckers. Good in school and whatnot.

But I never took no class on flying saucers, William says.

He laughs and Charlie does, too. Then Charlie gives a left turn signal and navigates the pickup from the blacktop to a dirt-packed and rock-strewn pathway that will deliver them to the potato field. William opens his eyes to see where they are, looks out the window at the sawtooth horizon, watches Japanese beetles die on the windshield. He can hear them popping.

The shocks and struts of the antique pickup are tested on the bumpy road and William's teeth knock together when the left front tire bounces into and out of a deep rut. Charlie spits tobacco juice out the window and downshifts from the column, and just on the other side of a slight rise, looming in a midmorning mist, there's a fancy new Haith grader situated alongside an older and smaller version of itself. William whistles at it. Like something out of a science-fiction movie.

Fuck the Puerto Ricans, he says. You'll soon have robots working them fields.

Ha. Charlie laughs. That's my new toy.

Sure is pretty.

Cost me a pretty penny anyhow, Charlie says. Let's see if she puts out hey.

He parks where tire tracks have scarred a small clearing in the brush and kills the engine that diesels for a bit before it shuts down all the way, which pisses him off to no end. Charlie is the type of man who likes for things to function properly.

Fuck me, he says under his breath.

He leaves the key in the ignition and gets out of the pickup and William does too. The ground is hard under their rubber-soled work boots. The steel toe of William's right Dunham is exposed and peeling back in the shape of an eye. He soft-kicks a fat tire and a loose side rail on the rusted potato grader as he passes it and imagines the old and tired machine moaning and breathing unevenly, like a cancer patient under a tender hand.

What about this one, William says.

Trying to sell it in auction but probably part it out some.

Together they walk around the retired heap and Charlie mounts the Haith, shows William how to access the platform where he'll be leaning over the roller bed to remove clods of soil and stones and undersized spuds. He gives him a pair of gardening gloves.

Watch your sleeves, he says. Don't get them stuck in there.

Oh, all right.

I'm serious, boy, Charlie says. Take your arms clear off.

William tucks the sleeves of his long undershirt into his gloves. Then Charlie gets the new rig running and he cups his palms at his mouth and hollers for William to hold on, and he manipulates it into position at the northern base of the furrows. His crazy cousin Ted arrives soon, drinking his first morning can of Budweiser and smoking the fattest cigar William has ever seen. Ted's driving a John Deere tractor that's hauling a galvanized steel container and he waves his free hand at Charlie and nods his stubbled chin at William, lines up the container under the chute of the grader so it can catch potatoes. Ted'll follow along like that, slow and straight as an arrow, all damn day long.

CHAPTER TWENTY-FOUR

Hoyt points out French Diego at the Seven O's. He says how he one time watched him carry a refrigerator up two flights of stairs. He doesn't have many teeth left and he stinks to high heaven. He's well over six feet tall and has a green teardrop tattoo. Applejack knows this bad man has made other bad men cry. Everybody at the bar has kicked in to watch French Diego fight Applejack in the back lot, which smells like last night's vomit fest and wet cardboard boxes. The odds are stacked against Applejack. Frank Olzewski Senior is holding the money because Hoyt doesn't trust Frank Olzewski Junior for some reason. Applejack stretches and sticks his T-shirt in his back pocket. He puts a roll of quarters in his goofy fist.

The match lasts longer than usual, maybe ten or eleven minutes. Applejack gets hurt but French Diego yields when his right shoulder pops out of its socket. He's clearly impressed with Applejack's ability. Hoyt collects the soiled bills.

That one, French Diego says. He can still fight.

We call him Applejack, Hoyt says.

Call him whatever you want, French Diego says, his right arm dangling.

Hoyt laughs until he coughs. He licks his thumb and counts the money aloud like a carnival barker, describing in detail and at the top of his lungs his favorite parts of the contest for anybody who will listen. Applejack sits on somebody's bumper to catch his breath. His nose is bleeding and his left eye is leaking yellow fluid. His brain feels as though it's swelling inside his battered skull. Strangers slap him on the back and chant his name. Hoyt is full of adrenaline, images of his friend's performance, and brown booze. Frank Olzewski Senior gets Applejack a dishrag that smells like mildew.

MAY 22, 3:07 a.m.

Applejack smoked a Swisher Sweet and listened to the radio in the limousine. He had been chain smoking, the ashtray full, overflowing. The window was open a crack and some rain blew into the car but he didn't mind. When the door to room number three opened and Jill slipped out he sat up straight. Something was wrong. She paused under the overhang for a couple beats. Then he watched her duck and make a beeline for the car, one hand holding her purse over her head, the other clutching her shoes. He leaned across the seat and opened the door for her. She got in. There was blood on her hands and face and her makeup was running. She looked like shit. Some kind of demented female jester.

    What the fuck hey, Applejack said. That's blood all over you.

    Yeah.

    The fuck happened in there.

    She looked at her hands and rubbed them on her coat.

    Did he hit you, Applejack said. And where's the kid. He looked her over, trying to see where she was maybe cut. Where's that Peanut, he said.

    She's gone.

    Bullshit. I been sitting right here the whole time.

    She's fucking gone gone.

    What're you saying.

    He killed her.

    Applejack slapped her. It caught both of them off guard and he regretted it instantly. Jesus Christ, she thought, putting her hand to her cheek. First the Greek and now this dude. What am I, a motherfucking punching bag. Then Applejack twisted away from her to get out of the car. Looking for somebody else to hit. She figured she knew where this was headed and she grabbed onto him with both hands, trying hard to hold him back.

No, wait. Stavros says we got to get some things.

He shrugged her off easily and without another word.

They're fucking crazy, Applejack, she said. Please don't go in there.

Applejack took long strides toward the door.

Stavros and the Selectman hauled Peanut's body over the side of the bathtub. Stavros had her arms, the Selectman her legs. They dropped her in carelessly, clumsily. Her head smacked against the porcelain like a gong, echoing in Stavros's ears. A total fucking mess.

This is some shit, Stavros said. This is really some fucking shit this time.

Not what I need, the Selectman said. Not right now.

He was thinking about his position in the community. Stavros was thinking about drilling him in the face, making him tell when is a good time for this fucked-up shit.

They both grabbed towels from the rack on the wall and wiped as much blood as they could from the linoleum and floorboards, but that only made it worse, spreading the mess around.

Fuck this, Stavros said. We got to get you cleaned up.

He took the towels from the Selectman and chucked them, along with his and the soiled throw rug, into the tub on top of Peanut's pale corpse. He jerked the curtain closed roughly, tearing it from the rod at one end. They left the bathroom together, entered the bedroom where they were met with a heavy, quick pounding on the door. The Selectman backed away from the sound.

I'm not here, he said as he choked on a rough whisper.

That fucking cunt, Stavros said. What'd she forget.

Stavros opened the door expecting Jill, but Applejack burst into the room.

Applejack, Stavros said. What the fuck.

Where is she.

Applejack looked around the room, taking it all in—the mess, the men, no Peanut—and then he quickstepped to the bathroom. Stavros and the Selectman heard him pulling the shower curtain aside. After a minute he came out and headed straight for the Selectman. He caught him hard under the jaw with the heel of his hand, sending the Selectman crashing over the table, knocking over bottles of booze and sending plastic cups flying. The Selectman landed on his back, tasted his own blood. He sat up and sobbed, trying to regain his senses and prepare for whatever Applejack was going to bring next. Stavros got in front of Applejack and put up his hands.

Don't fucking do this, he said. Listen to me.

Applejack swept the Greek's legs in a single motion, leaving him in a heap as he pinned the Selectman with his eyes. Calm and certain, focused. A lion studying his prey before the kill.

You fucking did that to her, he said. She's just a kid.

He lunged and kicked the Selectman's face, steel toe against nose, putting the back of his head through a spot in the drywall. Fucking please, the Selectman said.

I bet she said please, Applejack said. And begged you to stop. He stepped back like to swing his leg again.

It wasn't his fault, Stavros said, slowly getting up on one knee.

Applejack stopped and looked at Stavros.

It was that shit she was taking, Stavros said. Whatever the fuck.

Applejack turned back toward the Selectman, did a little dance to get his hips aligned, clenched and unclenched his fists. He could feel a big headache coming on.

Mixed with drinking, Stavros said. That's what probably did it.

A bad cocktail, the Selectman offered. But I didn't kill her.

All that blood, Applejack said. The cut in her head.

I know.

And he dumped his mess all over her.

That was after, Stavros said. She was already gone.

That was after, you say, Applejack said. After what. He ran scenarios in his head, none of which he liked.

I know, Stavros said. I'm not saying he's not a sick fuck.

And nobody does anything, Applejack said. Makes a call for help.

It isn't a thing where she got killed, Stavros said. It's just a thing where she died.

She's bleeding out and this sick bastard fucks her like that.

Stavros let out a long breath.

Is that what you're telling me, Applejack said.

I don't know, Stavros said.

Jesus Christ, Applejack said. I'm calling somebody.

The Selectman started to protest.

Don't you open your fucking mouth, Applejack said, or I'll shut it for good.

The Selectman raised his hands. And did he just fucking smile at me, Applejack thought.

He made a move for the telephone but Stavros beat him to it, pulled it out of the wall and threw it across the room. The phone dead-centered a cheap painting and fell with it to the floor. Pieces of both scattered about now.

Stavros was breathing hard. Call who, he said between labored breaths. For fuck sake.

Applejack stabbed a finger toward the Selectman.

We're all in the same boat here, the Selectman said. Don't nobody need this.

I warned you keep your trap shut, Applejack told him.

So the poor kid died, Stavros said. It's too bad but it is what is.

People die every day, the Selectman said.

This is wrong, Stavros.

Where you been all these years, Stavros said. Most what we do is wrong.

But this is way past wrong.

We take care of this right, the Selectman said, and it ain't so wrong.

And you don't want the stink of this on you, Stavros said.

Applejack got past the Greek and put the boots to the Selectman again as he slithered against the wall. The outside door was still open and hail the size of riverbed stones was now falling beyond the overhang. Jill came into the room, saw Stavros struggling with Applejack, and she bent and grabbed the empty Old Crow bottle from the carpet and raised it high and brought it down hard on Applejack's head. Lights out. Stavros caught Applejack on his way down and eased him to the floor and looked at Jill.

I see you got your mind right now.

I heard what you all said. That this thing is my fault.

The Selectman spit out a yellow tooth and smiled.

I'm not going down for this, Jill said. Nobody's landing this on me.

CHAPTER TWENTY-FIVE

Cass likes to cut herself. The first time was in high school when she scratched the name of her then-boyfriend onto the inside of her forearm with a beer bottle cap. He called her a stupid bitch and dumped her because of it. So she cut her other arm with an X-Acto, careful slits in honor of the fucking prick. And then she was done with him, never spoke his name again, but it felt good to watch his life slowly go to shit until he went off to the Army and got his leg blown off in Bosnia or some-fucking-where. In honor of nobody now she uses a razor blade and is careful not to cut a vein. She doesn't want to die or make a big mess. She just wants to feel something, anything. She covers up with long sleeves even in the warmer seasons so nobody will notice, but of course Applejack sees when they wake up together. She's been trying to seduce him for forever and a day but he treats her like his kid sister, although she finds comfort just sleeping with her head on his chest even if he won't touch her. She figures it's just a matter of time.

What the fuck is that, he says. On your arm.

Oh that's nothing.

They're lying on a mattress and she pulls the blanket around herself. She's not showing yet and he is not aware that she's pregnant.

Did you try to do a suicide, he says, tugging at the blanket so he can see the fresh scabs.

Don't be stupid, she says. She hates that word. It's just so trendy and that isn't what she's all about.

Well what then, he says.

Cass starts to cry. You wouldn't understand, she says. What it's like to feel nothing.

Fuck you say, Applejack says. Then he takes her hand, traces the scars on his arms where his father used to stub out his everyday smokes and his goodtime cigars. The old man had always been impressed with his son's unusually high threshold for pain. That's me in you, Applejack says. That's what the old man would say to me. He tells her how it eventually became a thing of pride between them.

Cass turns away from Applejack. She loves him, and after she fucks him he will love her back. That's how she thinks it works. And so to her it's easily worth the wait. Applejack doesn't say anything for a minute or two but she knows it's a temporary reprieve. This man doesn't give up that easy, not over something like this.

He lifts her arm gently and inspects it again. Jesus Christ, he says, is that my name. And she can smell his breath sweet with Southern Comfort. He's in big-brother mode again. You'll catch a vein one day, he says.

It's a full-on cry now. She tries to hold back but just can't do it anymore.

CHAPTER TWENTY-SIX

Later that same week Applejack smokes on the rooftop outside his apartment. It's unseasonably cold and he can't tell his breath from the smoke. There's television noise from the bar downstairs. Some drunks pour out of it and move as one along the sidewalk like salmon swimming upstream. A pickup stops at the corner of South Main Street and about half a dozen skinny Puerto Ricans jump out the back.

Applejack closes his eyes and listens to the Spanish chatter.

Donde esta, a voice says. Where is it.

Les siguen, says another. Follow them.

Es en el cielo. It's up in the sky.

Applejack opens his eyes and looks up at the sky, nothing but the early moon and stars and night clouds, and then Suzanne joins him. She's eating a piece of dry toast.

What you doing, she says.

Having a smoke.

Give me some.

All right.

He hands her the cigarillo and she stands right up against him.

Where they all going, she says as she indicates the crowd of people down below.

They seen something, he says. Up in the sky.

She coughs into the inside of her elbow when he says it and then takes another long drag of his cigarillo and considers the far-off horizon for a while.

Who did.

Somebody.

Shit, she says. That's just folks talking.

Applejack reaches for the cigarillo and she gives it over. He takes a short puff.

They ain't out there, she says. I'd know if they was.

How's that.

I'd feel it, she says. I think sure I would. She nods her head and eats her toast.

The crowd is getting restless and beginning to disperse.

Anyhow, she says. You gone to tell me where you been.

He doesn't say anything and a blood-red sun descends behind the mountain.

Dipping your wick, she says, trying to sound lighthearted about his infidelities.

Are we on that again.

Neither one of them says anything for a while.

You taking the car, he finally says.

Unless you can drop me.

Whatever, he says. Six of one, half dozen of the other.

Her shift starts at eight o'clock. She'll make a hundred bucks on a good night. Applejack isn't often the jealous type and she appreciates that about him. He'll still stop in to see her routine from time to time but never for very long. Especially if Stavros is around. She doesn't begrudge him the necessary distance.

How much you drink tonight already, she says.

A couple.

And what.

A shot of whiskey. That's all.

How's your head.

Hurts like hell, he says. But I took some them pills.

From over there. She indicates the pharmacy across the street.

Yeah, Applejack says.

How much that cost.

He just gave them to me.

All right then, Suzanne says.

She knows Billy, the local pharmacist, is fond of Applejack. Most everybody is. Elgin over there fills prescriptions in the back sometimes. He has never been to pharmacy school but Billy taught him how. He helps Mrs. Padykula with her diabetes medicine and Rocky with his blood pressure pills. Big Al from Oxford Pickle needs something for hay fever, Hoyt has an upset stomach, and Stavros has irritable bowel syndrome.

Well, Applejack says. Let's saddle up.

They go downstairs and back behind the bar in the dirt lot, and he backs the ATV into the stone driveway and turns the key and nothing. He curses and tries again and again until the engine coughs. Finally it fires up. Suzanne hops on behind him. She puts her arms around his middle and brings her head in close, shuts her eyes, smells his beard. It's a happy smell to her. He aims his rig up the hill to the end of North Main Street.

At the club she gets off the four-wheeler and removes her helmet and so does he. She gives him a kiss on the lips. Be a good boy, she says.

What else is there.

She laughs.

You know what else, she says.

All right then.

I'm done at two.

All right.

Should I get a ride.

That might be better.

Suzanne is disappointed because she's worried about his health as well as his tomcatting around. She shrugs her shoulders at him and he hits the throttle.

Hoyt meets him at the Seven O's. That's going to be their starting point anyhow. There is zero parking because of excavation work so he creates a spot for himself. Hoyt is at the bar watching television and Applejack claps him on the back.

Hey, he says.

Back at you, Hoyt says. Your girl working tonight.

Yeah.

You got yourself a good one there hey.

Well, he says. There's good and then there's good.

Hoyt laughs. He has this way of laughing that folks call contagious.

Applejack buys the next round. An older Polish woman brings a tray of microwave food. Hoyt gives her a good tip and says thank you in her native tongue. She smiles and returns to the basement. The bartender is protective of his mother and he watches them watch her while he runs a cotton cloth over a martini glass. He makes a comment that Applejack ignores, but the bartender is nothing if not persistent and after some amount of confusion Hoyt breaks an empty Bud bottle across the guy's forehead. Somebody calls the cops from the payphone and Applejack slugs his way outside.

CHAPTER TWENTY-SEVEN

Applejack wakes up when Cass knocks on his door. Suzanne is working, he says, but you can't just come here like this.

I need a ride to that doctor in Indian Orchard, she says.

Two hours later religious fanatics are holding handmade signs and dolls wrapped in blankets and poster-sized pictures of aborted fetuses. Applejack shoves them aside to clear a path to the double doors. He waits in the lobby and listens to the god-awful bullshit music they pipe in.

When the procedure is completed Applejack and Cass sit in the MGB in the parking lot and Cass cries and Applejack does a bump. You want some, he says. She declines. The crazies are milling around and staring at them so they leave. Applejack takes 91 North. The highway is slick from a first rain. A couple troopers on bikes with sirens blaring go flying by in the fast lane. Traffic comes to a standstill because of an accident. There are train tracks alongside the highway and a coal line races past them.

Did they have to cut you, Applejack says over his shoulder, keeping his eyes out the windshield.

No, she says after a minute or two. They just stretched me and put tubes in me.

Applejack imagines a vacuum cleaner sucking things out of her.

But did it hurt.

No, she says. Not really.

He's glad they didn't hurt her. Now he'd like to put his hands on the guy got her that way and left her to deal with the situation on her own, but she refuses to give up a name. Applejack acknowledges he's no saint, but that's some fucked-up shit in his book.

There's an eighteen-wheeler flipped over on its side near the Lyman Street exit. Thousands of gallons of milk spilling onto the highway, a fire truck and ambulance already on the scene, three foreign sedans and one minivan smashed all to shit, too. Emergency crews working frantically with the Jaws of Life to pry open the back passenger door of a shiny German car with a yellow sign that says BABY ON BOARD. The smell of gasoline and antifreeze and burning tires and water. The rubberneckers are in full force. For fuck sake, Applejack says.

Cass snaps out of a daydream and looks up at the mess for the first time and she starts to cry again. She puts her head on his shoulder and closes her eyes. Applejack thinks of the words to an old Johnny Cash song.

CHAPTER TWENTY-EIGHT

William has Charlie's pickup parked in a barn. The hood is propped open with the engine running, a plastic protector draped over the fender. Standing on a cement block, he reaches in and twists the wing nut from the top of the air filter housing to access the carburetor that he feels has been running rich, judging by the sooty residue on the spark plugs he switched out earlier. He uses a screwdriver to adjust the needle valve and then his thumb to test the throttle, slanting his eyes, listening for the sucking sound of the air and fuel mixing optimally.

There's an old billy goat, skinny like a bag of sticks, wandering the grounds. It pushes its nose against the back of William's knee. He tries to swat it away but the goat won't go. He steps down from the block and crouches with his cupped hands out. The goat sniffs his palms and looks at him.

See, William says, I ain't got nothing for you.

The goat sneezes at the gasoline smell and sidesteps into one of two stalls.

William laughs at the yellow snot on his hands and wipes it against the front of his dungarees, spits, and returns to his task. He gives the valve a couple more turns. Satisfied, he kills the engine. Charlie is paying him for a general tune-up: change the plugs, distributor cap, and wires; replace the air and fuel filters; tighten the alternator belt; change the oil; switch out the thermostat because the rig's been running hotter than hell; top off the radiator, brake, and wiper fluids; and adjust the carburetor. He's just finishing up now, pleased to have put in a good day's work.

Less than two miles away as the crow flies, a woman named Kat sits with Applejack in his MGB. This is a bad fucking place, she says. I can't hardly stand it no more.

She used to be an office manager for a dentist in Bucktown but then she formed a habit and now she sucks dick to support it. She has tried rehab but that only ever lasts a minute. Now she's a real mess, her nostrils caving in on themselves. Applejack doesn't know how she finds work looking like that but she seems to do okay. She operates mostly out of the bathroom at the Outpost Bar. The owner is a little guy with an attitude, one of those Napoleon complexes, and he likes to knock Kat around to keep her honest and that doesn't help in terms of her deteriorating physical appearance. But it's dark enough in there with all the bad lighting so a pretty face doesn't really matter. It's more about willing and able.

Applejack gives Kat twenty bucks just to ride around with him a while, to get her out of the weather for a spell. They drive down toward the Dwire Lot and it's all lit up for some kind of party. He gets her a black coffee with two sugars from the pharmacy. She says, please don't talk about God or any of that other shit these hicks try to force on me.

Well what then, Applejack says.

So she tells him about a yahoo from just the other night who was into receiving pain and he paid her to stick sewing pins in the eye of his pecker. He kept them in a jar, all different sizes. She could only do two and then her stomach turned so she barely even got paid for that. Another time, this was a few months back, a black guy asked her to carve her initials in his shaft with a rusty old utility knife.

Where you find these sick fucks.

Don't worry, she says. They find me.

Applejack makes a face, takes a pull from his bottle.

But there are normal ones too, she says.

Oh, I'm sure of it.

Don't get on your high horse now.

I hope you're careful at least.

Well, I don't sell my body, she says. She only does blow jobs and kinky requests like pissing on them.

Applejack parks under Stillwater Bridge and Kat puts some more of that shit up her nose to get herself right. He watches the river snake along as she talks and talks, she's really grooving now. An awful and rotten smell is coming up out of her. Applejack closes his eyes, has one of his spells, dozes off, and then she wakes him.

Come on, she says as she unzips his fly. Let's get that juice out of there.

Applejack pushes her hands away.

Oh, too good for me now, she says.

They drive back to the Outpost in silence and she gets out without saying another word.

CHAPTER TWENTY-NINE

Hoyt is waiting patiently, parked outside the town hall in a handicapped space in his fastback, sipping a cup of coffee and flipping through the sports section of the local rag. There are three large inner tubes on the roof of the car held in place with bungee cords and a topless Styrofoam cooler filled with cans of beer and ice secured on the trunk lid.

One story above the street, J. Meredith Jones, Applejack's parole officer, is sitting on his windowsill smoking, blowing near-perfect smoke rings out the open window. Bags under his eyes, his gray hair is coarse as straw and tied with a blue rubber band into a rough ponytail. The room smells like the incense Jonesy likes to burn, that he feels has a calming effect on his clients.

An oscillating fan blows in the corner nearest Applejack, who slouches in an aluminum chair with his legs outstretched and crossed at the ankles, his hands behind his head. His eyes are closed. Jonesy looks at him for a moment and smiles and then shakes his own damn head.

Fucking humidity. Jonesy tries to strike a casual tone. Not so much the heat today.

Applejack doesn't respond.

Jonesy looks at him again and squints, really regards him. All right, he thinks. Fuck it. Down to brass tacks then. You been going to meetings, Jonesy says. I ain't seen you at none of the spots.

Applejack doesn't move. Shit yeah, he says. I been going.

Jonesy laughs. All these years of practice, he says, and you're still a shitty liar. He puffs on his cigarette, blows more smoke rings.

Anyhow, I thought it's supposed to be anonymous, Applejack says.

Anonymous don't mean you're invisible.

Well, shit.

Listen, Jonesy says. I'm going to bat for you here with the judge and all.

Uh huh.

In case you forgot.

He stares at Applejack for a couple heartbeats, recognizes that his client is not present. Jonesy gets a little annoyed and his tone shifts. Get your shit together, he says, and I might can keep you out the Junction.

Right.

Ain't that the thing, Jonesy says. A clean slate and all.

Fuck, Applejack says.

Ain't that what you want, boy.

Applejack fidgets in his chair and opens his eyes. Yeah, he says. You know that's what I want hey.

Well then what's the fucking problem.

No problem, Applejack says. And I already told the Greek I'm out.

How'd that go.

How you think.

Well, Jonesy says. At least that's a start.

Applejack sits up abruptly and absolutely eyeballs Jonesy now. Fuck your start, he says. It ain't that easy for me.

Jonesy takes a puff and waits for Applejack to continue, to get it off his chest.

This is where I'm from, Applejack says. This is who I am.

Jonesy is getting pissed now too. His message doesn't seem to be sinking in, and he clears his throat noisily, hocks a loogie into the small, metallic trashcan near his desk. It sounds like a small stone hitting the bottom.

Nobody said it was gone to be easy, he says.

Applejacks settles back in his seat and folds his arms across his chest. But this is all I know, he says. This world I'm living in now.

All I said was keep your damn nose clean.

I know, Applejack says. Stay away from Stavros and them.

Your little fucking crew.

My little fucking crew.

Stay away from the Castaway Lounge. Your new girl up there.

Oh, right. That'll never happen.

All the rough stuff, Jonesy says. That thing you do.

Applejack snorts air through his nose. Well I don't do that no more, he says. The fighting.

Jonesy shakes his head and chooses to ignore that particular lie. Because one more fuck-up out of you, he says. Even a little one.

This is horseshit and you know it.

Even if it's not your fuck-up.

Complete horseshit.

You happen to be nearby when somebody else farts.

And what.

And you're serving that nickel plus some.

Horseshit.

Horseshit nothing, Jonesy says. You can bet the ranch on that.

Applejack closes his eyes and breathes deep, trying to regain his composure, to get hold of himself. But fuck this group therapy shit, if he wants to get something right and be heard, he'll throw a goddamn left jab. He needs to punch to have an impact, because only in violence can he correct his mistakes in the same instant he makes them. The room fills with smoke from Jonesy's cancer stick. Applejack opens his eyes and puts his hands behind his head, interlocks his fingers.

Fuck that, he says. That's all horseshit.

It is what it is.

Half a bag I was gone to smoke myself, Applejack says. And you know it.

Okay.

Everybody knows I stopped selling last time.

Jonesy laughs through his nose and crushes out his cigarette on the brick façade of the building just outside his window, leaving a yellow-brown stain the size of a dime.

Hoyt's car still down there in the street with the radio going.

Well, that on top of everything else, Jonesy says. You made your own damn bed.

The oscillating fan gets stuck and Applejack reaches over and fixes it.

Best-case scenario is Stavros's place fails, Jonesy says.

The fan gets stuck again and clicks three times.

Your fan sucks, Applejack says.

Jonesy shakes his head. I know, he says. Annie gets them cheap over to Caldor's.

She should get a new one.

Don't hold your breath. She's tighter than bark on a tree.

Applejack fiddles some more with it.

Your boy, the Greek, getting run out of town I hear, Jonesy says. He's trying to get the conversation back on track.

Applejack looks at him for another heartbeat and then away.

Either by the real mobsters, Jonesy says. Or the Staties who been coming round.

Applejack is still trying to get the fan going.

One or the other, Jonesy says. Just a matter of time.

It really sucks, Applejack says about the fan.

Are you listening to me, Jonesy says. Because I hear what he's up against. You caught up in something big.

Horseshit.

The fan clicks. Jonesy produces a soft pack of Salems from his pocket.

You don't know nothing about it, Applejack says. You got no idea.

Tell me then.

Fuck you.

Applejack wishes he could tell Jonesy about that night, just to let off some pressure in his brain. But it's a problem he must solve on his own. He stands and walks to the door. Jonesy taps the pack of smokes against the corner of his desk until the end of one pokes out far enough for him to get. He sets it on his bottom lip and lets it stay there.

Applejack, Jonesy says.

Applejack stops at the door and looks back over his shoulder at Jonesy, who smiles like a man trying to sell him something, trying to bring him back around. Just stay clear of the Castaway Lounge, he says. My brother.

Your brother now.

That'll go a million miles for your cause, Jonesy says. If you can do just that.

When Applejack emerges from the town hall, Hoyt's out front in the car. He starts the engine and punches the gas pedal so it roars and barks and stutters a bit, trying to get a reaction out of his boyhood chum. Hoyt hands over a cup of coffee and Applejack takes a sip and gives Hoyt a dirty look, spits the coffee back into the cup.

That shit is fucking gross hey, he says. He looks out the window at the storefronts across the street, Michelle's Cafe.

What'd fucknuts have to say, Hoyt says.

The usual bullshit, Applejack says. Fuck the Greek and keep it clean.

Get a real job, Hoyt says. Stay clear of the club.

Applejack looks at Hoyt. Right, he says. Go to a fucking meeting for once in your life.

I guess I know the drill by now too.

Applejack chucks the coffee out the window, cup and all, and Hoyt backs up and starts to pull away, tires blazing and white smoke building up beneath the Mustang, billowing outward and forming a wake behind the car as it fishtails away. Across the street, newly anointed Officer Blake Gillmore is about halfway through a Western omelet at the counter of Michelle's, but now with the commotion outside and everybody looking at him expectantly he's going to have to give chase to another simple townie fucker.

CHAPTER THIRTY

Bright white light flashes behind Applejack's eyelids. He jams his hands deep into his pants pockets. Dennis sells dope in the shitter. Applejack tells Grandma to bring him a beer and a shot. Then he waits a half hour, which is the deal, the agreement. Time's up and he's about to leave when a husky woman in a long blue coat taps him on the shoulder.

Are you Applejack, she says.

He looks at her. Who wants to know, he says.

I'm Lila.

He holds her stare.

From the phone, she says.

Oh okay.

Lila removes a white envelope from her purse. Applejack looks it over but doesn't really feel the need to count the money, takes the thin stack of bills from the envelope and folds it down the middle and puts it in his shirt pocket. He drops the envelope on the bar and she snaps it up. She's nervous and he offers to buy her a drink. She declines.

It's all there, she says.

Okay.

He's wearing a red coat, she says.

All right.

He's got on sunglasses, she says. Even at night, the fucking dickhead.

Ah, one of those.

He's over to the Hollywood.

I know the place.

You should hurry.

All right.

Lila notes that Applejack is not hurrying. His name's Joey Brock, she says.

Joey Brock.

Tell him I sent you because I want him to know.

All right.

Either this is from Lila or Lila sent me, she says.

Lila sent me.

That's right.

Applejack finishes his drink and wipes his mouth with the back of his sleeve. He leaves without saying goodbye.

Lila watches him go. He's still not in much of a rush and she wonders if she'll really get what she paid for. Outside she leans against a telephone pole until a brand-new Chevy with a lift kit pulls up for her. Applejack recognizes the driver from around town. Then a little bit later, inside the Hollywood, he picks out this Joey Brock, listening to music, drinking alone. Applejack orders cocktails and smokes cigarillos and waits.

Maybe it's an hour or more when Joey Brock walks outside and Applejack follows him. He pulls the hood of his cotton sweatshirt up over his head and blows warmth into his square-knuckled fists. This shouldn't take long, he thinks. He enters the dirt lot behind the bar where all the yahoos park their rigs.

Joey Brock, Applejack says.

Yeah, the man says.

I got something for you.

Who the fuck are you.

It's from Lila.

Oh, that no good fucking cunt hey. He says it in a conspir-atorial tone, not really sure what's happening here. What's about to happen.

Applejack drives him against an overstuffed dumpster with his shoulder and he feels the wind leave the larger man's body. Joey Brock goes down easy and barely even puts his hands up to defend himself. His sunglasses fly from his face and land in the dirt, cracked. Applejack bangs his head against the hard ground like trying to open a coconut, using his ears as handles until all this brain-knocking activity renders him unconscious. That should be sufficient for what the woman paid, Applejack thinks. He leaves the man like that and goes back inside and buys another drink or two, feeling good and alive now.

Then against his better judgment he goes to the Castaway Lounge.

Suzanne is surprised to see him. She smiles. He offers her a ride home.

But there's this afterparty, she says.

Oh, he says. All right.

I'm going just now.

Got it.

A hundred bucks plus tips.

All right. That's good dough.

That's what we want right, she says. Fast money.

Sure we do.

So we can fuck off out of here. The plan.

That's right, he says. What we been saying all along.

Well, don't be sore then.

He tries to smile, to look like he's not sore. But he hates to be away from her now.

So I'll see you later, she says.

So see you then.

He turns the key and his ATV comes to life.

Hey, she says. What happened to your hands.

He regards the cuts on his knuckles, his fingers all puffed up like sausages from rapping them against Joey Brock's skull. Oh, that's nothing, he says. Fast money, right.

She puts her soft lips against his damaged hands as though that can help. The limousine is in front of the club and the driver's tinted window rolls down and Hoyt is behind the wheel, smiling, a fat wad of chewing tobacco swelling his bottom lip. Hoyt shakes his head and rolls his eyes at Applejack, like to say I'm really fucking sorry about this. Some college boy pokes his head out of the sunroof. He sizes up Applejack and smiles at Suzanne.

Girl, you got the address we told you, the college boy says.

I know where it's at.

Sure you don't want to ride with us.

I best not.

But we'll behave.

I got my ride, but thanks.

That your father or something.

Nah, this is my friend, she says.

Friend.

He's a fighter.

No shit.

Maybe you heard of him.

He looks at Applejack. The kind of look that will get him hurt someday. Nah, he says.

Applejack spits in the dirt.

Well don't worry mister, the college boy says. We'll take real good care of her. Then he laughs and there is more juvenile laughter from inside the limousine.

Applejack pictures pulling the college boy out of the car by his neck, working him over right there in the middle of the lot. Putting his fist through the college boy's mouth and out the back of his head, ringing out his textbook-filled brain like a sponge. Then the smartass ducks back inside and the sunroof closes, and Hoyt shrugs his shoulders again and tells Applejack the dumb fucking kids are paying him cash money, too.

That's all right, Applejack says. Don't sweat it.

I'll make sure nothing stupid happens, Hoyt says. You know.

Applejack nods at his friend, feels a little better now. Then Hoyt's window hums shut and the stretch drives off slow.

Suzanne tells Applejack it's some kind of fraternity party nearby the campus in Amherst. She says it'll be harmless. They just want to look at her tits and squeeze her ass a little bit. Applejack knows all about those harmless kind of parties—the kind that start out that way, anyhow—but he isn't in a position to judge her. He tells her to please be careful. She kisses him on the mouth and their teeth clack together.

Jesus Christ, he has fallen hard for this one.

Then his head hurts. It takes a minute for him to collect himself.

Are you okay, she says.

Right as rain.

Is it your head again.

Yeah.

You got to get that looked at.

They already looked at it, he says. And I look at it too every fucking day.

You know what I mean hey.

Yeah, sure I do.

Well, I don't know you should be driving that thing across them fields.

Yeah, he says. Well.

Stick to the roads is safer. You'll end up in a ditch.

All right, baby.

Will you wait up then.

Sure I will.

Then we can go to breakfast.

All right, he says. What's the address.

The address.

For the party, he says. Just in case.

10-J Brandywine.

All right.

Will you remember it.

Sure, he says. 10-J.

I love you.

All right then.

Her ride pulls up, another of the girls, and she gets in the car and waves.

Applejack goes to the BP for black coffee and a bacon sandwich. Mercier is in there and they avoid eye contact. Then he leaves and the valley reeks of a wet dog and Applejack breathes it in because it smells like home to him. He cuts across 116 and passes by the plastic shop and the candle factory and turns right onto King Street.

There's a bonfire where Hoosac Road ends in a turnaround and it's just some of the regulars getting high. Applejack lets them alone and he sits on a stretch of curving rock wall that overlooks the river. A wooden sign posted nearby warns of certain death with a single misstep. Water slaps against stone. When it's light enough to make out the grand silhouettes of the tall ferns on the distant ridge, he smokes one more cigarillo. The bonfire is just smoldering embers now, and blue smoke and the smell of melted plastic, and black ashes that had drifted up are now falling from the sky, wafting heavily downward like fallout from something awful that hasn't quite reached Franklin County. But it soon will. The party is over. Applejack spits on the abandoned fire pit and listens to it sizzle like eggs in a pan.

Applejack is sleeping on the couch when he hears Suzanne's key in the door. He sits up and rubs sleep from his eyes as she enters the room and drops her duffle on the floor.

Hey, she says.

Back at you.

You were gone to wait up.

Well, he says, I'm up now.

You always say you will but you never do. She sits on the couch and puts her hand in his hair and he closes his eyes. You look like dog shit, she says.

He laughs.

Well, that makes sense, he says, 'cause I feel like dog shit.

Well, she says, I want to call that doctor right fucking now.

Applejack hushes her, tells her to relax.

Don't hush me, she says. I'm fucking worried about you.

I'm right as rain, woman, he says. Just a little tired is all.

We should fucking call him, she says.

Maybe later, after we get something to eat.

Well, she says, in a quick uncoupling from her worry, I could eat a horse.

Let's go then.

They cross the street kitty-corner to the pharmacy where the breakfast counter is open before dawn to accommodate early-bird farmers and late-to-bed strippers. She talks about the party but spares him the details. She says the frat boys were mostly gentlemen. They paid cash in the amount promised plus a little extra. She says they kept their hands to themselves and Applejack knows that's bullshit.

He doesn't want to think about them groping her. He doesn't want to think about her enjoying being touched by somebody else. He orders a ham and cheese omelet with hash browns, wheat toast, and a short stack of blueberry flapjacks on the side. Suzanne gets eggs over easy and a can of peaches with cream. They drink black coffee and tall glasses of orange juice, squeezed fresh out back.

The worry drifts back. She doesn't ask about his head again but he catches her looking at him.

You see that Nick, she says.

Sure, I saw him.

Well, she says. How's he.

Oh, you know. He's just Nick.

I guess I know all right.

Not really, she doesn't know shit. But Applejack wants to change the subject.

What'd you all do, she says.

Not much, he says.

She doesn't like his friends. She thinks they're going to get him killed.

We watched the game, he lies.

The game.

Sox lost.

Like you care for a game. Then what.

Then nothing.

You had some drinks though.

Yeah, he says. We had a couple three drinks hey.

Suzanne figures Applejack is fucking a few somebody elses on the side. She's not naïve. She's heard all the stories. It just drives her a little crazy. She doesn't know what she would do if she were to catch him with his actual pants down around his ankles. She suspects Applejack doesn't even consider it cheating because in his eyes there have to be rules in order to break them. And he's not big on rules, this much she knows to be true. And she understands that with what she does—Stavros and the club and everything that goes with it—maybe she's not in any kind of position to assert moral authority. But she's actually working for a paycheck and he's just dicking around.

Then they walk home and she gets in the shower. She cleans herself good for him. He's asleep on the couch again and she puts him in her mouth and of course he wakes up. She finishes him like that, with the bright new sun practically bursting through the timeworn bed sheet that hangs over the window for a makeshift curtain.

You're a real professional, he says when she looks at him for approval.

It isn't so much the words, but his tone that strikes a nerve with her.

What does that mean, she says.

Nothing.

You didn't like it.

I didn't say that.

You sure seemed to like it.

I said I didn't say that.

I've got proof right here in my hair that I just fucking washed.

I didn't say I didn't.

What then.

He wants to punish her for working the private party, for being so fucking lovely.

You just know what you're doing, he says. That's all.

And.

And nothing.

Say what you mean.

Practice makes perfect, he says. That's all.

What the fuck is that now.

Take it as a compliment.

You're a real asshole.

Well, he says. At least we agree on something.

He wraps her up tight in his arms until she calms down. He wants her all to himself. He's discovering that she's truly damaged, too, but he can handle that. He knows he brings crazy out in women. It can't be helped. Then she unplugs the phone and gulps some pills. She goes to the bedroom and tells Applejack that she's going to take a nap and not to wake her even if the building is on fire. He tucks her in and pulls the blinds. He pictures the apartment going up in flames with both of them trapped inside.

He can't help it. These thoughts he has.

Slams his eyes shut.

There's a jackhammer pounding between his ears.

MAY 22, 3:52 a.m.

Stavros sat in the basement of the Castaway Lounge on a stack of cases of Miller High Life. A single light bulb hung down in the center of the room among cobwebs from the unfinished ceiling and exposed beams bristling splinters the size of railroad spikes. The bulb swayed like one of those pendulums that tells of distant earthquakes. Deep in thought until movement, voices, and soft curses disturbed him, Stavros looked up at Hoyt holding a couple gallons of bleach, one in each hand. Nick stepped out of the shadows with a box of garbage bags and a handful of surgical gloves. He had blown air into one of them and then stretched it over his scalp so the fingers stood erect like some cartoon mohawk. He clucked like a chicken and did a little two-step. Then they each held up the items to Stavros and waited for a response. He looked at them.

These fucking clowns, he thought. Where's fucking Rodney when I need him.

This is the shit we use for the bathrooms hey, Hoyt said.

Stavros was quiet, vacant and still.

Hoyt and Nick looked at each other and then back at their boss.

What the fuck, Hoyt said. You gone to tell us what happened hey.

That new girl get sick all over, Nick said. Or what the fuck.

Stavros finally snapped out of it. Yeah hey, he said. Or what.

Stavros watched as the bulb swung to and fro, a perfectly formed cobweb next to it. A moth fluttered across his cheek, bounced off the bulb, and got stuck in the web. A black spider began to move methodically toward its prey.

CHAPTER THIRTY-ONE

A painted woman licks cocaine off Applejack's dick while her Basset Hound barks behind the closed door. Applejack watches her from where he is, like it could be a movie. There are smells in the room, too: a burning candle and a just-struck match and unwashed linen and the earthy bouquet of the whore, like the sea and the earth where they meet. The moon outside the second-floor window illuminates the bad town like a dim bulb—its shadows and alleyways and the dark gash of its big river all welcome poor souls with threat and promise. She finishes and he pays with a wad of cash and sips Jack Daniel's from a metal flask. They sit like old lovers and talk about her dog and her car and the corn beef she has to slow cook for her godson's baptism. There's a haunting and familiar emptiness to the transaction. He first met her when she was dancing for Stavros. It doesn't matter to her that he has a girlfriend, or that she knows his ex-wife from elementary school.

What else, she says.

I don't know nothing else.

I hear you on a tear, boy.

Well, Applejack says.

Well shit.

She laughs and he does too.

Same old shit then, she says. Just a different day.

I'm trying for something different-like, but don't know I can do it.

You are what you do.

Come again with that.

Well, she says. You can't change who you are unless you change what you do.

Let me think about that a minute.

Jenny Two Drinks gets dressed while he fixes his pants. She jokes that she's coming out of retirement, doing a shift at the club tonight. The apartment needs air but the windows are painted shut. Downstairs at Grandma's the jukebox plays Elvis. Jenny kisses Applejack at street level and her lopey hound sniffs between his legs at some slow-drying memory of the breedings it's bent to in its day, and they laugh about that and other small things. Then she's gone and Grandma pours him a strong one. He loses a game of eight ball to some yahoo and steps outside for a smoke and to watch the fog.

Hoyt gets him high and they sit on the bench in the town common. Chickens dance around them and stumble over busted bottles for the opportunity to shit on each other. The sun at dusk hangs like an old hubcap. Hoyt has the fastback tonight and he drops Applejack nearby Mary's house because he wants to talk and that's about it. But she's sure off the wagon and, never a happy drunk, she throws an ashtray that nicks him in the ear. She finishes a bottle of Jim Beam and lobs that in his direction as well. When he gets too close, she stabs at him with her lit cigarette until he departs with some of his belongings. All this without ever leaving the couch and one eye on her favorite show.

He wonders what got her drinking again. She was doing so good.

Outside now with a garbage bag of his old stuff, he closes his eyes, and when he opens them he's in a strange place. These damn blackouts, he thinks.

Puerto Rican words and red and yellow fruits spill into the spaces around him. He feels like a stranger here. A dirty pickup stops and he climbs in the back. Then the driver shakes him awake and tells him to sleep somewhere else. He has a heavy hand.

Applejack is back where he started, which doesn't matter anyhow, and a state cop chases two long-legged spics down Sugarloaf Street and then it sounds like the Fourth of July. Somebody is parked in a Malibu and watching his apartment. It isn't that fucking Rodney character but maybe it's Ricky Simpson, who has been known to do odds and ends for the Selectman. Applejack lets the air out of his rear right tire while he's reading the newspaper and eating a strip of jerky. Then he hugs his knees against the wind in the doorway to Rogers and Brooks. Stars are pinpricks and a horn warns pedestrians away from the road, an ambulance siren screams. Must be the Statie shot somebody, he thinks. He closes his eyes.

I guess that sick fuck is worried about me, he thinks. Sending Ricky way out here.

Bad move to tell Stavros he was quitting the life. He should have just up and left without a word. Maybe a good move to disappear now, he thinks. But where to.

It's not in him to step back from a fight, but this hunt-and-peck stalking shit is a fucking hassle. And he surely doesn't want any harm to come to Suzanne.

When he opens his eyes he's standing before Ricky in the hallway outside his apartment. He works on the kid's kidneys until he can't possibly take it anymore. Ricky calls Applejack every name in the book and tries for the buck knife he keeps in his boot and so Applejack hits him one last time, knocking his lower jaw off its hinge. He won't be able to speak for a while, but the message he'll deliver isn't about words.

———

Mercier takes the call around nine, some asshole at the club getting rough with one of the girls. Mr. Childs who teaches science at the high school. That fucking guy again, Letorneau says.

She only had two rules and I broke both of them, Mr. Childs says when Mercier gets him in the room. This should be a love story instead of what it is. I was that excited about the way things were going. She thought I was the funniest thing since, well, I can't think of what right now because I'm nervous in this setting.

We're just three men talking here, Mercier says.

Come on, Mike. The fucking police station.

Relax. Just tell us what happened.

Mr. Childs straightens his bow tie.

All right, he says. The place was packed but like it was just me and her all alone in there.

Go on.

So to answer your question, that's how we first met.

Love at first sight, Mercier says, sneaking a look at his partner.

And it wasn't just physical attraction either. Not on my part.

Oh no.

She had a beautiful mind.

Of course she did.

We really connected.

Examples. Letorneau coughs, shaking his head and trying not to smile.

You want examples. Like we talked about everything under the sun. For example, my shirt, this one that I'm still wearing right now. She thought it was silk but I told her it's actually a polyester blend. They do nice things with polyester now. Here, it feels just like silk. Go ahead.

Letorneau keeps his hands in his lap, doesn't want to touch the fucking shirt.

Don't be shy, Mr. Childs says. I don't bite.

Well, Mercier says, as he reaches out and rubs some fabric between his thumb and finger.

Innocent until proven guilty on that one, Mr. Childs says. I mean really.

She's got your tooth marks on her arm, Letorneau says.

Yeah, I suppose that particular piece of evidence is pretty damning. Mercier shakes his head.

But doesn't that feel nice, Mr. Childs says. Doesn't it feel like silk.

Sure it does. Now what else can you tell us.

And my keys. She asked about my keys. Wanted to know why I had so many and if I could move them to my back pocket so she wouldn't get poked. Occupational hazard, I guess.

And so that's it. What you talked about with this girl.

No, of course that's not all. I'm just giving you the examples that are fresh in my head. I asked her stuff about herself too. I understand that healthy relationships are about give and take.

Like what, Mercier says. What'd you ask her.

Letorneau stifles a laugh and Mr. Childs throws him a quick schoolteacher look.

I asked her, for example, how old she was.

Oh, Jesus, Letorneau says. I don't even want to know.

Was she one of your students, Mercier says. From the high school.

No, she was not.

Well, what else then.

I asked what she had planned for the weekend.

And.

She told me she was going to slow cook a corn beef for her godson's baptism on Sunday.

Fuck me, Letorneau says, laughing. I can't take much more of this shit.

What is this now, Mr. Childs says. What's funny. I don't see anything funny.

You silly fuck.

Mercier puts his hand up, telling Letorneau to back off.

All right, he says, looking at Mr. Childs. What's your point.

My point is that everything was going in a really good direction, Mr. Childs says. None of what happened was any kind of premeditated or anything like that. It was a thing of a passion.

Crazy about her.

That's right. My point is that I'm not the bad guy here.

Technically, Letorneau says, you are the bad guy here.

Well, that's right, Mr. Childs says. I guess technically I am.

So she told you about her rules, Mercier says.

That's right. No rough stuff and don't touch my privates, is what she said.

Letorneau laughs so hard he's afraid he'll piss himself.

You think that's funny, Mr. Childs says.

Go on, Mercier says. Ignore him.

You see my dilemma. I had to break the first rule in order to break the second one.

Sure you did.

But we were way past that stage as far as I'm concerned.

How long did you know this girl.

You mean specifically. Because like I said before, we were really connected.

Be specific.

Do you believe in love at first sight. It was like that. So I'm not sure how important that is in terms of the ways we normally measure time. Not sure how that'll help you in your investigation. Our investigation, really. In many ways I'm the victim here. Well. No. You're right. Not in that all-important way. What was your question.

How fucking long did you know her, Letorneau says, losing patience again.

Well. From the first time I went up to her until Nick and that fucking Hoyt came to get me and made me sit on the curb outside the club to wait for your guys, it was like three or four minutes. No more than five because we walked straight to the VIP area and her song hadn't even finished yet. So in terms of actual time, I knew her for a couple minutes or so. But if you've been listening to me at all you'll see that this is bigger than that and I've really known her my whole life. Or longer. Because she was the one. And I have to tell you—truth be told, all things considered, no regrets—better to have loved and lost or however that goes. That was no-holds-barred the best three minutes of my life. Now can I call my mother for a ride or what.

CHAPTER THIRTY-TWO

Ray behind the bar looks at Applejack. It's the Rod and Gun Club. Applejack tries to get his bearings. His ATV is outside in a ditch. Okay. Ray fills a glass with beer from the tap. There's a girl working the bar, too. Her name is Amber Lee or something. Lynyrd Skynyrd is on the jukebox. Rain falls into Lake Pruitt.

He's been on a real bender, the girl says.

Yeah, Ray says. I been hearing about that.

They talk about him like he can't hear every fucking word. It makes him laugh.

Drinking the county dry, Amber Lee says.

Knocking heads all over town.

Like he's counting the days.

I'm counting them, all right, Applejack thinks.

He sits there and minds his own business for the most part, but surely missing Suzanne something awful. Then it's dark and the girl tells him it's time to go. But he doesn't want to leave and so he breaks some furniture and whatnot until Ray eventually gets up the courage, comes around the bar with his sawcut nigger beater and he hits him square on the chin. Applejack had seen him coming and figured let the man have a story to tell if he wants. Ray puts everything into it and Applejack leaves his feet. The girl screams and Applejack laughs and Ray helps him up and walks him outside, apologizes, and sits Applejack against a tree in the wet grass and mud near the ditch where he flipped his ATV. He locks the door from the inside, and even though Ray's married Applejack thinks he's banging that girl in there, that's the big rush to get him out.

After a little while, Applejack rises and walks into the lake, past the shed where the fishermen stow their gear and the dock boats. Doesn't even remove his boots. They'll be out here before sunup, he thinks. Somebody'll find me. The water doesn't feel like anything to him. When it's over his head he dog paddles until he runs out of breath. His clothes and Dunhams weigh him down some. He thinks about dying and how it's going to feel. Underneath is warmer and thicker than he expected, and quick he touches the bottom, raising mud. He watches the waiting last forever and then it's over just like that.

His eyes go closed.

I'm no fucking shark, he thinks.

Then one comes to him like in a dream, flashing rows of razor-sharp teeth and getting closer, circling, the force of its roundabouts lifting Applejack to the surface.

He opens his eyes.

Not ready to die today.

Ray pushes on his chest while the girl standing behind him cries. His neck and shoulders hurt, his lungs are burning. Engine thirty-three brings volunteers, he recognizes one or two from the annual firemen's muster. He can smell their rubber coats and they do a fine job with him.

The chief writes down what Ray tells him about Applejack's behavior leading up to the event. Then they stuff him, bitching, thrashing about, into a white ambulance. I don't need this shit, he says. They strap his arms and legs to a gurney and give him oxygen through a plastic mask. It smells like medicine. He watches Ray and the girl and the Rod and Gun and the lake and his ATV in that goddamn ditch disappear through the little square window.

When he opens his eyes again he's in a hallway at the hospital next to a farmer with a kitchen knife handle protruding from his skull. The nurse has a Puerto Rican name and smells good like coconuts. He tells her so and she laughs. She wheels him to a room and hooks him up to wires and tapes needles with tubes onto him. There are machines and it's all very impressive. He wants a cigarillo in the worst way. The nurse asks him about his jaw and he had forgotten about that, about Ray coming at him with the damn stick. He laughs a little and tells her it's a separate incident from the alleged drowning. She shakes her head. They talk about rain after a few minutes of silence while she plugs him in. She says her mother once told her that rain was all of the angels in heaven crying at the same time. Why would they go and do that, he says. That gets to him, he doesn't know why, but he reaches out and she lets him hold her hand for a minute or two.

CHAPTER THIRTY-THREE

Two undercover troopers and a severe-looking woman in a navy-blue business suit come into Grandma's and so Applejack departs, thinking oh shit. He sits on a rock because he can't see straight and he closes his eyes and when he opens them Benoit is drinking a beer with him at the river. Benoit played fullback at Westfield State. That was before the service and way before the penitentiary. Applejack almost doesn't recognize him with his head shaved.

What the fuck, Applejack says.

It's hot and some other yahoos are down there, too. They're mostly watching kids jump from the bridge. Benoit takes off his T-shirt and he has not gone soft at all. He has the brand of a notorious bike club inked on his right bicep. There are a couple townie girls he's rapping to and Applejack listens to him run his game for a while. He hasn't lost his edge. They smoke a little reefer that somebody is sharing around. It's pretty green. The McNulty brothers pass with their thick-shouldered dogs and they come back to shake Applejack's hand and shoot the shit.

You still slugging hey, Benoit says after the McNulty brothers leave.

Yeah, Applejack says. Sometimes.

Not like back in the day though.

No, Applejack says. Nothing ever is.

The townie girls disappear and Benoit asks Applejack more specifically about the fights, the blackouts he's heard about through the grapevine. Heard you had a little stroke or some shit, he says, genuinely concerned.

Applejack laughs and denies it and assures his old friend that he's fine.

That's good to know, Benoit says.

I can still bring it when I need to.

Shit, Benoit says. I used to get down back in the day, you might recall.

It was true. Benoit broke some serious bones in the 1970s.

It can get plenty rough down there by the river with everybody trying to beat the heat. Too many opposites in one place: the Sugarloaf Boys and Main Street and Turners Falls. Lots of posturing, but Applejack just sits back and watches. Benoit talks about his job folding towels at the Greenfield YMCA. It isn't much but keeps him out of trouble.

Applejack walks over to the package store to get more beer and a bottle. John John Bartos is wearing a wife-beater. He was a badass once too, but now he's gone spiritual. There's a picture of Jesus on John John's abdomen that he likes to show off. It isn't bad for an amateur job. He drinks with Applejack and Benoit for a little while and they talk about all the sweet meat out on the riverbank. He's happy to reflect on old times with people who had been there.

Benoit likes to rib John John about finding God but only when it's convenient.

You know why Jesus'll never come to Mill Town, he ribs.

Why's that smartass.

No wise men and for sure no virgins.

John John doesn't see the humor but Benoit laughs just the same.

Tina comes by. She is sure poison and liable to get somebody stabbed. Her shoulders are sunburned. Applejack can smell how horny she is. The four of them end up at John John's apartment and then they each take turns with her on the couch with the others right there and a porn flick on the video player. She cries afterward and says she feels like a whore and Benoit laughs. Applejack tells her she isn't a true whore because they aren't going to pay her. John John zips his fly and tells her not to worry because she couldn't sell that ass if she wanted. She goes from sad to angry and she throws a porcelain statue of the Virgin Mary at Applejack and it breaks into pieces on the floor.

Applejack is naked, his clothes torn from his body during this combat, and from a crouching position he springs at the man they call Bear. Bear rears up and overpowers him, but he manages to come back with a quick locking of his jaws on Bear's neck. Black fluid flows from Bear's throat. The mad crowd cheers wildly and yells out wagers, splattered with urine and saliva and blood. Applejack holds on with all his might. The men flail back and forth, relentless, neither willing to accept defeat. Then Applejack shifts his position and bites the larger man's ear and pulls it from his head and spits it out like a stale apricot. It bounces and comes to rest on the pavement. He brings his knee up and connects with something soft and he does it several times until Bear finally collapses.

Applejack falls on top of his opponent. Then he chews on the man's other ear but without much conviction. Bear doesn't move. Applejack can hear the low roar of a hundred hands clapping. He closes his eyes and takes a deep breath, feels his bowels shifting, slips further into the abyss.

CHAPTER THIRTY-FOUR

They had to cut through a cornfield and hop a fence to get to the river. Applejack and Nick are in inner tubes, floating near Red Rock Crossing. Nick has a cooler in his lap. The ice has melted and most of the beer is gone. An empty inner tube floats between them. Hoyt lets out a Tarzan yell and cannonballs into the water from a rope swing tied to a tree along the bank. He clambers into his tube as Nick throws him a beer.

You guys coming to the ballet tonight, Nick says.

Fuck no, Applejack says.

We can take the limousine, Hoyt says. I got it for a thing tomorrow.

Who died now, Nick says.

Ask me if I care.

Or can even keep track, for that matter, Nick says.

Well, Applejack says, I'm supposed to stay away.

Lots of new talent, Nick says.

Whatever. Don't even try to sell me on it.

What the fuck, Nick says. Can't just go cold turkey.

Oh yes I can. You guys are holding me back.

Back from what.

Exactly, Hoyt says. And according to who.

According to fucking Jonesy, Applejack says. Plus, Stavros's pissed.

That you're leaving him.

Like a spurned lover.

Applejack laughs at that comment. Or my ex-wife, he says. Nah, he thinks I'm gone to flip. He cups water in his hand and brings it to his face. His buddy's worried I'm a rat, he says.

The shit from the hotel, Hoyt says. You mean the Selectman.

I'll select that motherfucker all right.

I hear the Staties are on top of all that now.

Like flies on shit.

We should all maybe take a step back.

Applejack nods his agreement.

Well shit, come by for one last hoorah then, Nick says.

We could hit the Westview first, Hoyt says. Scare up some of that college pussy.

Applejack shakes his head.

It ain't just pussy he needs, Nick says. It's strange pussy.

You boys ain't listening, Applejack says.

You got to get back on that horse sometime.

What horse is that now.

The one where you're the Lone Fucking Ranger.

And if a horse don't work, Nick says, you could try a pig or a cow.

Suzanne has been gone a few days, disappearing like she does, going on these little trips with Stavros. Excursions, she calls them. Applejack understands it's part of the deal they have, that it's only temporary. But that doesn't mean he has to like it.

Well, Applejack says. No way I'ma go to the club tonight.

Ah too bad, Hoyt says. Jill the Pill is dancing.

He looks at Nick when he says it.

I'd eat a mile of her shit just to see where it came from, Nick says.

Would you eat the corn niblets out of it too.

Yes, sir, I would.

Boy, Applejack coughs. She been serving you nothing but shit for ten years.

Nick flicks his mirrored shades down from the top of his head. Applejack's distorted face is reflected in them. Hoyt gulps his beer. The prominent knot in his throat moves up and down, sharp barbs of hair around it like metal shavings on a magnet.

CHAPTER THIRTY-FIVE

There's a big storm coming, building out over the Atlantic Ocean, one hundred miles off the Massachusetts coast, where wind and water conspire to unmake things made so careful and strong by man. They get on television and radio and name it after a woman and say to get the hell out of the way. Weekend renters flee and homeowners bang ten-penny nails into four-by-eight sheets of plywood to cover bay windows and protect precious views of the same Mother Nature who would just as soon kick their asses and make them like it.

The hurricane swells in velocity and scope as it moves west, a whirling dervish whose wild dance topples longstanding remnants of Yankee ingenuity, folds in long barns and prefabricated log cabins like so many decks of cards, snaps hundred-year-old oaks like dry sticks, and rolls thousand-pound cows like toys booted across the floor by some twisted kid. Then the storm goes north and eases back on the throttle wind-wise, but cranks down rain like soggy curtains and every now and then throws it all sideways in sheets. Driving a car is impossible and traffic stops on 116, 91, and along Routes 5 and 10. There's a smell blown over the countryside like fresh-dug dirt and maple branches and something pungent, almost electrical. A wet chill cuts quick to the bone and the air doesn't feel like summertime anymore. It doesn't feel like much of anything.

Then the rain stops just like that.

A pink plume of fog stretches thick across the Franklin County sky like strawberry taffy. Suzanne is having car trouble again. She wishes she never even heard of the MGB. Some days she wishes she never heard of the man who owns it. Applejack smokes without using his hands and looks under the hood while she paces back and forth and checks her thin silver wristwatch, the one that fucking Stavros gave her.

I have to go, she says.

Not in this you're not.

What is it.

Coil wire is fried. He removes the wire and holds it up so she can see the burnt, frayed ends of it.

Shit, she says.

Come on.

I thought you had a thing.

I do, he says. But if we leave now I can still make it.

What about this piece of shit.

I'll look at it tomorrow, he says. No big deal. He's trying to avoid Stavros and the club, but what the hell. Best-laid plans and all that.

The ashes of his cigarillo stick out past his face and he lets them fall. Then he takes her to work on the ATV, across alfalfa fields and down firebreak roads, and on the proper street he runs a couple stop signs and she's a nervous wreck the whole time. Then they park in front of the club and she shoves her helmet into his gut.

I'll fucking walk next time, she says.

Come on, he says, laughing. It wasn't that bad.

Oh my God.

All right, he says. All right.

That's why you get stopped, she says. Driving like a fucking asshole.

All right, he says.

This won't work if you're fucking locked up.

What's that now, he says. What won't work.

Whatever it is we're trying to do here.

What exactly is it, he says, that we're trying to do.

Shit, I don't even know anymore. You tell me.

Far as I can tell, he says. What you're trying to do is give everybody a turn.

Be careful who you call black, Mister Kettle.

Applejack looks away from her and lets out a breath he'd been holding in.

This ain't the time or place, Suzanne says.

All right, he says. All right already.

Some of the other girls are standing by the door and calling out to Suzanne, teasing her about being late for her shift. The Greek will have your ass and that kind of shit. One busty little Oriental broad who picked Jaguar for her stage name winks at Applejack and flashes her goods. He smiles until Suzanne calls her a fucking cunt bitch. Applejack considers going back later so he can take the Jag for a test drive. Suzanne knows what he's thinking and grabs him between the legs and warns him against it.

You're an asshole hey, she says.

Ha.

She's got crabs, she says.

Applejack laughs at her insecurity and loves that she's jealous.

Serious, she says. Plus the thing with Stavros.

Okay, he says. I get it.

Please stay away from here or you'll be sorry.

Maybe I am already.

What.

Sorry.

She picks up her duffle and turns away from him and he leaves on two wheels.

———

Then he's sitting in the basement of an old refinery in the center of Turners Falls. There are twelve guys and Applejack recognizes a couple of them. Everybody kicks in twenty bucks and it's a winner-take-all type deal. The ring is just ten feet by ten feet so there is nowhere to hide or dance around like a faggot. Each bout lasts maybe five minutes. The only rule is when your opponent submits you have to stop and that is it.

Some six-foot-four farm boy challenges Applejack for the first fight. Applejack breaks his arm at the elbow in two minutes. Then he sits down and watches some skinny Polack versus Hollywood Johnny. At the end of the night it's Applejack against Bloody Knuckles for all the marbles. It lasts maybe ten minutes, which is like forever, and his lungs are burning. Then he splits Bloody Knuckles's nose open with a headbutt and the old-timer can't see through the mess. Applejack collects the purse and somebody hands out stolen towels.

CHAPTER THIRTY-SIX

Some hook-nosed bitch tries to steal a customer from Suzanne. He has become a regular of hers and everybody knows it. Comes in maybe twice a week and drops twenty or thirty bucks each time and never wants anything extra. One time he snapped his radish while she undressed but he's never touched her or tried. Suzanne doesn't know the nose girl's name, she's only been around a few weeks. I'll give her the benefit of the doubt, she thinks. Catches up with her in the makeup room. Gets in her face a little bit, just enough.

That one's mine, she says.

The girl rolls her shoulders back and sticks out her witch-dimpled chin.

Which one's what.

That one you were just with, she says. That one you won't be with again.

Fuck you say.

A couple other girls are in there changing and smoking. Bored, they perk up at the smell of violence.

Bitch, Suzanne says, I will knock you the fuck out.

The other girl backs up and turns her torso, elbow bent and fist cocked, like she's going to throw a punch, and then the Greek's guy Rodney whatever-the-fuck walks in. Suzanne and the other girl settle down at the sight of him.

What the fuck, he says.

Nobody else says anything.

I can hear you bitches all the way out there, he says.

Suzanne looks at him and fake smiles, adjusts her earrings, all innocent. Oh, don't worry, she says. It's nothing.

The hook-nosed bitch walks to her footlocker.

The other girls go about their business.

Come on, Rodney says to Suzanne. The Greek wants to see you.

Suzanne knocks on the door to Stavros's office. She can hear him closing out a phone call. It's fifteen minutes before her next three-song set and there's a good crowd for a Wednesday. A crew of excavators from Karl's unable to work in the rain has stopped in for a taste. Two-for-one lap dances on the half hour. It's a gold mine if you know how to work these guys the way she does. Come on Stavros, she thinks, hurry the fuck up. She checks her nails and snaps her gum.

Stavros sits in an old wooden chair on casters behind his desk. He's talking to his representative from the beer distributor in Athol about a better rate for Budweiser products, but it's going nowhere. There are three neat piles of cash and an adding machine with a ticker tape streaming out the back end and a green-shaded accountant's lamp with a short pull chain. There's some fine white dust on a *Car & Driver* magazine and a straw and a credit card. When he hears the soft knock on the door he opens the middle drawer and shoves the cash inside, wets his finger and dabs at the powder remnants, rubs it on the inside of his mouth across his gums. A huge wad of Kleenex shoved up his left nostril for a nosebleed. He ends the call by banging the rotary phone into its cradle repeatedly, and you motherfucker this and you motherfucker that. The vein in his temple throbs.

Yeah, Stavros says to the closed door. Who is it hey.

Suzanne turns the knob and pushes the door open a bit. Hey, Stavros, she says.

Look what the cat dragged in.

He always says stupid shit like that. She flashes the smile.

With his thick accent and same-same lines, Suzanne thinks, it's like this clown learned most of his fucking English from television shows and advertisements, radio jingles. She slides inside and closes the door, arches her back against its frame, brings one knee up. It's a considered pose Suzanne uses when she wants to make an impression.

That's a good look, she smartasses as she indicates the tissue jammed in his nose and hanging over his lip. He gives a weak laugh and removes the tissue. You wanted to see me, she says.

Yeah shit, he says. Come on in.

She steps forward.

Sit down, he says.

She sits.

All right, girl, he says. Here's the thing.

Fuck, Suzanne thinks. Here we go. She snaps her gum loud enough he blinks.

How long you been here with me now, he says. Dancing here.

Two months.

Two months already.

That's right. It was raining when you started me.

Fuck, it was raining cats and dogs. I remember it now, Stavros lies.

Spring showers. I didn't have an umbrella.

Stavros laughs, puts his feet up on the desk, hands behind his head. That's right, he says. You were all wet.

Yeah hey.

Like a stray pup you were.

They sit in silence for a minute or so, music from the club area.

So what's up, she says. Snap goes the gum.

Well, he says, things are better for you now.

True.

Your situation has improved.

You're my God and savior, she thinks, get to the fucking point.

All right, he says. So here's the thing.

Dramatic pause as he shifts in his seat, adjusts his balls.

Stavros tells her he wants to take her out of the lineup. Put her on the shelf, doesn't want to share her anymore. There's a trailer in Whitebirch where she can live rent free and he'll double her money and buy the best shit for her, jewelry and clothes, a car, and take her on nice vacations up north. They'll go on a date once a week, either Friday or Saturday, depending on his wife. Do an overnight thing at the Motel Six.

Suzanne doesn't exactly jump for joy, he notices, and he wonders what this two-bit fucking cunt is thinking, what she expects from life. This is about as good a deal as she'll ever get, he's certain.

She doesn't say anything at all. Chews her gum loudly. Applejack will fucking rip this guy's limbs off, is what she's thinking.

I know what you're thinking, he says.

How could you. Are you some kind of psychic hey.

He's no good for you anyhow.

Says you.

That one, Stavros says, he's probably no good for nobody no more.

What's that mean.

It means what it means.

Talking like that about your boy, Suzanne says. You got some history.

He was my boy one time, but I don't know where his head's at no more.

Right there where it always was.

Yeah, okay, but all those years of violence catches up to a man, Stavros says.

Is that right.

And I don't just mean about his proclivities.

That's a big word.

He's punch drunk and you know it.

He did it for you.

Bullshit. Maybe I paid him, but he would've done it anyhow.

Well.

So about what I said.

Well, she says, a girl should be able to make up her own mind about these things.

Don't you like our little trips we been taking.

Sure I do, Suzanne lies.

If you think he'll be a problem, he says, I got people take care of problems.

Yeah, she says. I been seeing those people come around.

Stavros looks away from her and whistles.

The kid with his mouth wired shut, she says, for instance.

He looks at her now. That wasn't even me, he says with a laugh.

Well I guess it doesn't matter.

Is it true love then.

What.

What you and him got going.

Jesus, Suzanne thinks, ignoring his question. I really didn't see this coming.

So, he finally says. What you think.

She doesn't know what to say—but now she wants to get the fuck out of Stavros's office, out of this fucking place. She wants to find Applejack and just get all the way gone from here forever. That's the plan but they just need a bit more time. Or maybe the clock is running out.

Let me sleep on it, she says.

Sleep on it, he says. All right hey.

That's a lot to think about, you know.

Sure, I understand, Stavros says. In the meantime I got another private for you, he says. Expose her to some nasty shit and make his deal look even sweeter, he figures.

Rodney smokes under broken clouds outside the club. There's a girl named Nancy he's waiting on. She needs a ride home and is taking for-fucking-ever. He misses Springfield, the action down there. He had learned boxing in the city and was known as an up-and-comer, fighting mostly Puerto Ricans and blacks at the Chestnut Street YMCA. He even went to Worcester once and did five rounds with Gerry Cooney. Almost five rounds. To this day Rodney will say that Cooney cheated him with a headbutt. The referee called the fight halfway through the fifth, saying he was going to bleed to death. Rodney got pissed and caught the referee with an uppercut and that was the end of his career in the ring.

Nobody would give him a shot after that. Promoters wouldn't touch him. They said that kind of controversy with a proven talent might be good advertising, but with a kid just learning the ropes it showed immaturity and unprofessionalism. So Rodney's mother's cousin got him work where his talents wouldn't be wasted. Too much standing around, though. Rodney needed fucking action. He was restless and earned a reputation as somebody who'd jump the gun in a situation. Nobody wanted to work with a guy like that. They said he was dangerous even to himself. So to get him off the streets the boss had him take a two-year hit for an arms deal went to shit. The hope was he'd learn some patience in the can. But what he learned is life's too short to fuck around. Now this. This one-horse town is fucking slow.

The back door opens and Nancy comes out with her duffle.

All set, Rodney says.

Yeah hey. Thanks for the ride.

All right, he says as they walk together to the car. But I got to make a stop first.

Whatever.

It'll just take a minute, he says.

He appreciates what Stavros is doing for him, he does, but the old man turns pussy sometimes, the way he handles things. Like with the stupid girl who took all the pills. Stavros said to get rid of the body, throw it in the river with the car. But Rodney figured cut her up and spread her all over Franklin County. That way nobody would find her, not like that they wouldn't, and nobody could hang it on them. And so that is what he did. It was messy business, though. When Stavros and the others came in and said to stop with the fucking chainsaw he didn't want to stop, and nobody'd step in close enough to try to stop him. He was making a signature move is how he saw it, like the sports announcer said about the shortstop, his signature move where he threw two dudes out and the whole fucking place went nuts with close-ups on faces and shit. But then pussy-ass Stavros embarrassed Rodney in front of the others, made him look stupid standing there when the saw just quit, out of gas, and the Greek whipping him with the telephone cord, having a change of heart. And then Applejack clobbering him with a monster haymaker out of nowhere. The Greek had untied the fucker and sicced him on Rodney like a Doberman.

Rodney feels robbed of his bold move and knows Stavros'll never give him his own thing to run. But the fucking guy is getting old. You never know with old people. Accidents happen all the fucking time. And so he left with a knot on his melon and the girl's mostly intact body wrapped in a bed sheet and the chainsaw in his trunk, because it was too late to turn back now and the others simply didn't have the stomach for it, and he finished what he started standing by a light pole on Claymore Road with his high beams going and nobody around he guessed, but didn't really give a fat rat's ass at that point.

PART TWO

"Dying changes everything."

— Stavros

CHAPTER THIRTY-SEVEN

Cemetery Cyn pedals her three-speed bicycle up Mountain Road. The old woman's only got one speed left as the rusted shifting mechanism long since refused to split the gear wheels. The stiff chain is another problem, and she lifts her ass from the seat for leverage, grunting with each push. Her black boots have no laces and their loose leather tongues flap like a pair of silent mad-panting dogs giving chase. And although it's summer, she's donning a heavy flannel dress and overcoat, timeworn and weather-beaten.

She rides these back roads during daylight hours because bored town boys in niggered-up cars delight in regaling her with harsh words and throwing frappés and eggs and brown apples and all manner of shit at her. So she's content to stay out of the way.

A glint of light off to the side there. Goddamn. She sees it again, something sparkly. Cemetery Cyn stops pedaling and brings the bicycle to a standstill and gets off, scans the cunt grass and cattails. A whippoorwill calls and she spots the nightjar on a branch among tree shadows, displaying black and gray mottled plumage, expanding its wing chord in preparation for flight. It signals again and the old woman sets her mouth and echoes its melancholy refrain as best she can and then the bird swoops down and captures a departing human soul and disappears like a dream, a slower and low-pitched version of its infectious song alive in the throats of an invisible flock. Cemetery Cyn has followed its fleeting trajectory with her eyes and now they get caught on something.

What you trying to show me, she says. Then on a slight rise the delicate foot of a girl turns up its toes from the brush, a thin gold band displayed upon the wrong-twisted ankle.

Mercier puts on the hazard lights and parks the cruiser alongside the graded shoulder. The trunk lid is bungeed down to keep Cemetery Cyn's bicycle from bouncing out. He turns off the ignition and pockets the keys and gets out of the car, realizing the old woman has fallen asleep in the passenger seat. He smiles and spits tobacco juice on the blacktop and unhooks the chord ends from the bottom part of the bumper, swings up the lid. He's careful with the bicycle, leaning it against the fender, and then he winds the bungee cords into a tight circle and places them back inside an orange plastic box. He closes the lid that's warm to the touch, puts his hands on his belt, sighs.

Shit, he says, and spits again.

He finds the disembodied leg pretty much where she said he would. Cemetery Cyn startles him when she appears like a shadow by his side.

Jesus, he says. You scared me.

Maybe there's other things you ought be more scared of.

So, he says, you didn't see nothing unusual.

She lets loose a throaty cackle and shakes her head like he's an idiot.

You mean besides this here, she says, indicating the leg that almost looks like it's from a tattered store mannequin.

Right, he says. I mean in terms of how it ended up way out here.

She shakes her head. Nope, she says, some spittle flying from her prune-skinned lower lip.

Mercier takes a knee to inspect the body part and the area around it, careful not to touch anything, looking for any kind of evidence. A cigarette butt or a gum wrapper. A footprint would sure be nice. Tire tracks like in the movies.

I'ma go now, Cemetery Cyn says.

Mercier stands up and faces her, extends his hand. Well, he says. Thanks for telling me, I guess.

Cemetery Cyn regards his hand until he puts it away and then she goes to get her bike. Mercier spits and watches her and he puts a finger in his ear and wiggles it around.

How many is that now, Cemetery Cyn says over shoulder.

How many what.

You know, she says. The pieces of that poor girl.

Shit, Mercier thinks, everybody knows. The talk of the fucking town. Well, why not. And he figures now is as good a time as any to call that pushy broad from the state.

CHAPTER THIRTY-EIGHT

Peanut's father and two brothers break Boy Country's leg with a four-way lug wrench and stuff him in a front-load dryer. He tells them what they want to know even though Applejack made him promise never to mention Stavros. So now they're surely gunning for the Greek, Rodney, and the Selectman. Boy Country spilling the beans will get back to Stavros and then he's going to want to set an example.

Applejack tries not to get mad about it. He tells Boy Country he has to get out of town though, for his own safety. Tells him he should go visit his aunty in fucking Sturbridge or wherever.

But look my leg, Boy Country says. Them boys wilder than fuck.

You would be too.

How I'ma get around now.

On crutches I guess.

You should've heard me, Boy Country says. Screaming like no tomorrow.

Might not be for some of us.

Don't say that.

Funny though.

What is.

A young girl working at a place like that.

Yeah. I know what you mean.

If they cared so damn much.

Oh, right. You mean like too little too late.

They like to cut her off when she was alive. Now she's dead and look. Why do folks do stuff backward like that.

I don't know, Applejack says. But we'll read about them soon enough.

They gone to settle up with Stavros. Called him the Greek nigger.

Shit. They might could do it, too.

But first they want Rodney and that other fuckwad.

Right, Applejack says. And I expect they'll come calling on me too.

Tim Kelly is eating a jelly donut from Hebert's when the flatbed pulls up and parks in front of the store. He recognizes the man behind the wheel and his two grown sons in the back—a rough bunch that hails from Bernardston. His understanding is they like to do things the old-fashioned way and don't have much need for the conveniences that modern technology can afford so he wonders what piece of equipment they want to rent. The string of rusty cowbells jangles when they open the front door and Tim wipes his hands on the front of his blue work pants, leaving white powder stains from the pastry.

Morning, he says.

Need a chipper.

What size job.

Normal size. Something I can tow maybe with a tractor.

Clearing some land are you.

Sure. Like that.

All right, Tim says. Let me show you what we got.

He shows him the Valby CH140, a machine for people who need a small, durable chipper. Roller bearings enable it to run at speeds up to one thousand RPMs under a load.

Built to last, Tim says.

Well, the man says. What's that one hey.

The 160 model.

Tim crosses the floor and the man follows him. This one can chip soft and hard woods, he says. Then he goes through his pitch even though he can tell the man is disinterested: it can produce uniform chips suitable for burning, landscaping, animal bedding, and mulch.

The man coughs and Tim stops talking. Something across the showroom has caught the man's eye. What's that, he says.

My personal favorite, Tim says. I call it Big Daddy.

The Valby CH260 has two sets of blades and an optional crusher screen. The solid construction of the rotor allows for trees up to ten and a quarter in diameter. The desired chip size is preset and determines how fast the trees are pulled into the machine.

Again, Tim says. Not knowing exactly what you're gone to tackle.

Let's take that one then.

All right. I'll get the paperwork started. Cash or credit.

This here'll be cash.

All right then.

What's the cleanup.

Just hose it down before you bring it back, Tim says.

Anybody ever fall in.

Tim looks up at the man. What, he says. You mean like a person.

Yeah. By accident.

Not that I know. But that would be a mess.

The man coughs.

Want me to show you how to run this thing, Tim says. Safely I mean.

Nah. I'll just learn her as I go.

MAY 22, 3:57 a.m.

The digital clock hanging over Pioneer Bank read four in the morning. The town police cruiser was parked and idling across the street from the Bloody Brook Bar. The rain had let up a bit. Neon beer signs were being turned off two and three at a time. It was way past the legal closing time but the Brook was well known around town for its after-hours parties, and some of its ragtag clientele were just now spilling out into South Main Street, staggering to various American-made cars and pickup trucks and Jap-made ATVs. Nobody seemed especially bothered by the fact that the cops were on the scene. Some folks even waved and called out friendly greetings. No problem driving drunk.

Chief Kevin Helbig, off duty, fumbled with his large ring of keys and looked up and saw the cruiser. He mumbled something under his breath and made his way toward his employee, walking as straight as possible. The driver-side window of the cruiser rolled down and there was Letorneau on a solo patrol, wearing a shit-eating grin.

The chief leaned against the car and looked up at the sky. Think the rain's gone to hurt the rhubarb, he said.

Letorneau laughed. Looks like it already did, he said. You want a ride home.

Nah, the chief said. I'm good—just down the road, you know.

All right, Letorneau said. Any luck in there tonight hey.

I need more than luck at this point.

Just a slow drizzle now. The chief slapped his hand on the roof of the car and turned around to cross the street. Suddenly an engine roared and

the limo sped through the intersection, barely missing the chief, splashing
him as it shot through a puddle. Sonofabitch, the chief said.

Letorneau adjusted the rearview so he could watch the car drifting
away.

One of Griswald's, the chief said. But who's that driving.

Probably that fucking lead foot, Bowers.

Looked like Stavros behind the wheel.

Jesus, the chief thought. What's that fucker up to now.

Both men watched the limousine fly past Holiday Pizza and Leo's TV
and Boron's Market, cross the train tracks just past Elder Lumber, and
pause at the stop sign at 5 and 10. The stop sign was hung upside down,
one screw winning a battle with young vandals. After barely hesitating,
the limo took off. Letorneau turned back to face the chief.

You all right.

Just a little wet is all.

Want me to get after him.

Fuck no, the chief said. I don't really want to know what he's up to.

He made an exaggerated display of checking the intersection for
any more oncoming traffic. Then he gave the thumbs up sign and went
toward his truck. Letorneau tapped the horn twice, put the cruiser in
gear, and slowly drove in the opposite direction.

CHAPTER THIRTY-NINE

Rodney doesn't hear the pickup. Or if he does he figures it's just somebody coming to enjoy the shaved beavers and why even bother turning around. When the tire iron makes contact with his skull there's a sharp crack like a Jim Rice home run at Fenway. His eyes roll back in his head and his three-quarters-smoked cigarette drops to the ground. Elroy and Cornfed grab him, toss him into the truck like an oversized sack of cement.

The ex-boxer wakes up, if you can call it that, in the back of the flatbed on a bumpy road. He's wrapped up in duct tape so he can hardly move and breathing is difficult. He has a worse headache than when he fought Gerry Cooney at the Centrum that one time. The back of his skull feels wet and warm. There's a lot of bouncing around, driving over potholes and whatnot, branches scraping against the side of the Ford. The truck comes to a stop and it's dark so he can't see, but he can smell somebody not too far away.

And he can hear him. Sounds like he's trying to sing a song but doesn't know the words. Then Rodney feels a tap on his forehead, maybe metal. Maybe the toe of a boot.

The god-awful attempt at singing stops.

Morning, sunshine.

Rodney doesn't recognize the voice, but it sounds like one of those backwoods types who fucks up a perfectly good evening in the club all the time. Fucking redneck motherfuckers, and why did Banana Nose send him to work for Stavros in Stillwater in the first fucking place. Yeah, he was born and raised in the area, but he would've preferred a gig in Springfield or even running a book in Holyoke.

A tap on his cheek this time. Definitely a boot. Smells like a boot with some cow shit stuck in its treads. He can't remember how he ended up here in the back of this truck and now he's beginning to get pissed off. And wouldn't he like to twist the leg that owns the boot. But he can't hold the anger because he's so goddamn tired. He shuts his eyes and goes back to sleep.

After drinking a bottle of whiskey and each man in turn pissing on their captive, and after their father on his knees waking the man up and putting words to what's going to happen to him next, Cornfed and Elroy shove Rodney into the rented wood chipper like they would a small tree or large shrub, except with the added bother of his flopping and twisting and humping, trying to get out of this fix. They stick him in feet first so to watch his face, his eyes big as plates. A discount silver mummy in duct tape. They barely hear him scream because of the tape and also the motor. The man at the rental place was right—it is a real mess. Elroy jumps up and down like a high school cheerleader and can't stop laughing. Then he starts to cry and the old man wonders is the fucker that drunk that he can't make up his mind anymore.

Suddenly, Elroy stops, a rundown devil toy. His arm comes up and he points.

Pa, look.

I'm looking.

But look. He got stuck.

Jiggle it.

Cornfed jiggles it.

Oh, there he go.

The motor whines and the revolutions of its gear wheel slow around some kind of thunderous groan and the machine almost stalls before Rodney goes all the way through. It's gagging on him like a dog with a splintered chicken bone. It stops, then catches and revs to full speed, and then he's gone. And that is that. Elroy's shoulders slump.

Shut her down.

Pa, look.

I see.

What a tub of guts he was.

Even with all them fake-ass muscles.

You smell that.

What is it, Pa.

That's death, boy. That's just what death smells like.

Then Cornfed gets sick on the tractor. Elroy laughs like everything's funny or maybe something horrible is coming his way and it's the best thing he can think of to do.

The old man rolls a joint and tells his boys to shut the fuck up and let him enjoy the moment in peace and quiet. He opens his mouth slow and wide and smoke pours out. He feels a little better, but it isn't settled completely in his mind yet, the whole thing. There is more work to do and he knows it so he can't really get logjammed with this one small victory. One down and two to go, he thinks. He watches his overgrown boys wrestle in the tall grass, headlocking each other and shoving dirt into one another's mouths. The energy of children trapped inside the bodies of men. These are sure throwbacks, the father thinks, dumb as a couple stumps but loyal as any daddy could want from his sons. Better than dogs, them boys. He spits on the ground at his feet and feels the hot sunshine pushing on him like the fevered heel of some massive hand.

CHAPTER FORTY

Mike's Westview Bar is packed with UMass students and locals. It's not hard to tell the difference. Applejack and Hoyt enter through a side door and head straight for the bar.

Jill and Cass are sitting at a table near the front door, drinking vodkas mixed with cranberry juice. They had met through Peanut in the spring, at the pharmacy, and Jill remembered that Cass had shown an interest in dancing, said she wanted to make some real money. So Jill got her an audition with Stavros tonight. It's the first fresh face she's bringing around since the shitshow with Peanut, different than running a retread like Honey through the meat grinder, and Jill is feeling off her game for certain.

The girls are just getting settled, sipping at straws, looking around, checking the crowd. With the jukebox cranking "Summer of '69" and all the coeds singing and laughing and shouting over each other, it's impossible to hold an actual civil conversation.

Frat boys chug pitchers of beer, townies shoot pool, and a chubby girl in a pink sorority sweatshirt retches in a plastic trashcan in the corner. A couple clean-cut jocks exchange looks with Jill and Cass, getting ready to move in. Jill notices Applejack and Hoyt standing at the bar. Oh shit, she says, using her drink to point them out.

What.

Jill brings her drink back in close and sips it through the straw. A couple guys, she says between sips. They do some things for Stavros.

Cass looks where Jill points and smiles when she sees Applejack even though she knows he won't be so pleased to see her. Not in this environment, not fixing to do what she's fixing to do. But that was her motivation all along, trying out this dancing naked business. Not so much the money but more to position herself in need of saving.

All she's ever wanted is for Applejack to rescue her.

Maybe they won't see us, Jill says.

Hoyt sees them at that very moment, of course, and he waves from the hip.

Fuck, Jill says. She puts her glass on the table and leans forward, wonders how this will go.

Cass can't stop smiling at Applejack. Oh yeah. I seen that one around town.

Jill makes a face and rolls her eyes. Have you now, she says.

Yeah.

Well, be careful, she says. He's on Stavros's shit list hey.

The college athletes finally get up their courage and make their way over to the table but before they can spit out an opening line Hoyt blocks their path, gets in their faces. Applejack lingers in the background, sipping at his bottle of Bud—maybe nonchalant, maybe with the eyes of a snake watching a mouse take its last few breaths.

Get lost, Hoyt says to the boys.

At first the young men consider a challenge, but then they really size up Hoyt and Applejack and decide against getting tangled with these grown-ass dudes over pussy—more fish in the sea and all that— so they ease back and disappear into the smoke.

Hoyt turns toward Jill and Cass. Young and dumb and full of cum, he sings.

The girls laugh.

So what brings you to this fine establishment, he says.

But wait, Jill says. How you know they ain't with us hey.

Those young boys there, Hoyt says. You'd have to strap a board to their ass.

The girls laugh and Jill flips Hoyt the bird in a good-natured way. Hoyt extends his hand to Cass, takes her fingers like they're at some fancy dance hall, and bows. I don't believe I've had the pleasure, he says.

Not yet you haven't, she says.

He trips over a little laugh and wonders did she mean what he thinks she meant.

Cassiopia or Cass, she says. That's my name.

Hoyt, Hoyt says. And this here is Applejack.

Yeah, Cass says. I seen him around hey.

Cass keeps Hoyt's hand but doesn't pull her eyes off Applejack. He's looking at her too. Jill senses something between Applejack and Cass, and maybe she's jealous.

This one strips with me at the club, she says to try and break that damn connection. We're just doing a little warmup here is all.

She glances at Applejack to gauge his reaction. As though he'd give two shits about that. But Jill is surprised to see a change in his face that makes her think twice, watches him take a good long pull from his beer. Then Jill looks at Cass.

Hoyt looks at Cass, too. What's a matter girl, he says. Cat got your tongue.

It's just so loud in here.

Well, Hoyt says. Come on then.

He jerks his head toward the front door. Cass looks at Jill and she shrugs her shoulders, nods. The girls stand and pick up their drinks and follow Applejack and Hoyt.

We'll make sure you get to work on time, Hoyt says.

Applejack rolls his eyes and gives Hoyt a hard look that lasts a couple steps. He's torn. He knows he should avoid the Castaway Lounge but Jesus Christ here they go.

He looks at Cass and she looks at him. What the fuck is this now, he thinks. He's got to talk to this girl. Talk some good sense into her when they get a minute alone.

Yeah hey, he says. We'll get you there all right.

Hoyt motions to the bartender that the foursome are taking their drinks and leaving the premises and the old fucker shakes head and smiles and licks his mustache, and sticks a finger in his mouth like to suck a dick. He laughs when he does it, spitting little bits of pickled egg onto the bar that he then wipes with a rag from over his shoulder.

Ten-foot hedges have been planted in lines and rows with corners and openings, and trimmed carefully to form a labyrinth at the north end of the University of Massachusetts campus. Over the years the maze has become a popular make-out spot for students and locals alike. The limousine is parked on the side of the road nearby. Loud music and laughter inside. A teenage couple emerges red-faced from the bushes looking grass-stained and untucked, holding hands. They see the black stretch car and hear the wild partying going on inside so they scurry in the other direction.

Hoyt sits in the driver's seat with Jill beside him. Applejack and Cass are in back. Empty bottles of beer, a half-empty jug of orange juice and a half-empty bottle of vodka on the seat between them. A handheld mirror and a razor blade.

They all raise their glasses in another toast.

And here's to naked women and free booze, Hoyt says.

Hear, hear.

Everybody takes a drink. Cass spills a little down her chin and

Applejack reaches over slowly and wipes at it with his thumb. She bites his thumb a bit, smiles at him. He pulls his hand away.

So listen, Jill says. Stavros'd be pissed if he knew we was drinking.

Oh right. The rules.

So it'd be nice if we could keep this quiet. You know.

Your secret's safe with us, Hoyt says. And then he looks over his shoulder. Right, Applejack.

Whatever, Applejack says.

Hoyt moves his hand across his lips like he's closing a zipper and turning a lock, and then he runs down his window and throws away an invisible key in dramatic fashion, really hamming it up. Then he runs up his window and whispers something into Jill's ear and she finishes what is left in her cup and slides closer to him. Her head disappears when she goes down on him and Cass notices what's happening up front and gets flustered, fidgets like she wants out of the car but stays put. Applejack looks out the window. In the distance, a lightning bolt rips the sky. After a minute Hoyt adjusts the rearview so he can catch the action in the backseat, see if Applejack is having fun too.

Y'all hear that, he says, faking what he imagines to be a Texas accent.

Jill is really slurping on him now.

Sounds like a cow pulling its foot out a the mud, Hoyt says.

Applejack shakes his head some more. What the Christ am I doing here, he thinks.

Hoyt sees in the rearview that nothing is going on between Applejack and Cass. He taps Jill's shoulder until she comes up for air, strings of saliva attaching her to him.

Come on, baby, Hoyt says. Let's you and me get lost in the maze.

Jill's out of breath but agrees with a nod of her head.

Leave these two chatterboxes alone, Hoyt says.

Jill looks into the backseat, wipes her mouth with the back of her hand.

Whatever, she says. Just don't make us late or Stavros'll go apeshit.

Hoyt chuckles and mumbles something about Stavros the Freak, fixes his pants, and reaches back and grabs the bottle of Ketel One and gets out of the car, holds the door for Jill.

Cass slumps in her seat, chews her thumbnail nervously for a second or two. She knows Applejack must be pissed. He's going to give it to her good now that they're alone. The lecture about she's just a kid and should leave grown-up shit alone.

Applejack clears his throat to break the silence. Don't worry, he says. I ain't mad.

Cass lets out a long breath. Why not, she says, unable to hide her disappointment. She wants him to have a stronger reaction, to blow up and even put hands on her.

Well, he says, I just never figured you for this life.

Really, she says. What kind of life you figured me for.

Applejack shakes his head. I don't know, he says. But not this one.

You don't make it look so bad.

Jesus, he says. Don't I though.

No, you don't.

And besides, he says. When were you gone to say something.

I knew you'd find out sooner or later.

Did you now.

Yeah hey. I know how people talk.

I guess that's right.

You're gone to let me do it then, she says. Let me dance over there at that place.

Applejack laughs and looks her in the eye and then he looks away. Dancing ain't the half of it, he says.

Well whichever you want to call it.

Well, he says. You're gone to do what you want anyhow.

Cass fake laughs and chews on the tip of her thumb. I'll do whatever you want, she says. Just tell me what you want. She puts her hand on his leg, hoping that's what he wants now.

Nah not that, he says.

But she keeps her hand where it is just in case.

I do want to get a little high though, he says after some amount of silence.

All right, then. Me too.

He digs a joint out of the right front pocket of his dungarees and they smoke it some, then tap their cups together and take a drink. Applejack looks through the window. In the darkness outside, Jill laughs hysterically, shrieks with pleasure. Applejack puts his forehead against the glass. Thunder in the near distance is getting closer.

There's another storm coming, he says. Tis the season, I guess.

Cass leans over and puts her head on Applejack's shoulder. She likes being with this strong man who is not pawing at her but better seems to give a shit what becomes of her. Down the road, you know. It's rare for her to spend time with any man like that. Applejack is still looking out the window and she follows his gaze, their heads touching, their breath fogging the glass.

He figures this could be a second chance for him. He wasn't able to save that Peanut, but maybe he can keep pretty young Cass out of harm's way. He has no intention of letting her dance for the Greek—a fucking audition or whatever they were calling it—or even letting her set foot inside the club. Not tonight or any other damn night. He feels a fresh-stoked fire in his belly about settling up with Stavros and that other sick twist. And maybe, just maybe, he can get to them before Peanut's people do.

MAY 22, 4:02 a.m.

Applejack was out cold, lying on his side on the bed, curled in the fetal position. His hands tied together behind his back with telephone wire and his feet bound with a lamp cord. The Selectman was fully clothed, his nose and both eyes badly swollen red and blue. He was going to have a couple nice shiners for a while. He held a wet, bunched-up towel to his face. Jill had fixed her makeup but still looked like a walk-off from a car wreck. She chewed her shirt collar, avoided looking at the Selectman. Drummed the table with her fingernails. They sat in chairs at the broken table that was upright again. The radio played Patsy Cline's "Crazy" and outside the rain and wind wailed like backup.

The Selectman poured two drinks. He always believed good strong whiskey helped any situation. Stavros tell you who I am, he said.

Jill took the drink he handed her, looked at him briefly, and shook her head. She looked away. She was not scared of him anymore.

Suffice to say, he said, you don't want to fuck with me.

Jill snorted. Suffice to say, she said, you're a sick fucking puppy.

She downed her drink. Applejack moaned and stretched his legs out. Jill and the Selectman both looked over at him.

You and your boy there, he said, I can make you both disappear. He snapped his fingers. Like that.

Jill snorted again and pointed at his nose. Aw, poor baby, she smartassed. That looks like it hurts.

The Selectman put his hand to his nose and winced. Fuck you, he said. And I need more ice.

Jill laughed. You don't really think I will get shit for you, she said. So he took the towel and left the room, making sure the door didn't close all the way. Jill rushed over to Applejack. He stirred but didn't open his eyes.

Applejack, she said, wake up hey.

He opened his eyes.

What the fuck, he said.

He struggled with the wire but it was no use, good and tight, cutting his circulation. He closed his eyes against the pain for a few seconds. His head hurt like hell.

I know, Jill said. Sorry I clocked you.

He opened his eyes and looked at her. All right, he said. Unfucking tie me then.

Not until you promise.

What the fuck. Promise what.

That guy's a fucking menace but Stavros's right about this. We got to clean it up.

Unfucking-tie me, Jill.

The Selectman came back into the room with more ice in his towel. He nodded at Applejack and Jill, closed the door and locked it, sliding the chain in place. Hey, hotshot, he said. You really did some damage hey.

Fuck you. Untie me.

Be nice, the Selectman said. The position you're in.

Oh yeah. What position is that.

Tied up.

Motherfucker.

I don't know, the Selectman said. Might want to watch what you say.
Really.

I was just trying to explain to your girlfriend here.

How important he is, Jill cut in. How he can make us disappear. She snapped her fingers. Like that.

Okay, smartass, the Selectman said. Let's keep this whole thing in perspective.

This should be good, Jill said.

She was just a whore and not even a good one at that.

Oh, that's fucking priceless.

There's always a price, baby.

Applejack struggled against his restraints, white-knuckled, red-faced.

Somebody better untie me, he said.

CHAPTER FORTY-ONE

The first shift is just getting started. Applejack drinks a beer and smokes a cigarillo, has a hard time watching a big-boned girl try to groove to "Don't Come Home A-Drinkin'." She's clumsy and uncomfortable, front and center, and it's no wonder she's not working later when the real dancers come on. But she has fake blond hair and a good attitude about the whole thing and Applejack gives her a couple bucks in between routines. When she finishes her three-song set she goes into the changing room and comes out in a new outfit and sits in the empty chair next to him. He ignores her and watches a black broad with huge tits and heels flop around. She scoots up the brass pole so her head is just about touching the ceiling, pauses to survey the room and try to make eye contact with some horny fuck, slides down and lands awkward and loud doing the splits. Applejack wonders where the Greek finds these goofy, uncoordinated girls willing to do some naked clown dancing on his stage.

Or where Jill finds them.

The fucking Greek's savage little headhunter.

You want company, the big-boned Polish girl says.

Applejack looks at her up close for the first time. She's pretty in a simple, country kind of way when not stomping boards and twisting her ass. Sure, he says.

What's your name.

They call me Applejack.

Applejack, she says. That's a kids' cereal.

He gets that a lot and he tells her as much. Stavros around hey, he says.

Nah I ain't seen him today.

Applejack decides he'll either pretend to mend fences with the Greek or bust his fucking chops straightaway as soon as he sees him. He doesn't know which yet. It all depends on how his old friend comes at him, this follow-up to that dress rehearsal for hell. He can sense the pills from earlier starting to really work now, what he calls the second wave. He can't stop his knees going up and down like windup legs on a doll. His heart bouncing around inside his ribcage. Perspiration building on his forehead. The girl recognizes his increasing agitation.

You all right, she says.

Yeah, he says. I'll be all right.

Well then, she says. You want to go back there with me. She nods her head toward the curtained stalls.

What for. Applejack plays stupid.

Oh, she says. Just about everything.

Everything hey.

Anything you want pretty much.

He pictures the scene back there. He smells past goings-on like old tree sap, can practically hear long-ago dick scuffings. She puts her hand in his lap. He ignores her, chugs his beer until it's gone, then gets up and leaves her sitting there all alone. Applejack goes outside and takes his ATV fast down Christian Lane and past Holy Ghost Cemetery. He's really flying now. He goes to the Tobacco Shed but they won't serve him because he nearly killed Tom Ford in there last year. He gets back on his four-wheeler and speeds past the used car lot and the Bucktown Inn and the church. He takes the back roads. Then he's at the sawmill looking through the hurricane fence at the river, dusk fog a curtain thrown over the world.

It's past midnight at Grandma's. They're sitting around bullshitting and playing chess. Grandma is on a tear, nobody can beat him. Hoyt is getting pissed because he doesn't like to lose. Applejack arrived after everybody else so he has some catching up to do. They're drinking Jack and smoking, and Nick has a plastic bag full of the Greek's coke.

Stavros set me up nice, he says.

Fuck Stavros.

Hoyt gets up from the table and calls Grandma a fucking communist motherfucker, always saying political shit like that now. He flips the chessboard off the table and sends the black and white pieces flying and Grandma laughs at him. Then Hoyt introduces Applejack to a man named Ian who sells tools out of his truck. Applejack had noticed him staring and figured he was a three-dollar bill and that doesn't trouble him much. He has nothing against the gays. He will set things straight if it comes down to that. Ian tries to stand up to shake Applejack's hand but he's too far gone. Hoyt says he got an early start. Ian has a silver flask that he doesn't share with anybody. It doesn't matter, they all drink something.

What we need is another Holocaust to finish the job, Ian says apropos to nothing, trying to get a rise out of somebody, anybody. Applejack knows the type.

Then Hoyt is singing Elvis Presley too loud and the lights are low and nobody is playing chess anymore and a couple girls from town stop over to party. Grandma is brooding because he wants to keep the streak alive and also because he gets nervous around females. The girls, Sherry and Peg, are wearing halter tops and short jean skirts and no panties. Nick shares his blow with them and Peg sits on Applejack's lap. She isn't good-looking, not even close, but she knows what she's doing and Applejack likes her tongue in his ear. Ian is still watching him closely and that makes the girl nervous. Applejack tells her not to worry, that Ian's just a pole chugger and he isn't interested in what she has to offer and she giggles. Ian wants to know what's funny and Applejack tells him to mind his own goddamn business. Then Peg gets up and grabs Sherry, and they thank Nick for the bump and leave. These girls have been around, can smell trouble from a mile away.

Ian tries to stand again but he's still too damn drunk to get his legs under him. He starts spouting crazy shit at Applejack from his seat.

Hoyt tries to warn Ian away but it seems his mind is made up. He has the intense but resigned look of some movie-made kamikaze pilot closing in on his target.

I heard about you, he says. Some kind of badass.

Grandma slaps his hand on the bar to try to snap Ian out of it. But there's no stopping him now, and the drunk looks up at Grandma and smiles wide and crooked.

He don't look so badass to me, he says.

Applejack long ago tired of the type of man who feels the need to challenge him as a measure of his own fortitude, so he can come away with a story for his buddies. A straight fight for money or over a personal beef is fine. But this other thing is bullshit.

Then Ian wants to know where Applejack is from. Not where he was born but where his parents are from. Grandparents. Trying to figure out a breeding line and if it's good or bad. Some kind of Arian Nation prick. Applejack has dealt with his kind before at Cedar Junction and other places, too. Tells him fuck off. He's a big blond-headed goon. Applejack advises Grandma to be more picky about the kind of people he serves. He stands up and cracks his neck side to side.

Hoyt sees that Applejack is getting pissed so he says fuck it and drags the stranger through the door by the armpits and puts boots to him in the street for a while. Not enough to do serious damage, though. Applejack thinks maybe he hears a couple ribs snap and his face looks pretty busted up. Ian tries to fight back at first but ends up curling pretty tight on his side, his left arm bent backwards at the elbow in a horror-show way.

There's a crowd at the fry house next door and nobody even bothers to look up. Applejack smells patties on their grill and deep-fried fish and chips. A Cadillac honks its horn and slows down, a concerned citizen perhaps, good for him. Then Grandma shoves Applejack, Hoyt, and Nick back inside, locks the door. Nick has white powder on the tip of his nose, paranoid that Ian might come back with a gun. He's not the only fucker owns a gun, Hoyt says. Outside Ian gets into a crouching stance and spits blood onto the street and eventually hoists himself up, staggers to his little red pickup and drives away. Applejack watches him go and wonders at how shit everywhere seems to be falling apart.

CHAPTER FORTY-TWO

Applejack wakes up in the dark, already fucking. It's not Suzanne. When he finishes he wipes himself off and looks at the girl in the light of the bulb that hangs from a wire in the bathroom. It's Alice from behind the bar at the Bloody Brook. She's a beautiful French Canadian girl. Even though he's a broken man his medicine is still strong, which he sees as maybe a blessing and maybe a curse. He gets dressed and she's sleeping again in her one-bedroom in the worst part of Mill Town. Not that there's a best part anymore.

Then Sam Chesla picks him up at six o'clock. Sam is an older guy, a friend of Applejack's father from back in the day. Truck full of tools and ductwork and leftovers from past construction projects. He honks the horn when Applejack is sitting in the reclining chair in the kitchen smoking one of Alice's cigarettes. There's a sheetrock job in Chesterfield, honest work. The man'll pay eight bucks on the hour. They get coffee and eggs at the pharmacy. Fat Mike smells like the public landfill. Sam covers the tab and agrees to let Applejack close his eyes in the half-ton pickup, but just for a minute.

Just for a minute, he says. We got a full day of work hey.

But when Applejack opens his eyes they're already driving home.

This was your last chance, Sam says. The sun is fading, Sunsick Mountain shoulders a blanket of mist. I don't know how anybody puts up with your shit no more.

Applejack looks at him, bored. Only half listens to the broken-record speech he's heard a million fucking times before. Sam parks the truck and looks at Applejack, even leans his reddening face toward him as though he has something really important to say.

Be careful what you say next, Applejack says like to draw a line in the dirt.

He waits for Sam to settle back in his seat, to calm down and get his mind right. Then he gets out and shuts the door, conscientious about it, almost polite.

Sam doesn't say anything else, knows better, but he puts the truck in drive and with one foot on the brake and the other on the gas he squeals its tires and fishtails. Applejack stands in the middle of the street and watches him drive away like that.

Mary is on the sofa drinking Maker's Mark through a red straw that bends. They go for a ride in his MGB like when they were kids and before there was the great space between them that quick fills with mean-ass every time they get close to each other. It's cold but they roll their windows down. He tells her he and Suzanne are leaving town together and she doesn't get mad. She even holds his hand. The radio plays songs they can sing together. She could always carry a tune and sometimes, some songs, just plain sing really nice. It's a moment they share. She sits against him with the bottle between her legs.

They kill it and go by Whitmore's for another. Rich Kellogg is in the back of the store bench-pressing three hundred and fifteen pounds, three forty-five-pound plates on each side of the bar. He bangs out ten reps before he realizes he has a couple customers.

Holy shit, he says when he sees Applejack and Mary. Blast from the past.

Mary laughs and Applejack closes his eyes.

Hours later he opens them and he's alone on the bank of the river under Stillwater Bridge. His bones shiver, rain falls, black water swirls around the chrome bumper of something familiar. The twisted guardrail and a strange green stain. Applejack tries to piece together in his mind what has happened here. He calls her name again and again and again. There's nothing. He tastes his own blood and something else, too. He follows the tire tracks from the road as skid marks and then down the bank and into the river itself, and he swims to where the car went nose down, its rear bumper just barely breaking the water. He ducks under and grabs hold of the roll bar and pulls until he is half inside the MGB, the British beater, his pride and joy. No sign of Mary. If she's not trapped inside the car he now worries she was flung. His head hurts so fucking bad. He swims to shore and kneels on the dark hard ground and asks the moon and stars to forgive this trespass. Then Mrs. Olzewski reports the skid marks and Mike Mercier arrests him.

Mary was with me, Applejack says from the backseat of the cruiser.

She's fine, Mercier says. You dropped her home.

Applejack sinks down, drops his face in his hands. Soaked to the bone, he shivers.

Jesus, he says. He rubs his temples and closes his eyes, opens them after a minute. Listen, he says. I know you got a job to do.

Mercier sees where this is going, has been down this road before.

But I'm really up against it right now, Applejack says. Trying to fly right and all.

So this is how you fly right then, Mercier says. Drunk driving cars into rivers.

Applejack lets out a long breath he'd been holding. Fuck me, he says. My head.

He explains to Mercier that he's leaving town for fucking good this time and the cop sure likes the way that sounds, to have this particular menace out of his hair.

There was property damage, Mercier says after some seconds.

What property.

Guardrails and whatnot.

Maybe I can work that stuff off. You know, before I cut.

And get your fucking car out of there. Call Fisher's or whatever to tow it.

All right. First thing.

You're lucky nobody got hurt, Mercier says. Just sleep it off in the tank tonight.

Jesus, Applejack says. I sure owe you one this time.

CHAPTER FORTY-THREE

After Mercier springs him, Applejack walks home and takes his ATV out so he can clear his mind. Past the Railroad Ridge there's a long stretch of road in front of him. It's straight and black and not a car in sight. He opens it up as much as he can and feels the four-wheeler shake beneath him. Wind feels good pushing against the skin of his face. He runs a picture in his head of himself on that ATV hitting a tree stump and then his broken body careening hundreds of feet in the air, cartwheeling, landing boneless in an empty field. It bothers him but not enough to ease up on the throttle, and the next mile brings another version where he takes a face plant on the blacktop and leaves a human stain the length of a football field and the rig follows him, end over end, until it catches fire.

Then he smells gasoline and he stops on the shoulder of the road, pops the shell. Everything's hot to the touch but it appears to be a corroded fuel line. Goddamn shit, he thinks. Sits his ass down in the dirt.

You got a problem there, buddy, a voice says.

Applejack looks up to see an old farmer in an even older Willys pickup, stopped right there in the middle of the road, four bald tires straddling the dotted yellow line.

Yeah hey, Applejack says. Sprung a leak.

Gas line.

Yes, sir.

Need a lift anywheres.

No, I got it.

Well.

It shouldn't be a big deal.

The farmer chews on his thumb and looks from Applejack to his four-wheeler.

There's a station up the road, the farmer says. Maybe they could help.

Nah I should be all right but thanks just the same.

You could throw it in back, the farmer says. Get out of this heat for a spell.

Applejack could use some shade. Well, he says. Hell's bells.

Let it cool down some before you get to tinkering.

You know what.

Come on then. Got a ramp back there for my mower.

There are sheets of plywood in the bed of the pickup and Applejack and the farmer make the ramp and together push the ATV up into the back of the Willys. The farmer chews a cigar the entire time. When they're done Applejack catches him looking at his trembling hand so he jams it in his pocket. You said there's a station, he says.

Yeah hey.

They got us a cold beer or two up there.

Maybe so.

Where we at anyhow.

Southfork, the farmer says. That's what they call this place.

Applejack can tell that the old farmer likes his drink too. He has that pincushion nose. His name is Roy. The radio is busted and he hasn't much to say but that's all right. They take a couple left-hand turns and there's a rusted Texaco sign swinging from a chain. They pull in and Roy gets out and nods at a thin young boy at the pumps. Applejack follows the old farmer inside and it smells like rubber and grease and gasoline and hand goop. There's a live bait machine and Roy kicks it open and inside loose bottles of beer stand among the small cartons of night crawlers. He bites the cap off one and hands it to Applejack and then he bites the cap off another and takes a good long pull.

Ahhhh, the old farmer says.

That hits the spot.

Yes, sir.

This your place.

Nah, the old farmer says. My brother's.

Oh, all right.

That's his boy out there too, he says. But he's got some issues.

Don't we all, Applejack says.

He looks outside and watches the strange boy chase a fruit fly or something. Roy gets two more beers. Applejack keeps watching the boy. Roy keeps on talking.

Deaf and dumb, the old farmer says.

No shit.

A two-time loser or twice blessed, the farmer says. I never know which.

The farmer laughs when he says it but Applejack can tell he's got love for the kid. He looks at Roy and also laughs to be polite, takes a sip of his beer. Roy calls out loudly to the boy. Stomps his feet and waves his arms when it's clear the boy can't hear him. The boy does look up after a while.

Hey, Pudge, Roy says, waving. Come on in here, boy.

Pudge, Applejack says.

That's what they call him, the old farmer says.

Applejack takes a tug from his bottle.

The boy gives up on chasing bugs and comes inside. Roy tosses his hair.

This here is my new friend, Roy says.

The boy reads his lips and looks at Applejack.

What's your name, new friend, Roy says.

Jackson Woods, Applejack says. They call me Applejack.

The farmer raises an eyebrow when he hears the last name. Ah, Woods, he says. Then you're kin to them DuBois by the river.

Applejack doesn't say anything, knows the weight his name carries. His lineage is well known in this county. Generation after generation of fuck-ups and ne'er-do-wells.

So is that your clan.

Applejack looks him in the eye, yet enough answer for any man. Roy averts his gaze and shakes his head and allows himself a little chuckle. Applejack starts to smile.

All right, the old farmer says, turning back to the kid. This here's Applejack.

The boy looks at his feet and Applejack feels bad for him. Nice to meet you, he says.

Roy lets Pudge go back outside and then they finish their beers. Applejack asks about the tools and any spare parts, and the old farmer shows him where his brother keeps them all locked up but lucky enough he has a key. There is an old Studebaker in the garage, jacked up and missing a wheel, so they roll his four-wheeler into a shady spot under a maple tree so he can mess with that fuel line, get it right for the long road home.

Roy watches him for a few minutes with the boy by his side. Shit, the old farmer says. I got to get now.

Applejack looks up at him.

You under control, Roy says.

Yeah, sure.

Okay then.

Thanks for the beers and everything.

All right then.

What about them tools.

Lock them up when you go.

And the shop.

Pudge'll stay right here.

Okay then.

He'll watch over it.

And I mean he's okay by himself.

As okay as he is when he's not. Roy laughs.

All right then.

I'll see you when I see you.

The old farmer leaves.

Applejack takes his time because it's so hot and his head is pounding. He gets another beer from the bait machine and figures that's not going to be a problem. Roy won't give a shit. He leaves a few bucks folded up in there just in case. Pudge wanders around the perimeter but doesn't ever get close to Applejack. It's a game to him.

Come on, Applejack says. I won't bite you.

The boy stops in his tracks and stands stock still until Applejack looks away. Applejack laughs and the kid smiles.

All right, Applejack says. I'll leave you be.

He finishes up on the ATV and rides it around the gravel driveway and up the road just a bit to test the fuel line out, check for leaks. Everything seems to be in working order now. He gets it up on two wheels, hollers for show. Then he puts away the tools and locks them up and puts his empties in the trash. Over by the sink, as he's washing his hands with pink goop and tap water, Pudge pats him on the arm and it surprises him, that the boy sneaked up on him so close and also the softness of his touch, like a butterfly landing. The boy has something in his hand and he gestures for Applejack to take it.

What you got there, Applejack says. He dries his hands on the front of his pants.

It's a folded-up page from a dime-store magazine, a cartoon cowboy roping a steer in an enclosed pen. Hot dust blowing from the bull's nostrils. The boy points at Applejack. He laughs and tries to give it back but Pudge won't take it, flat-out refuses.

Boy, I'm no poke, Applejack says. That's not me by a long shot.

Pudge runs and hides. Applejack puts the paper in his back pocket and rides off.

Armpits and forty-weight motor oil, a sour stench. Peanut's father is perched on the edge of the bed when Applejack opens the door to his room, and her brothers pass a bottle of Jack back and forth. The old man looks at Applejack and points a finger at the picture of Elvis on the wall.

The fucking king, he says.

Yeah.

He really was that fucking guy.

Yeah, he was good.

A pickle smoocher, how he danced, though.

Right. Elvis the Pelvis they called him.

But he was great.

Blue Suede Shoes, Jail House Rock.

Love Me Tender.

Applejack stands in the doorway and considers hightailing, knowing these men are here to visit a shitstorm upon him. He's never been a runner but this day is maybe a good one to start. He could sure beat them down the hall, down the stairs, to the street.

Then what.

Problem with running is at some point you have to stop.

Fuck me, he thinks.

Peanut's father regards the poster for another moment or two.

Well anyhow, he says. Close the fucking door a minute.

Applejack closes the door.

You were there.

I was there.

And let them do what they did.

Wished I didn't.

I know, the old man says. I know about you.

I seen what you done to Boy Country's leg.

Yeah, well, he got off easy, too. Peanut's father coughs into the inside of his elbow. We're gone to really settle up with that Greek nigger, he says.

Get in line.

The old man takes the Jack from the knuckleheads and puts it in Applejack's hand. Applejack tugs at the last little bit of whiskey, considers smashing the bottle against the wall and using the jagged neck as a weapon, open up the big one to his left and then stick it in the other dude's jugular. Square off with the ropey old man while his sons bleed out.

He pictures it going down that way, plays it out in his mind.

But instead he lowers the bottle to the floor and straightens up, hands at his side, relaxed.

All right, he thinks. I'll take my fucking medicine.

Cornfed makes the first move, slow bringing a big ham-handed haymaker that Applejack sees coming from a mile away but rather than duck or dodge it and use the attacker's clumsy momentum to his own advantage he absorbs the blow, leaning into it even, with the side of his head. However predictable, the boy is strong and it rattles Applejack, yet he remains on his feet. Elroy produces a length of metal pipe maybe eighteen inches or so that he whacks against the back of Applejack's legs. Fuck that hurts. Again there's an opportunity to counter but against all instincts he yields. And here comes Cornfed with a running-start uppercut, a primitive blow from the center of the earth that explodes through his fist. Every muscle and every fiber in his being fast-twitching and rippling in propulsive harmony. Applejack sure appreciates a shot such as that and his head snaps back like a ragdoll and his body falls limp. The boys go to town on him with steel toes and stomping his back with the thick rubber heels of their boots.

He waits it out.

Then they depart without using words. His head on carpet, Applejack one-eye watches them down the hall, barely lifting their feet off the floor, a silent, strange shuffling trio of ghost men. Downstairs at the Brook, Chink Stankowski is having a bachelor party and he's really whooping it up, sounds like. The music is too fucking loud.

A game of eight ball being played.

Somebody slams a shot glass on the bar and roars like a lion.

Applejack closes that one eye.

CHAPTER FORTY-FOUR

Hoyt thanks Stavros for helping him out of a jam. There's a court date set and he's going to clear it all up, some fucking thing with a warrant over past driving shit, so that it won't come back to haunt him. He promises as much. They're sitting in Stavros's office.

Stavros likes Hoyt, he really does, and wants to groom him so that he can someday evolve. That's what he says: evolve. Kid like you, a part-time driver and errand boy is a fucking waste. You give up that farming bullcrap and maybe help run the business a little bit someday. Now that Applejack is a turncoat piece of shit, Stavros says.

Out of loyalty to his friend, Hoyt feels uncomfortable even having this conversation. Applejack was once the heir apparent, or so it seemed to everybody.

And what about that Rodney, Hoyt says. Ain't that what he's about.

Well, Stavros says. To be honest I don't know where that fucker's at.

He wonders about Rodney, if he tired of this one-horse town and sneaked off to the city. It's got him worried. Feels like everything's slipping through his fingers lately.

All right, Stavros says after a minute or two.

Hoyt takes his cue and stands up.

So bring the car at around ten, Stavros says. She'll be out front.

All right.

Drive her there and stick around till she's done.

All right, Hoyt says. The usual.

And on the off chance that there are any complications.

Got it.

Can't be too careful these days, with all the whack jobs out there.

Hoyt likes working the private parties. Not just the extra money, but the opportunity to be around Suzanne. He doesn't have much of a chance with her—she's Applejack's girl and all—but stranger things have happened, and that's his frame of mind. Especially if the client is maybe a little rough on her and she needs a shoulder to cry on, he thinks. That kind of thing could really work out for him, not that he would ever betray Applejack in such a way. He wouldn't ever make a move on her, but if she were to put it out there, well, who could blame a man.

Stavros doesn't offer much information on the guy who called so Hoyt doesn't have a read on the setup yet, if he's some kind of weirdo or what. Usually the privates have some real quirks. Crazy motherfuckers.

Suzanne's waiting out front just like Stavros said, fighting off the bone chill with a ratty pea coat from the Army/Navy in Brattleboro. She'll ditch the outerwear before she meets the weirdo. Hoyt wishes she'd take it off for him right now. She's smoking, chatting with another girl. Hoyt guides the limo to the front door of the club.

He hits the button to run down the front passenger-side window.

Going my way, he jokes. An ex told him once that women like a sense of humor more than anything. Even dick size, but he's not buying it.

Suzanne looks up and sees him. She finishes whatever she's saying to the other pole dancer and gives her a big hug. I'd love to get caught in the middle of them four titties, Hoyt thinks. Every man's fantasy. He gets out and goes around to pop open the door for her but by the time he's made his way to her side of the car she's already sliding into the back. Pure queen bitch move, he thinks. She knew he was coming, his routine. What is up with this cunt. Pisses him off a little bit, but he isn't one to hold a grudge. It isn't his nature. He's already over it by the time he buckles up his seatbelt. Hoyt fixes the rearview mirror so he can make some eye contact with her.

Safety first, he says as he tests his own seatbelt.

Oh fuck, she says, dropping her hands in her lap. I forgot something. Then she fastens her seatbelt. I need rubbers, she says as she slumps in her seat. Or at least one.

Let's see what I got.

Hoyt snaps open the glove compartment and reaches in and feels around: three grape-flavored lollipops, various loose papers proving registration and insurance, a flathead screwdriver, a plastic packet of tissue paper, a book of matches advertising Rick's Pot Roast on Federal Street in Greenfield, and—bingo—two lambskin cock covers. He's been saving them for a rainy day but this favor could pay off for him.

He tosses them back to Suzanne. Your wish is my command, he says.

She mumbles thanks, puts them in her purse, settles the purse in her lap.

Suzanne unbuttons her coat partway and then buttons it up again.

Nervous, Hoyt says.

Let's just go.

Okay, fuck it if she doesn't want to talk to him. He fiddles with the radio dial. Kind of music you like, he says.

Suzanne slaps both hands down on her thighs.

Country, pop, easy listening, he suggests.

Just drive, she says. For fuck sake.

Oh my God, he thinks, this one is ice cold tonight.

He shifts into drive and checks oncoming traffic over his shoulder.

Suzanne lights a cigarette as Hoyt merges onto 5 and 10. Using controls on the center console, he runs her window down a crack so the car doesn't fill with smoke. Must be trouble in paradise with her and Applejack. She definitely needs to get screwed. That's just exactly what she needs tonight. He suddenly feels even better about the job, the service he provides. Everybody wins in this deal here—either getting paid or getting fucking laid. He thinks about what Stavros said, about him eating a bigger slice of the pie someday. Maybe be in charge. He sure likes the way that sounds. The radio's on reggae, Bob Marley or some shit. Hoyt taps fingers on the steering wheel and hums along.

The guy who answers the door looks normal enough. Maybe in his mid-thirties, skinny, prematurely bald, probably shy as hell so he has to pay for his pussy. Suzanne smiles and makes sure he can see Hoyt with the engine running behind her. Double-parked and hazards flashing. The guy says his name is John, which is really fucking original. Suzanne wants to laugh but she holds it in. He invites her inside and she says sure, what the hell.

Raindrops pelt the tin roof.

The trailer is small and clean and warm and barely furnished. A rental. This guy's not from around here, she thinks.

Candles are burning, guitar music on the boom box. John is treating this like a date. That's fine with Suzanne. Play along, give him the girlfriend experience. So far so good. She checks out his wall-hanging art scotch-taped to the wood paneling. Mostly black-and-white photographs of hungry-looking people, Puerto Ricans and Jamaicans and a few local boys she recognizes working in the fields she has driven past maybe a million times in her life. But she's never really looked at them, not like this. Each photo is dated and titled. *Picking Strawberries* and shit like that. She looks at him watching her and he's smiling now, and she notices he has a gold tooth, right there front and center.

Where'd you get these photos, Suzanne asks as she stares at his tooth. She wonders is it real gold or some phony shit.

I took them.

You took these pictures hey.

Um, yeah, that's what I do.

So you take pictures, she says. Like for a job.

Yeah.

You get paid good for that, she says. For taking these pictures like this.

Well, I do other stuff to pay the bills.

Oh, I see, she says. I guess I know how that is.

But yeah, he says. Hopefully someday.

Okay.

I'm trying to set something up with a gallery.

What you mean.

To show them to people.

Hang them up so everybody can see.

That's right.

Where would you do a thing like that.

Maybe Hamp or something.

Suzanne is impressed. And she wonders how much that gold tooth is worth.

I'm working on this other project just now, he says, that I can't really talk about.

Then why bring it up, Suzanne thinks but bites her tongue. That sounds cool, she says.

It's going to put me on the map.

Cool. You mind if I look some more.

No, he says. Go ahead.

She puts her purse on the floor and fixes loose strands of hair behind her ears. Checks out four or five pieces, one at a time and carefully, making small sounds with her tongue against the roof of her mouth. Stops at a close-up shot of an old brown woman with a toothless grin and deep lines in the baseball-glove skin of her face. Jesus, she says. This old woman's eyes are so fucking alive. I mean, that's the only way I can describe it.

This one is so fucking good, she says. Excuse my French.

Thanks.

Knowing, I mean. She's not really alive but look at her fucking eyes.

She's alive.

You know what I mean.

John inches closer to her and she notices, it's not her first rodeo after all, and she turns her hips toward his center, bends away from him with her hands on her knees, arches her back. Let him imagine what it'll be like, she figures. Give him a little taste.

How'd you do that, she says to the wall. Capture her eyes.

Suzanne can sense him go from staring at her ass to looking over her head at his own work.

Well, he says. You just got to be there when she opens them.

A pile of photographs on a foldout table in the kitchen catches Suzanne's attention. She stands straight and looks at John and he hesitates but shrugs his shoulders and nods at her like to say go ahead, take a look. Maybe ten shots, different angles but all the same subject matter, no people in these ones. And of course Suzanne recognizes the scene. The goddamn crop circles where she got abducted from. This must be some kind of a joke. She's so fucking tired of all the ribbing, drops the pictures on the tabletop.

What the fuck, she says.

You're the one, right, he says like a kid caught in that old cookie jar.

What one is that now.

Claiming flying saucers and whatnot.

Not claiming shit. I just told what happened.

But I want to shoot you out there.

Oh Jesus, she says. Is that what this is hey.

I could sell them. We could sell them.

Who would give a shit about that.

Magazines would, he says. Could put us both on the map.

I don't want to be on no map.

Oh, I guess you got your Oprah money.

Shit, boy. Not everything's about money.

Ah, so you'll do me nice for free then.

No. This thing here tonight *is* about money.

John breathes out and his shoulders slump.

So that's all this is then, Suzanne says. She picks up her purse and turns toward the door.

No, that's not all, John says. I want the other thing now too.

And you'll pay.

And I'll pay.

Enough of this horseshit, Suzanne thinks as she whips back around to face him. Her goal now is to ride him so raw he'll have to sit down to piss for a week. She wants to get down to business, steps right up to the sneaky little prick, so close she can smell him. A combination of Old Spice deodorant and the wine he'd been drinking all fucking day. Stares at that shiny tooth, pictures prying it out of his head with channel locks. She could sell it at the pawn shop in Bucktown.

Listen, she says. Forget about that other shit.

All right.

I have no fucking interest whatsoever.

John contorts his mouth in a funny, nervous way. Nods his head.

So just drop it.

All right, John says. He's got to get that three inches of flesh. Desperate for it now.

Stavros tell you how this works, Suzanne says.

Stavros.

From the club.

Oh, right, he says. The guy from the club.

So if you can give me the cash, she says, I'll deposit it downstairs with my man.

Of course.

He has money in his pocket. Wrinkled bills folded over once. She takes it from him and he opens the door so she can go and give it to Hoyt. She tells John or whatever the fuck not to go anywhere, to hold that thought. The limousine hasn't moved. The passenger-side window opens. She sticks her head inside. It smells like antacid medicine, the pink bottle in the cup holder is empty. An open packet of Rolaids on the seat.

Stomach acting up again, she says.

Just a bit, Hoyt says.

Something you ate.

Or somebody.

You're a fucking pig, she says. You know that, right.

He laughs but she doesn't so he catches himself. Nah, it's fucking ulcers, he says.

You're worse than Stavros now.

No shit, Hoyt agrees. He's happy to see her at least acting civil now.

Water with fresh lemon is good for that, she says.

Oh yeah, he says. I remember you told me.

She has homemade recipes for every kind of ailment, says she learned them from her mother. One of the cool things about this one, he thinks. Got some old-school in her and'll make a damn good wife someday.

Everything okay in there, Hoyt says.

Yeah, she says. Easy money. She gives him the cash.

He looks at it and slips it in his pocket. Okay, he says. But I'm right down here.

All right.

Just in case, he says.

Suzanne rolls her eyes at him, doesn't want to tell him about the pictures. These men, she thinks. Always trying to save the day.

John is waiting patiently just inside the doorway, hands in his pockets. He shuts and locks the door behind Suzanne, throwing the flimsy deadbolt, which she registers, and he asks her if she wants a glass of red wine. She considers but then shakes her head.

Red wine gives her a headache. Something a little stronger, maybe, she says.

He shrugs his shoulders, stands on a chair, looks in a cabinet above the fridge.

Some kind of whiskey, he says.

What kind.

Let's see, he says. Heaven Hill.

That'll do it.

He gets down the bottle of black bourbon and pours some into a glass with ice cubes.

She takes a sip. So, she says.

He looks at her over the top of his plastic cup, doesn't say anything.

Suzanne lets him hang there for a minute but then she saves him. So how you want to do this, she says.

He nearly chokes on his wine, tries to speak but has a coughing fit. She allows him to collect himself. He apologizes and she laughs it off and tells him not to worry.

Happens all the time. I mean, she says.

He looks at her.

What you like to do, she says.

Well, he says, and then he loses it again.

Jesus Christ, she thinks. This could go on all fucking night. Since there's a time consideration, she says, and I got other shit to do.

He gets it together and looks at her.

How about you let me take the lead for now, she says.

All right.

She puts her drink away and it feels good and warm going down her throat. John finishes what's left in his cup. She takes his hand and tells him to show her where the bedroom is. Coming on softly now, Suzanne is slipping into character. She practically glides with him down the hall. John sits on the edge of the mattress as she pulls the curtains closed.

CHAPTER FORTY-FIVE

Mary isn't happy to see him again. She tells him his damn dog died and she buried it out back past the well. Ah shit, he says. That was a good damn dog if I ever seen one. He gets his International from the barn where she's raising a pig that she named Oscar Meyer. It's full grown now, nearly two hundred pounds, and if the original plan was to butcher and consume it, well, Mary simply doesn't have the heart any longer. She follows Applejack around and asks about the bruises and scrapes on his face, more curious than concerned. She laughs and sticks the business end of a cigarette against his neck when his back is turned. He can tell she's still on the sauce and she's about the meanest drunk he has ever known. Oscar Meyer blows snot at him and Mary laughs some more and the truck fires up on the third try. He starts to ride off and without looking back he knows she's standing in the middle of the street, straddling the broken center line, giving her lungs a good workout. He knows every word of her usual rant and so he's glad he can't hear her. Applejack disregards speed limits for a mile to blow her the fuck out of his head.

Back at Grandma's the cross-dressing accountant puts his wig on the bar. Applejack stares at it. Mollie shoves drinks into him until he's thirsty again. It's just a matter of time. She lets him run up a tab that he's not sure he's good for anymore.

CHAPTER FORTY-SIX

Applejack is sitting on the couch. There's a bag of frozen peas set across the knuckles of his left hand. He holds it in place with his right. Suzanne stands in front of him, smoking a joint and swaying a bit to the jungle music coming from the Hot L across the street.

That's some music, he says.

You gone to tell me how you did that, she says, even though she knows exactly how he did it.

He lifts the bag of peas and inspects his knuckles. The swelling is going down.

I fell down the stairs, he says, chuckling.

She clicks her tongue and shakes her head at him. You're a terrible liar.

That used to be a compliment.

She holds the joint toward him until he sticks his chin out and she puts it on his bottom lip. Then she gets a two-thirds-empty bottle of Jack from the table that's cluttered with a full ashtray, a gossip magazine with dog-eared pages, and that photograph she liked so much of the old woman in the field, now in a picture frame. Suzanne took the shot from her trick as a sort of souvenir, left him sobbing in his miniature bathroom.

Want a drink, she says.

Applejack waves her over and she sits next to him and opens the bottle and takes a pull. The peas are melting, he says.

What.

The peas, he says. You might want to put them back.

He hands her the bag of peas that is starting to drip.

She cups her hands. Oh shit. I'll swap you some Jack Daniel's for them peas, she says, which he thinks is a fair trade indeed. He puts the bottle to his mouth and listens to her open and shut the freezer door.

Save some for me, she says when she plops back on the couch beside him.

Applejack gives over the bottle and leans in when he does it so he can smell her. He loves her scent: fruity and clean from the shampoos and soaps she uses. She's fresh out of the shower, too, wet hair clinging to her neck in ringlets, no makeup—perfect, just the way he likes her best. Her yellow T-shirt advertises Grant Elder Lumberyard. He caught just a glimpse of her white panties when she was standing in the doorway to the kitchenette, backdropped by the bad fluorescent lighting. The skin of her legs as smooth as polished wood. This girl is something else, he thinks. Jesus motherfucking Christ.

Jesus motherfucking Christ, he says.

She puts her head back and gargles Jack Daniel's, swallows it and looks at him.

What, she says.

You.

What about me.

Just you, he says.

Suzanne recognizes the look in his eyes—he's head over heels and so is she. It all happened sooner than she expected, but that is just fine with her. She recognized early on the power that she holds over men, calculated its advantages, and watched it get her into more than a small amount of trouble in the past. But this feels different to her somehow. Applejack is a different kind of man.

I showered for you, she says.

I know you did.

She swings her leg over his lap and straddles him, facing him, and she reaches down and puts his hands on her ass. He winces when she touches his sore fingers but he gets over it quick. There's a country western song pumping out of the Hot L now and she moves to it as she slowly lifts her shirt over her head, saying the lyrics softly.

You ain't woman enough to take my man.

God I love this one, Applejack thinks.

It'll be over my dead body, so get out while you can.

Her nipples are small and hard and pink as the erasers on the end of a pair of number two pencils and she presses them against his lips one at a time. She goes through a new routine she's perfecting for the club—it goes three minutes and some change.

Jesus Christ, he says again when she completes her practice set.

What's he got to do with it, she says.

Applejack laughs. Probably nothing at all.

No probablies about it, Suzanne says.

She smiles and they kiss for a long time. Then she gets up and stands him up too. He undresses while she watches, still careful with his left hand. Then she kneels and uses her mouth on him for a while. She knows it's his favorite. He closes his eyes and a pickup goes by with a motor he recognizes and a state police car siren wails and the smell of Wolfie's chickens. Piano music from another room, stopping and starting, maybe somebody taking lessons or practicing a new song. He doesn't know shit about that kind of thing but it sounds beautiful and he listens so he gets lost. Time has a way of slowing down when he's with her, it seems to him. Then he opens his eyes and guides her up by the shoulders until they're standing face to face again. Suzanne smiles and tells him come on, turns around, bends over the couch and puts him deep inside her, and they bump against each other like that for several minutes until they're both too tired to try anymore.

MAY 22, 4:02 a.m.

The limousine stopped at the flashing red on State Road.

Stavros was behind the wheel with Hoyt riding shotgun and Nick in the front middle seat with the bleach, trash bags, rags, and surgical gloves in his lap.

I called shotgun, Nick said. You're supposed to be riding bitch.

Stavros, Hoyt said, you almost ran over the chief about a mile back.

All I'm saying is fair is fair.

You gone to fill us in, Hoyt said, before we get there.

I'm always bitch, Nick said. And it's not fucking fair.

Stavros looked up at them, first at Nick and then Hoyt.

You two, he said. Shut the fuck up and let me think.

Hoyt slugged Nick in the arm and the smaller man tried to get his friend in a headlock, knocking the cleaning supplies to the floor on the passenger side. Stavros drilled a look at his pathetic crew again, wondered if he shot them both in the kneecaps would they still be playing grab-ass. Probably they would. He shook his head and sighed. He punched the gas pedal and the car lurched forward. An orange moon was high and full. The rain almost completely stopped. The limousine turned left onto Route 116, hit an oil-slicked patch, fishtailed, and then righted itself.

Fucking Rodney better be awake, Stavros thought to himself. I need that motherfucker like right fucking now.

Applejack was still tied up, propped against the wall at the head of the bed now. The Selectman and Jill still sat at the table. Stavros,

Hoyt, Nick, and Rodney stood around the bed. Everybody's attention on Stavros. Hoyt and Nick, wide-eyed, couldn't believe what they just heard, what went down in this room, and the shit they were all in because of it.

Bottom line, Stavros said, we got to clean this mess up.

Hate to sound like a broken record, the Selectman said, but I can't be here.

Stavros held up a hand. Wait, he said. I got an idea. He looked at Jill. Where's her car, he said. She has a car, right.

In the shop, she said. Down to Fisher's.

Stavros's idea was to stick the dead girl in her car, go over to Cheapside Bridge and run it down the bank, make it look good, like an accident. Disappearing a body is hard work, he explained. There will be a search and stones will get turned over, he said.

Instead, he suggested offering it up on a silver platter.

So that's the deal, Stavros said. She got drunk and drove off the road.

I like it, the Selectman said. Happens all the time.

Maybe smacked her head on the windshield. A real tragedy.

Genius. Nobody'll think twice.

Hoyt shrugged his shoulders and looked at Applejack and the Selectman grabbed his coat as though maybe he was going somewhere. As though his part in this was over.

Done deal.

Nick, Stavros said. You and her go clean the bathroom.

All right.

When you finish, he said. Take and dump all the shit in the reservoir.

Dump what shit now.

The towels and shower curtains and all that shit in there got soaked.

Jill started to protest but Stavros gave her a look. So she turned to Nick and he followed her, head down like a puppy dog, carrying the bleach, rags, garbage bags.

If somebody don't untie me, Applejack said, I swear to God.

Let's put this fucking guy in the car with her, the Selectman said, looking at Applejack as he adjusted the collar of his jacket. I see he's gone to be a pain in my ass.

Stavros gave the Selectman a look and then he turned to Applejack.

Listen, Stavros said. You think anybody counted on this shit. It's fucking terrible, but shit happens. This shit happened. Got to get with the game on the field right now.

This is no game.

But you saw the girl earlier. She was fucked up.

She had a seizure or some shit, the Selectman said, and banged her head.

Fucking tragic.

But I didn't kill her, the Selectman said.

We're all in this together, Stavros said. Like we always do.

This ain't like we always do.

Like I said before. You don't want the stink of this thing on you.

Turn the other cheek and all, the Selectman said like picking food from his teeth.

Applejack looked at the Selectman and wished for hands on him, boots on him.

That's right, the Selectman said. Stavros told me your sad fucking story.

You know he can help with that, Stavros said. All that shit.

Applejack looked at Stavros and then back at the Selectman.

Keep you out the Junction or wherever, the Selectman said.

That clean slate you been wanting, Stavros said. He knows the fucking judge.

Like this. The Selectman raised up his crossed fingers. Me and old Dan Swicker.

True fact, Stavros said.

But this gets out, the Selectman said. You're heading straight inside for a stretch.

This is some serious shit, Stavros said. A parole violation times ten.

Applejack swallows back the urge to roar.

This scheme you're cooking up, he said to Stavros. I help you then I'm out.

And then you're out, Stavros said. If that's really what you want.

Plus you got to keep your trap shut, the Selectman said. That's part of the deal.

It goes without saying.

Applejack looked at the Selectman.

And that other shit they got on me with the dope, he said. It just goes away.

Poof, the Selectman said. Like magic.

My swan song, Applejack said. Is what this is.

Whatever the fuck you want to call it.

Applejack looked around the room as though to weigh his options. All right, he thought. I'll go along with these fuckers for now. Get them to untie me. Roll with this thing until the moment is right to stick a screwdriver in the Selectman's ear canal.

Then he eyeballed Stavros.

All right, he said. Let's do it.

Stavros started to untie Applejack.

Rodney had been silent the whole time but he chose this moment to speak up.

Hold on, he said.

Stavros stopped untying Applejack.

I got a better idea, Rodney said. So as nobody finds her.

Stavros and everybody looked at Rodney.

What you mean, Stavros said. We just said we want them to find her.

They find her then maybe they find us, Rodney said. Don't you watch television.

All right so what then.

My way, Rodney said. They find the car but not the body.

But so they'll look for it.

Maybe, but they won't find it, Rodney said. Enjoying his moment center stage.

Why not, Hoyt said. Where will it be then.

A car in the river, Rodney said. The current might could take a body.

Take it where.

Who knows where it could end up. Stuck under a beaver hut. Or how many years would pass before they find it. Pieces of it.

No, Applejack said. Son of a bitch.

Stavros looked at Applejack.

Come on, Applejack said to him. Untie me now.

But Stavros looked away, figured best to leave him secured for now.

Rodney smiled and placed his gym bag on the floor. An unnatural heft to it but at that point nobody was thinking chainsaw.

Daylight leaked into the room in thick shafts. Nick and Jill scrubbed down the carpet just outside the bathroom. A full trash bag behind them on the floor, the big kind like you'd use to collect autumn leaves. Stavros and the Selectman sat on the stripped bed.

Can we trust your boy, the Selectman said.

He's just headstrong.

If he's a problem, the Selectman said, he's your problem.

Stavros looked at the Selectman and shook his head.

Add him to the list then, he said.

A soft knock at the door. Everyone looked at Stavros. Nick and Jill stopped scrubbing. Stavros put his finger to his lips and hushed them all, moved toward the door.

Another knock and then a voice on the other side.

Stavros, the voice said. It's Donald. Everything okay in there.

Stavros mouthed the word shit and then turned to the closed door.

Donny Boy, he said. Yeah we just had us a little party hey.

That was some racket you had going in there earlier.

I apologize for that, Stavros said. And will make it right with you in a little minute.

All right then. Sorry to disturb.

CHAPTER FORTY-SEVEN

Marie serves Bob the Fag some French-fried potatoes and a chocolate frappé. The Selectman can't eat because his stomach is in knots. He's worried about loose ends, anything that will implicate him. Top of his mind is Applejack, that barbarian fuck on his high horse. Hawk Wilson enters Michelle's drunk and the Selectman tells him go to hell, curses him up and down for being a lousy bum his whole life. He comes around the counter and pushes Hawk into the street. Mike B. and everybody laughs at the show. Then the Selectman sells Dutch Sanders Junior a six-pack of Budweiser on the sly because it's Sunday. The rule is no booze-vending on the day of worship so he stocks up during the week, stores cases in the walk-in freezer and charges double out the back.

He tells Ozzy make a run to the town dump. The pickup is piled high with cardboard. Chet'll charge him two dollars at the landfill and they'll drink a nip together, discuss pheasants. Afterward the kid'll drive along the river and Ridge Runner will be washing himself, he'll look up and watch Ozzy pass, and he won't even wave or anything. The kid will drive straight home because his mother is making stuffed peppers. There is a rhythm and predictability to this life that the Selectman finds comforting.

And now all this shit getting dredged up is like a wrench in the works. Putting everything he knows, everything he has built up, in jeopardy.

And he won't take it lying down.

Letorneau and Mercier are on duty. The Selectman asks what they want. They order coffee and sit in the booth. Marie won't wait on them because they arrested her son for drunk driving again. His name is Chris and everybody calls him Squid and he ran over Bruce Bohonowitz outside the Polish Club on a Saturday night last month. Bruce split his head open and got it stitched up at Cooley Dick where he spent twenty-four hours. Squid is still locked up for it. Marie smokes a Winston and stands as far away from the cops as she can. The Selectman doesn't say anything but gives her a look. She's been with him longer than anybody so he grants her a certain amount of leeway.

He pours coffee for Letorneau and Mercier. Free coffee for cops and they'll look the other way for the little shit, that's always been the understanding.

The Selectman wonders what besides a warm beverage he can offer them so they'll keep the state police at bay, get them chasing shadows out there in the hills.

Then a man nobody knows walks in. He's tall and dirty with black hair and a black beard. He starts pouring salt from the saltshakers into a paper towel he gets from his backpack, very deliberate about the process, this minor pilfering. The Selectman comes around the counter and tells him to hit the fucking road. When the stranger looks up to respond he sees Bob the Fag and gets agitated. He says aloud to anybody that Bob picked him up in Northampton and tried to make homosexual with him. That's how he says it. Like he doesn't know how to put the words together in a proper way.

That man there, he says. He try to make his homosexual with me. With that funny accent, so everybody looks at Bob the Fag and laughs.

After a while Letorneau and Mercier get up and make the stranger leave.

Come on, pal, Mercier says. It's time to go.

Working on his potatoes, dragging them one by one through ketchup, Bob the Fag is angry and embarrassed. Mike B. and all the rest make comments and laugh at him. He sucks his frappé through a straw, his face red. For the longest time he had kept his shit on the down low, but one time several years ago Boho witnessed him pick up a hitchhiker and he followed them to the infamous rest area off Route 91 in Northampton. He reported back of course and that's how it got out that Bob was gay. Or at least it became official.

The Selectman grabs Bob by the arm, pulls him off his stool and to his feet, and tells him to watch himself. Then, losing his composure with all he's got on his plate, he lobs his fist at Bob's nose, a clumsy tap really, but just enough shoulder behind it.

Pole smoker, he says, shaking the sting off his knuckles. What'd I tell you.

Jesus, Bob says, his eyes watering up from the goofy punch.

What'd I say, the Selectman says. You say it back to me.

Watch it. You said watch it.

That shit don't fly around here.

You think I don't know that. Jesus that smarts.

Jesus can't help you, the Selectman says. Not with what you do.

Okay.

You keep that shit to yourself.

Right.

Now, the Selectman says, yanking him toward the back, I got a job for you.

What's that, Bob says, fingering the space between his eyes.

I want you to do something.

The Selectman snatches a fat black horse fly from the air, shakes it in his hand like a pair of dice, and sucks it into his mouth, swallowing it whole. Then he reaches behind the counter and produces a brown envelope and extends it to Bob the Fag.

Go over to the bank, he says. They're expecting you.

Bob flaps open the envelope and sees it's empty.

You mean money. They're gone to put some money in here.

Fuck you think at the bank.

All right.

He tells Bob there's somebody needs a reminder about things.

What things.

Just how things work around here. Who's running shit and whatnot.

Wait a minute now, Bob says. I'm no heavy.

Not you, the Selectman says. You fucking faggot.

I was gone to say.

Call that Sambuchino from God's Country or whatever they call it up there.

Oh, you mean the Northeast Kingdom.

Whatever the fuck, the Selectman says. You still got his number.

William's daddy and Honey park in Charlie Smiaroski's crop-circled cornfield, but only because they're horny and it's convenient, not like they're looking for some otherworldly place to fuck. He puts his guitar in the back. The Impala belongs to her uncle who's dying of a cancer inside his lungs. Honey leaves the radio on and there's a little yellow light from it. Hank Williams Jr. sings. They listen to that shit for a little while. The moon is milk in a cereal bowl, how William's daddy describes it, trying to think of some cool lyrics for a new song that'll just kill the ladies at the club. Then they drink from a bottle of gin. They kiss and she tells him take off his shirt. She's got on a wife-beater and a short black skirt. Her tits are soft and perfect, unblemished. He plays with them while she uses her hand on him and she's chewing on about an entire pack of bubblegum, and the smacking sound, along with her nonstop chatter, practically drives him fucking crazy.

There's lotion in the glove box, she says. It smells like bananas.

Oh, for Christ's sake.

Reminds me of the beach.

Uh huh.

We should do that one day, she says. Go to the beach together.

William's daddy just rolls his eyes and doesn't say shit.

My uncle smokes to ease the pain, she says as she works William's daddy's dick.

Then she snaps her gum, which pisses him off even more and wouldn't he like to reach in there and snatch that pink glob of shit out of its misery. Out of his misery. Dope gets him through his weakest moments, she says.

She goes on and on, and William's daddy thinks calm thoughts, closes his eyes.

They met back in November at the Castaway Lounge, which was one of his regular gigs and she'd pick up a shift here and there. Honey started dancing for money at Anthony's right out of school. She's just two years older than his son. William's daddy doesn't want Honey to strip anymore, but he still goes to the club to play his songs most Friday nights, and he still runs his game on any bitch who breathes. He tells everybody he saved her, but she's not so sure, especially now since she has been with William.

Uncle Junior gets his treatments in Boston, which is like a hundred miles away, Honey says in the silence that's become as much a part of their secret rides as William's daddy's blistered fingers wiggling around inside of her. My mother quit cigarettes and cries on the porch every single night after her double shift over to the VFW, she says. It's her only brother and she's taking it hard.

William's daddy grunts and rolls his eyes again. Blah, blah, blah.

Honey finally hushes the fuck up and William's daddy lectures her about blue balls once more and she helps him take off his pants. He watches her slip her skirt down her legs that are tan and smooth and strong from lifeguarding part time at the Greenfield Swimming Hole. No real hair on those posts, just little blond fuzzies.

When she removes her panties the car fills up with the smell of her. He puts his finger inside and she closes her eyes and smiles. William's daddy plays her down there for a while like he would strum his six-string and the sex funk gets even stronger.

Then the steering wheel is in the way so they climb into the backseat. William's daddy's guitar gets in the way as well, so he moves it up front. There are mosquitoes, but they don't bother him much. It's too humid to close the windows and on top of everything else now he can whiff rotting relish from the pickle shop across town.

Then they take a breather to fire up another joint from her uncle's stash that's in a tin Sucrets box. She tells William's daddy again that Uncle Junior is going to die. She cries. The doctors gave him six months. He's lost sixty pounds and his hair is falling out. He collects disability from the railroad where he was a welder for more than thirty years.

Jesus fucking Christ.

William's daddy doesn't understand why she's telling him all this. Why she thinks he gives two shits about her stupid fucking uncle. Why she thinks she's the only one with a motherfucking cross to bear. She doesn't mean anything to him. Not really. He's just killing time. He thinks Honey must know this to be true. He's been honest with her all along, well, for the most part. And she is his son's girl now, after all. He's just breaking her in is how he sees it. Doing young William a solid. But he repeats every last word she says to give the impression that he's listening. It's a little trick he learned long ago.

Chemo.

Remission.

False hope.

Then he doesn't have a rubber because that's like taking a shower with a raincoat on so she begs him to pull out in time. Please, she says. Not like before, she says. I'm not ready for no babies. Her clothes are on the floor all crumpled and whatnot. Her breath is hot in his ear. She whispers his name over and over as though she's testing out the sound of it. They pound against each other for several minutes until they're slick and slippery with sweat and all the other juice. The noise they make is swampy and the stink is musty and wild. Then William's daddy finishes inside her because it feels better that way and she won't look at him now. Honey is so mad that she cries. She doesn't want to talk anymore it seems, which is fine by him. So he gets dressed and smokes a Swisher Sweet outside and he grabs his guitar and picks a little bit, trying to remember the words to the new song he wrote. He leans against the hood of the Impala, waits for her to stop.

I like to drink too much, he sings to himself. And I love a woman's touch.

He laughs at his own lyrics. Honey cries.

Jesus.

Go on and fix yourself now, William's daddy says.

She blubbers some more for what seems like forever.

Hurry the fuck up, he says.

This girl is really testing his nerves. He's supposed to play a show at the Seven O's in like twenty goddamn minutes.

MAY 22, 6:27 a.m.

The lot behind Fisher's Garage was surrounded by a tall hurricane fence. Standing under a yellow droplight hanging from a busted piece in the chain-link, Applejack and Hoyt spoke with a man in a blue jumpsuit who looked just rousted out of bed. Hair this way and that, eyes big, not blinking. He handed them a set of keys, Hoyt gave him cash, and the old man pointed the droplight at a blue Ford Pinto parked among several other vehicles in various states of disrepair and neglect, some of them up on cement blocks. Applejack and Hoyt walked up on the Pinto that looked like it had been sledgehammered.

The sun was slung low behind a canopy of trees and the limousine's headlights illuminated the scene on Cheapside Bridge. Applejack and Hoyt leaned over the railing, looked at the water, passed a bottle of Boone's Farm back and forth. Hoyt put the bottle down. The bumper of Peanut's car jutted from the surface as it sank into the river.

Not exactly a proper burial, Hoyt said.

No, Applejack said. Not exactly.

The car disappeared. The water rippled silently.

We're not talking about the car now are we, Hoyt said.

No, we're not. He really went to town on that poor girl.

Jesus, did he ever. Hoyt spit over the railing.

Just a fucking kid hey, Applejack said. He closed his eyes and rested his forehead on the inside of his elbow.

You all right, Hoyt said.

No. I'm not.

Well, what now.

Now, Applejack said, that sick fuck got to pay for what he done.

Which sick fuck.

Ah, right, Applejack said. All three of them, then.

And you don't mean the cops.

No, Applejack said. There's some other things besides the cops.

And you don't mean tonight.

My grandpa always said comeuppance serves best cold.

The local cruiser moved slowly through the center of town. Mercier and Letorneau making their rounds, discussing life. Letorneau ran down the list of women in town he'd either already bedded or would like to hop on someday in the not-too-distant future.

Then there's the Redmond girl.

You mean Myron Redmond's kid.

They drove by the common, the market, the package store.

Nah, not yet, Letorneau said. Myron's girl is only like twelve.

Oh, you mean his brother Mitchell's kid.

I hear she can suck a basketball through fifty feet of fire hose.

Shit, Mercier said, rolling his eyes. I never heard tell of such a thing.

The grapevine don't reach your house out there on Hillside.

Shit, we barely get electricity.

They drove by the post office, the local insurance agent, and the funeral home.

Smoke rose from the twin chimneys at Griswald's. With a sweeping motion of his hand, Letorneau indicated the vaporous emanations of a human cremation in progress.

Firing up the grill tonight, Mercier said.

That's one barbecue I'd rather skip.

Keep poking Frank Pekarski's wife and you just might get an invite.

The fuck you talking about hey.

Ah, maybe the grapevine reaches farther than you think.

*In the lobby of Motel Six, Donald Tanner sat behind the front desk
and bit into a battered leg of fried chicken from the Sheli Deli. The
telephone went off. He licked his fingers, wiped them on his pants,
fumbled with a greasy hand for a grip on the receiver.*

*The door to room three was open and Melinda Tanner perched on
the edge of the bed talking to her husband at the front desk using a spare
phone she kept in her cart. The smashed-up phone was in her free hand.*

That was one hell of a party, she said.

She listened but he didn't say shit back to her.

*They took everything, she went on. Sheets, towels, blankets, the shower
curtain.*

*She paused and listened to some more nothing, rolled her eyes.
Whatever, she said. And, Jesus, the bleach—gone to have to air this room
a week.*

*She continued to survey the room. The broken table and glass, the
telephone wire in knots on the floor, the picture, pieces of the smashed-up
telephone all over the place, the hole in the wall, and chunks of plaster
shit embedded in the crusty shag carpet.*

Well, she said. Good he paid you extra 'cause they broke some stuff too.

She held up the damaged phone as though her husband could see it.

*Sometimes, she said, I wonder what kind of joint you got us
running here.*

*Melinda moved the receiver away from her head as Donald began
yelling at her. Eventually she went off and it was clear that in a shouting
contest Donald didn't stand much of a chance. When she finished her
tirade she slammed the phone down once and then twice for good measure
and then she took a deep breath and dropped with a labored grunt to one
knee so she could inspect the broken table lying on its side. Wondering*

whose fat ass fell on it. An angry wind slammed shut the door and she jumped out of her skin. Goddamn motherfucking shit, she said, pressing both hands to her chest.

CHAPTER FORTY-EIGHT

They call the man Six Heads because he sticks and moves so fast. He's much younger than Applejack. He's another one wants to go professional as a boxer in the worst way and almost had a deal with a promoter in New York City one time. But this here isn't boxing. Not by a long shot. So he took a wrong turn somewhere. Applejack tapes his hands, drinks some water. He takes the cigarillo out of his mouth and smashes it under his boot. Six Heads is stretching his ropey muscles. There are a couple dozen old boys watching now and Applejack is the underdog again, like always with these celebrity types come rolling through town. It's not important to him anymore how the fuckers perceive him—and in fact he quite likes the long odds. He wants to put enough cash in his pocket that he and Suzanne can break away. All he can think about now is getting a fresh start somewhere.

The band stops playing. Six Heads is waiting for Applejack in the center of the makeshift ring. Dust swirls from between the cracked slats of exposed walls. They don't have a referee or feel the need for eyes on the dirty shit. They touch knuckles and start.

Six Heads has real technique. It's pretty to watch and he can connect five punches to every one of Applejack's, that's how quick his hands are. He ducks and fades and leans toward Applejack and then away. He's the kind of boxer that Applejack always wanted to be when his father first started showing him the ropes. But the kid has no power, his lands don't even sting. That's Applejack's real weapon. He absorbs body shots for a few minutes. He lets the kid dance around. All he needs is one home run. He waits and waits and waits for the kid to tire. Pukes in a wooden bucket. He wipes his mouthpiece on the leg of his pants.

That old sugarhouse smells like the sweat dripping off the fighters. Six Heads has got some stamina. He can't sit still during the breaks he's so amped up. Applejack needs to finish this shit because he isn't going to last much longer. In the fifth minute the kid pokes one of his six heads exactly where he shouldn't and for a split second Applejack can see in his opponent's good eye that he recognizes his mistake. It's too fucking late. Applejack catches him with a right uppercut under the chin that lifts him off his feet. He's on Queer Street for sure.

Applejack stands over the kid as he tries to get up but his synapses are misfiring, which is what happens. People clap Applejack on the shoulders and chant his name. He only wants to get some fresh air and pocket his winnings. There's a six-pack of Budweiser and he drinks four cans while Hoyt takes care of everything. The bandleader carries Six Heads and lays him down in the trunk of a 1973 Malibu. The kid doesn't look good but it's an important life lesson. A migraine starts in Applejack's temples.

CHAPTER FORTY-NINE

The cloudless summer sky is a cobalt eyeball on Franklin County. William and some of his running buddies are riding down an old logging road toward Walker Pond in the back of a red rusted pickup truck, each boy with a jelly jar of hard cider in his hand; Jiminy Flowers has been known to steal gunnysacks of apples from Holly Farms, scrat them into pomage using a homemade hand press, and secretly ferment batches of the cloudy brew in his grandfather's basement. And so here he is, driving too fast, rebel-yelling, bombing down the narrow dirt path, jolting his passengers six inches up from their seats with every rut and rock hump he bangs over. William maintains a precarious perch in the bed atop one of the wheel wells; Phillipe Chagniot is across from him on the other and Squawky Powers has the spare tire. Steve Fydo sits shotgun with Jiminy up front. Hardwired for fun and still too young to understand about grave consequences or the concept of cause and effect as it relates to their adolescent bullshit, these young men are wide-eyed and alive, adrenaline-fueled, by the time Jiminy halts crooked alongside a lightning-felled white birch tree.

He kills the engine and looks at Fydo. Here's to the old gal, he says. He takes a tug of his cider, and Fydo drinks too. Shit, Jiminy says and makes a face at the liquid. Goddamn.

That'll make your babies born naked, Fydo says.

Rogue seeds and chunks of pulp float in the cider.

Jiminy laughs and takes the lid from the center console and twists it onto his half-full jar, rests it on the floorboard that's been patched with scraps of sheet metal. Fydo takes a final pull and caps his empty, and then he puts both his hands out the open window and flat upon the cool roof, and he pulls his large frame out of the cab that way with remarkable farmboy grace. Jiminy's door groans and creaks when he forces it open with his shoulder. He steps out of the truck into the dirt and slams it shut. Their three bony cohorts jump out the back, all knees and elbows and long limbs at odd angles, while Fydo pisses on a clump of windblown cattails and Jiminy lights himself a cigarette. The day is sunny and clear but cold, and William shivers against it, his hands in his pockets.

It's colder than a nun's cunt up here, he says.

A witch's tit, Squawky says, removing his cap and pushing his hair back.

Molasses in winter, Phillipe adds. On my granny's nipple.

William spits and laughs. Squawky replaces his cap, finishes his cider, and puts his jar on the bumper. Phillipe reaches into the bed and produces a gunmetal tackle box. He unsnaps the double hasps and lifts the lid, exposing a top tray holding a variety of fish hooks, bobbers, lines, and lures. Beneath are leaders and sinkers, a little glass container of salmon eggs, needle-nose pliers, a flashlight, a Swiss Army knife.

Go look if you can see her, he says, waving at the pond behind him.

All right.

I'll get this shit ready.

Turtle soup for dinner then, Jiminy says as he takes a puff.

Bullfrogs sing their fuck-me song around the perimeter of the pond.

Get me one of them bulls, Phillipe says. And we'll use him for bait.

Their holy purpose today is to catch the turtle that tried to snatch away old Miss Stahalek's puppy Pekingese at the beginning of summer when she was out here picking blackberries for a pie. Nearly gave the woman a fatal heart attack. If they don't kill the damn turtle their aim is to paint its shell OSHA orange so at least it can't sneak up on a little dog anymore.

William and Squawky approach the narrow footbridge that cuts the pond about in half. Boards are dry-rotted and hopelessly helter-skelter from its original piss-poor construction.

I'm telling you, Squawky says, whoever built this shit was drunk. He tests it with the steel toe of his boot.

You go on, William says. It won't hold the both of us.

Ah, Squawky says. You're just chicken shit.

I'll nab that frog like he said, William says.

Squawky proceeds slowly to the highest point of the arched passage and then snaps to attention with both hands in mock military salute to shield his eyes from the sun.

You see her, William says. Swimming round out there.

Nah. Can't hardly see shit.

The sun reflects on the surface of the pond. A family of brown-breasted mallards that had been dabbling in the shallows scatters, takes a short flight and then touches down on shore as William picks up a long dropstick with a gnarled head.

Don't worry, he says to the ducks. It's not for you.

Unconvinced, the ducks quack nervously and finally settle in the grass several feet away, the larger drake warning off the intruder with a series of quick bobs of his glossy green head and a high-pitched nasal portent. The mud at the edge of the pond is thick and black, and William moves around the perimeter, the rubber soles of his oversized work boots making small sucking sounds with each careful step. He listens for some throaty bitchings from the bullfrogs.

He hears a big one and then sees it nearly within reach, and so he stalks up on it with the stick over his shoulder, and when he is in range he brings down the branch two-handed, hard as he can, and the bullfrog dies with a popping sound. Its bloated yellow throat collapses in on itself like a pin-struck balloon. It'll never beckon another female.

William drops the stick and scoops up the dead frog in one hand.

Fuck you got, Squawky says from the bridge.

William holds it up, dripping mud and slime and frog piss down his forearm.

Good one.

It'll do. You see that old snapper.

No.

Just as Squawky speaks his answer a board gives out beneath his weight and his left leg punches through the dry rot and is submerged in muck and water to the knee.

Fuck me, he says as he struggles to pull himself out.

William laughs and watches him.

She's gone to nip off your toes, he bluffs. I see her now.

Squawky's head jerks around to see how close the monster is.

I can't feel my nuts, he says as he continues to wriggle.

Numbnuts then, William laughs.

Fydo and Jiminy are laughing too from over by the pickup, the radio playing now, dueling fiddles from "The Devil Went Down to Georgia" by the Charlie Daniels Band. Phillipe looks up and smiles but remains focused on his task. Squawky gets his leg out of the hole and he pulls himself up by the handrail, makes his way to the end of the bridge and onto the dirt path, where he shakes his muddy boot and scrapes it against some brush. Squawky and William convene with the others at the truck.

Boy, Jiminy says to Squawky. What in the hell.

Fuck off then.

Give me that, Phillipe says, indicating the bullfrog.

William tosses it to him underhand and Phillipe catches and hefts the weight of the slick little corpse, then works a hook through the middle of its soft skull. The frog's legs stick straight out when he tugs on the line as though somebody had just run some electricity through its body. He swings the bull in a semicircle from his hip, like a legion priest with his incense-filled thurible over a dead man, chasing back old demons, splattering the other boys with flecks of algae and pond scum, and after three swings he lets go the frog and it arcs high and slow backdropped by the agate sky and it splashes down in the center of the pond. A red-and-white bobber perfectly centers in the disappearing ripples. The other end of the slackened line is wrapped around Phillipe's ballpeen wrist. He feels minor tugs as the bait settles deep among the undulating ditch grass and quillwort.

Now what, Squawky says.

Now we wait.

How long.

Squawky is not known for his patience. Phillipe gives him a look.

However fucking long it takes, he says.

He spits over his shoulder and lowers onto his haunches and looks out across the water. The others go to the back of the pickup and pass around whichever jelly jars have any cider left in them. They hoot and holler and carry on, smashing empties and wrestling and exchanging friendly blows, until Phillipe whistles at them. William gets to him first. The rest of the group, just behind, sees that the snapping turtle has taken the bait—the bobber is gone. They form a sort of bucket brigade with each grabbing hold of the fishing line and pulling. It cuts deep into the yellow-leathered flesh of their fingers and palms.

Fuck me, Jiminy says. She's a tough bitch all right.

Pull, boys, Phillipe says. Let's get her on land.

Resolute, the boys tug and struggle hand over hand until the bobber breaks the surface and then the head of the snapper appears and the beaklike jaw opens and then the carbuncled carapace is fully exposed. Out of the water finally, it's a beautiful and belligerent beast, hissing, pulling back against the boys' best efforts with its telescoping neck, raking at the dark earth with its sharp claws, releasing a musky odor from behind its thick rear legs. We've got her, William says. Somebody grab the paint. Fydo lets loose and runs to the truck for the spray can. And then the line breaks, the boys fall back on their asses and each other, and the turtle reverses into the pond with the hook still lodged in its lip and six inches of line attached to the bobber that floats ten feet out and vanishes.

We had her, William says.

Nah, we didn't have shit, Phillipe says. Motherfuck.

Should of grabbed her.

She was right there.

Fydo shakes the can and the little balls within clack around.

Phillipe lets drop the line and kicks at the mud with the toe of his boot. He wanted that turtle more than anybody. Fydo suggests coming back with a shotgun and tracing it with the bobber, blasting the fucker to kingdom come, but Phillipe shakes his head. Another day, he says. The boys load their shit and get back in the pickup and Jiminy cranks the engine over after a few tries. The smell of gasoline pooling in the carburetor. The truck serpentines as he pulls away from the pond.

Dusk settles on the little valley, that strange time of day when the moon and the sun are in the sky at the same time, broad brushstrokes of orange and blue. And not more than a mile down the road, where it forks off toward either the river in one direction or Mount Leverett in the other, a limbless human torso rests upon a pile of flat rocks, on display like a sacrifice to some ancient tribe of cannibals. Almost unrecognizable, its rotting gray flesh torn away in patches, a gnawed-on rib protruding from it like a handle.

Jiminy sees it first. The pickup is stopped, its motor still running, Jiminy's foot hard on the brake. Holy shit, he says, will you look at that. The other boys do as they are told. Jiminy figures it must belong to the girl on the posters, the one gone missing since springtime. Where's all the rest of her, he says as he scans the foreground.

He shifts into park and gets out and so does everybody else. They stand around the pagan shrine in a loose circle and remove their caps as though in ritual. Fydo balances on one leg like some strange bird and Phillipe puts a finger against one nostril and lets fly a string of snot out the other. William folds his arms over his chest. Squawky runs both his hands across his scalp at the same time and wants to know are they going to tell somebody. Fuck no, Jiminy says. We got to hush up unless we want to end up like that.

Fog falls like a dead dog on Phillipe. He's standing out in front of the Hot L waiting for somebody to sneak his underage ass in so he can shoot some stick. William double taps the horn and Phillipe looks up and then he gets into William's daddy's winter beater and they park in the alley between the twenty-four-hour coin-operated laundry and Boron's Market. They drink a couple longneck Buds he had on ice in a five-gallon pail in the backseat. Phillipe shows William how his hands and forearms and neck are brown and sticky from picking tobacco all day down to Hoyt Bowers' farm. He said it's true nigger work and Hoyt Senior is a senile prick. He hates it. They drink their beers in silence for a bit.

I hear they're finding pieces of that girl all over, Phillipe says.

Yeah well.

My old man says the Staties are putting her together like a puzzle.

Jesus, where would they do that hey.

They've a cold room or something.

Like the walk-in freezer at the package store.

Shit, I guess. And some female cop who's a expert on such things.

Have you told nobody.

I ain't about to say shit.

Then a couple yahoos from some other town come out of the bar shoving each other around and across Main Street right into the Malibu's pinned-down hood. William climbs through the open driver-side window and breaks his empty bottle on the one dude, who screams like a fucking woman and takes off running toward town looking over his shoulder the entire time, and Phillipe really loses his shit and gets the other one on the ground and goes to work on him, smashing his top front teeth against the cement curb.

They leave and take the back roads to Hatfield before Mercier and Letorneau get the call and come by in the black-and-white so they can toss somebody's ass in the backseat. Phillipe has some killer green. He rolls up a fat one to the blinking light of the stereo. His hands are teeth-cut and still shaking from thumping on the guy out in the street, but he does all right with the joint. He's a year ahead of William but he doesn't go to school anymore because of his temper. William is going to be a senior at Franklin County Tech in the fall. William's mother wants him to learn a trade and amount to something but isn't going to hold her breath on it.

They stop about a half mile up the dirt road to the reservoir and smoke with the windows all the way open to the smell of the corn harvest and cow dung and the rest of Johnny Baronas' farm. Phillipe tells William that a judge in Greenfield is making him stay with his grandma but he mostly sleeps in abandoned barns. William nods his head and blows smoke out the window.

What about a flying saucer hey, Phillipe says.

What you mean.

I been hearing talk.

Oh yeah. And me too.

Like maybe that's what took that girl and did her like that.

Cut her up. Shit.

Right, experiments, and just dropped pieces out the hatch as they hovered.

That would be some shit.

Well, maybe we should of told somebody.

Fuck that.

Still. It's got me all fucked up inside.

We didn't do nothing wrong.

Jesus, I only hope we didn't.

A spray of black bats that materializes in front of the windshield like an apparition startles the boys, and they drive around some more and park in the same spot across from the Hot L. Phillipe calls it the scene of the crime. The music inside is loud and it's hard to figure out from where they are what fucking song it is because of all the sloppy people talking and laughing and because of the buzz of the August heat, too. It sounds like ZZ Top. Phillipe says if he could just get one lousy game that would make his night. William tells him maybe on a Wednesday or something but they're really cracking down on weekends.

Kim Streeter from his driver's education comes out of the coin-op with some other girl. Hoisting wine coolers, they talk it up some with the boys and get in the Malibu. William moves the car back a bit to get out of the streetlight. Kim asks William about his girlfriend and the rumors she's heard. He just laughs and mugs on her in the front seat for a while and she's wearing one of those front-snap bras he likes. She gives him head while Phillipe gets the other girl high. William adjusts the mirror so Phillipe can watch.

Then Phillipe tries to kiss his girl and his sticky hand gets stuck in her hair and she freaks out and he hits her a little at first but he keeps hitting her with his fist like she's a man until William drags her out of the car and tells her and Kim to go the fuck away if they know what's good for them. Her nose looks broken. William says, Jesus Christ, and Phillipe sits in front with him and finishes his beer then gets out without saying anything else and then he walks straight through the main door of the Hot L. William wonders what the fuck. Everything all fouled up since the talk of flying saucers started. The whole damn town it seems. He watches the door of the bar for ten minutes and there's no sign of any trouble, so he figures everything is all right for the time being.

CHAPTER FIFTY

Bob the Fag offers Applejack a hundred dollars to take care of a certain problem. He's heard that's the going rate. He can pay half now and half later, after the thing is done. That's how he keeps speaking about it, hushed and cryptic, dodging his eyes all around, calling it the thing. Making this up as he goes along, doing work for the Selectman.

Nobody calls it that except on television, Applejack says. Don't call it a thing.

They're sitting at the bar at Grandma's. It's quiet, middle of the day. Grandma hired some new girl to watch the place for him. Blue eyes. Her name is Erin Gagner.

So you want me to beat the shit out of somebody hey, Applejack says to Bob, but he's looking at Erin. He knows who this man is, who signs his checks. He has suspicions about why he's really here today.

Bob the Fag continues to fidget, looking around all nervous-like. Yeah, he says. There's this guy.

Isn't there always, Applejack says.

But this one really crossed the line. He removes his sunglasses to show Applejack the shiner the Selectman gave him. Using his black eye as a prop in this small piece of theatre, to make the ruse conceivable. See what he done hey, he says.

Ah, Applejack says. That's a nice one there.

No reason whatsoever.

There never is. Applejack sips his Irish coffee, heavy on the Irish.

Bob fixes his sunglasses. He said I was looking at him funny, he says.

Well, Applejack says. Were you.

I look at everybody funny. But not everybody gives me a black eye.

Applejack laughs again.

You have a point there, he says.

Bob the Fag mixes half-truths and lies to explain there's some history with the guy. His name is Sambuchino. They took drunk-driving class together in Greenfield near the bus terminal, that's how they met. And then they would see each other around town at the local twelve-step hotspots, meetings in the basement of the church and such. He hired Bob to do his taxes. Sambuchino didn't know he was queer at first and then when he found out, well, he was pissed, felt duped, like he had been somehow taken.

So what, Applejack says.

He's a real homophobe, Bob the Fag says.

That means he's scared hey.

What.

I saw on television somebody is phobic about spiders it means they're scared.

Applejack is enjoying playing along now. What the fuck, he figures, have some fun with it. Is that what you're telling me, he says. This guy's scared of you.

Jesus, I guess if you say so.

Bob the Fag is caught off guard, perplexed, unable to tell from Applejack's straight face if he's fucking with him, trying to smash holes in his bullshit story. Not that it really matters. Then Erin behind the bar comes around and fingers her blond curls and starts to flirt with Applejack. I seen you looking, she says.

Bob the Fag tries to be patient but he wants to get back to the business at hand. He wants to do this job for the Selectman or it's his fat butt in a sling. And Applejack is so easily distracted with females around. A real grade-A pussy hunter.

Honey, Bob the Fag finally says to the little piece of ass, do you mind.

Erin pauses before looking at him. Applejack stares straight ahead. Erin lets out a long sigh and then goes away to the other end of the bar to wipe at it with a dirty rag.

So, can you do the thing for me, Bob the Fag says.

I said stop calling it that.

What do you call it then.

I don't call it nothing.

Bob the Fag slaps cash on the bar and slides it toward Applejack, the whole time looking around as though he's in some fucking movie about Cold War espionage.

Jesus fucking Christ, Applejack says. Take it easy. He finishes his drink and turns the glass upside down, places it next to the money. Where can I find this sack of shit, he says.

Tonight he'll be at Zeke's.

When tonight.

Pretty much all night, but try around nine, I'd say.

All right.

Bob the Fag gets up and leaves without finishing his drink so Applejack does it for him. Erin comes back over for more chitchat. It's just the two of them alone now. Rain starting up outside. Erin tells Applejack that she's always liked the smell of the first rain ever since she was a kid. Applejack pretends to listen, but he's thinking about Bob's tall tale, Stavros and the Selectman coming at him from a different angle now. Erin shares an apartment with a girl in Turner's and she knows he's been there before, stayed the night.

A couple underaged knuckleheads from two towns over hover in the doorway, trying to stay dry, working on a blunt. The smoke is coming into the place and Erin tries to shoo them away but they just laugh and ignore her. Applejack turns on his stool and they recognize him and whisper to each other and disappear. Then his head feels like there is somebody trapped inside it trying to claw his way out until he shuts tight his eyes.

Zeke's is a fine drinking establishment according to the sign on the door. But anybody who ever set foot in there would probably only say there are drinks to be had. The place is empty but for the man Applejack guesses is Sambuchino, throwing darts in the corner. Zeke straightaway ducks into the phone booth at the far end of the room and closes the door, pretends to make a call, which confirms to Applejack he had been fucking set up. Before Sambuchino can even turn completely around to face him, though, Applejack takes two long strides and in one motion grabs a chair and hits him with it. The man goes face down on the hard wood. His piece falls on the floor, too, and Applejack kicks it away and puts a knee in Sambuchino's spine. Pulls one of his arms back and up, and using the heel of his hand he pops the elbow and then drops it. Does the same to the other side. Sambuchino screams.

Nothing so useless as a triggerman can't pull a trigger.

Applejack rolls him over, takes a dart from the table, and sticks it in his eye.

Jesus, the noise he makes now.

And Sambuchino can't do shit about it with two broken arms. Can't even sit himself up. He uses his feet to slide away from Applejack until he reaches the far wall. Adjusts his hips to turn his body, hoping gravity will help his cause and the dart will simply fall out. He shakes his head, a dog breaking a gopher's neck, trying to get it loose. Then he stops.

For fuck sake, he says. Please take that thing out my eye.

Nah, let's just leave it in there, Applejack says. You're better off that way.

Sambuchino focuses his good eye on his attacker, calm, slipping into shock now.

Yeah, he says. You think.

Otherwise you're liable to leak all over hey. Do more harm than good.

Fuck me then.

Let a doctor take it out clean. At the emergency.

All right, Sambuchino says. Thanks for that.

Definitely in fucking shock, Applejack thinks, all polite and peaceable now.

I hope that fucker paid you good, he says as he heads for the door.

Sambuchino snorts. Not near enough for this, he says as he rests his head against the molding.

Zeke, Applejack calls out. Alert the volunteers for this poor fella here.

Still clutching the receiver, Zeke pushes the side of his face against the glass of the phone booth, trying to see is it safe to come out yet. Have these bad men completed their transaction. He'd wanted no part of it, but the Selectman holds the note to his bar. It has occurred to him that the Selectman has everybody over a barrel one way or another.

The confrontation happened just the way Applejack envisioned it going down as soon as he stepped foot in the place. It always does. Like he sees a piece of the future just before he puts violence on a man, the way the scene runs in his mind in flashes, how he premeditates every possible action and reaction in the split second before he lashes out.

CHAPTER FIFTY-ONE

Mercier gets the call. Beverly Hills is twirling a pistol around her finger in the town common. It's a clear night and he sees stars and smells smoke from an illegal burn somewhere nearby. The bartender from the Bloody Brook meets Mercier on the corner and tells him Beverly's been out there for an hour. Ranting and raving, sounding pissed off, but he can't really make out exactly what she's beefing about. People have gathered in the common and folks in the bar with window seats are laughing. A maroon sedan with a lift kit, sardine-stuffed with a road crew, pulls up to the curb, and as Rob Roy turns to greet the carload of customers he asks Mercier where she'd get a piece like that, an authentic cowboy-looking pistol like what Clint Eastwood totes in his fucking movies.

Jesus Christ, Mercier says. Who even knows anymore. He thanks Rob Roy and crosses the street.

Beverly Hills sees him coming and smiles. Probably off her meds. But he smiles, too, and puts his hands on his hips.

Beverly fucking Hills, he says.

Look at you with your long hair, she says.

He lifts his cap, runs his hand across his scalp like he's checking it. He tries to keep it high and tight as a general rule. Yeah, he says. I guess I need to come by for a visit soon.

Well, she says. You always know where to find me. Like he found her just now, she thinks and blushes. Mercier pretends not to notice.

There's a short stretch of awkward silence between them. An ambulance siren bleats and bursts on Route 5. Mercier's dogs are sure enough tired and he shifts his weight from one foot to the other. I'm going to have to get some new shoes, he figures.

Beverly Hills twirls the pistol almost as an afterthought.

What you got there, Mercier finally says.

She regards the gun in her hand and looks almost sheepish, as though she should tell him I'm sorry or some such shit. Sorry for making him drag his ass out here again.

Well, she says. There's some real assholes in this town.

Yeah.

Let's just say that.

She tells him about her slap-happy ex-boyfriend who just got out of Correctional, bitches for a few minutes about the woman who hated her perm and wanted a refund and is married to the bike mob, then the salon owner who wants to up her chair rental to cover some federal tax bullshit. Beverly Hills is having a very bad fucking day.

Mercier nods his head and looks away, feels he might be an imposter for wearing a badge when the shit in this town just keeps flowing and getting deeper by the day.

And that one almost put me in his trunk, Beverly says. You remember him.

Sure I do, Mercier says. And you got every right to protect yourself.

Damn straight.

Nobody'll argue that.

You catch that sick fucker yet.

Mercier inhales deep and lets it out slow. No, I have not, he says. No sign of him.

He takes a step closer and she doesn't seem to mind or notice. Why don't you give it on over just now, he says, extending his hand to her and moving to arm's length. And then we'll call it a night and I'll take you home, he says, and tuck you in.

She considers his offer.

The gawkers in the Bloody Brook Bar press their faces against the glass.

Fuck me, she says. I didn't want all this.

I know you didn't.

Beverly Hills exhales and when she does her shoulders slump. Just fuck it, she says.

She gives the gun to Mercier and he checks the chamber and sticks it in his belt and puts his arm out for her. She places her wrist inside his elbow and rests her head on his shoulder. They turn together and walk slowly across the town common toward his cruiser, and the booze bags at the bar clap and cheer like it's some kind of fucking show.

CHAPTER FIFTY-TWO

There's a hillbilly band playing at the Seven O's. One long-haired guy singing, another on the acoustic guitar, and some bald gal banging on the drums like they done her wrong. Applejack doesn't mind the music, but it surprises him to see that kind of thing on a Saturday night. They're charging five bucks at the door but Rex lets him slide. His twin brother Ty is slinging beers. Applejack bellies up to the bar. The moon isn't all the way up yet, it's early still, so maybe a couple dozen people in there. By midnight the joint will be wall-to-wall, a massive, heaving, pulsating, sweating fire-code violation.

Applejack drinks most of his beer in one swallow. He asks Ty to get him a pen and he writes a name on a cocktail napkin and shoves it toward him and taps his finger on it three times and then points at his eyes as if to say, I'm looking for this yahoo. Ty reads the name. He stays on it for a few seconds too long, seemingly not wanting to meet Applejack's stare. He finally looks up and jerks his head toward the back. Applejack finishes his beer and uses the side of his hand to wipe away the foam mustache. Then he wades through a vampire-eyed gaggle of town girls in half shirts and Jordache jeans.

The fighter is waiting downstairs in the basement with his handlers. When Applejack appears, they whisper to each other. There are cases of Bud and miscellaneous supplies. A single light bulb hanging from exposed wires and centered over a cleared ten-by-ten space on the cement floor, marked out with chalk. There's a mop in a yellow bucket filled with dirty water. Somebody jams the mop up under the door handle so that nobody else can come in. The fighter works his jaw and gives Applejack a look so hard it could cut glass, slips the fingers of his right hand into an old pair of brass knuckles. Oh it's going to be like that, Applejack thinks as he sidles up to his opponent, flashes what his mother used to call his hundred-dollar smile. Then quicker than a pig can shit he hits the fighter in the nose with his forehead that's about as hard as a chunk of maple wood.

Bone crunches. Blood splatters. Knees buckle.

He jams his thumb into the fighter's left eye and it feels like raw egg.

The downed fighter gets up and puts his hands to his face even though it's too late now. Applejack hits him in the sternum repeatedly, the kidneys, taking his wind. Breaks a rib or two, sounds like, feels like. Puts the brassed-up fucker back down on his knees, grabs a handful of hair and knocks two teeth out against his right kneecap. He lets go and watches him slip to the concrete floor in a puddle of himself, eyes rolling back into his skull. His handlers use smelling salts. They slap his face. It isn't something Applejack enjoys, he's simply good at this. He isn't angry or upset or emotional whatsoever. It's a business deal. That's how he sees it. Once he's sure the guy is toast, he washes his bloated hands with goopy pink soap at the sink, dries them on the front of his jeans.

Somebody pays him.

He takes a moment to put the mop back where it belongs.

A line is forming outside the bar now. Applejack can smell fresh-made bread from Hebert's. He gets on his ATV and rides down Sandhill Dune Road and up Red Gulley, the cool night air filling his lungs. He's going to have to ice his hands but the swelling will go down quick. He felt his right shoulder pop during a roundhouse swing and he's going to have to keep an eye on that, too. He thinks on Suzanne. One hell of a fine girl. But it's just a matter of time, he figures, before she's sick and tired of his bullshit. Not sure he's even cut out for playing house. And he thinks again on that Peanut getting caught up in the wrong life so early and what he could have done to prevent things going down the way they did. He stops and parks. His mind gets to wandering in such a way. Too many concussions'll do that, the doctor tells him.

CHAPTER FIFTY-THREE

Applejack sleeps, dreams a memory: For fuck sake, his father says, throws his playing cards down. He has the worst luck of anybody. Dutch folds too and Fat Mike laughs. Greg Goodyear buys a round of beers and Applejack's father tells him to sit still. For fuck sake, he says. Sit still there boy. He's smoking a long cigarillo like he is known to do. It's a party. Applejack is just a kid and he isn't supposed to be there but his mother took off to Florida with Jim the Barber. Applejack's father says she's a dirty fucking whore. He says they're all dirty whores. He also says Jim the Barber is a dead man.

They better stay down there in Florida, he says. For goddamn fuck sake.

Applejack's father keeps a loaded gun in his pickup. Everybody does. Roger Sadoski turns off the lights and the music gets loud. Applejack puts his fingers in his ears. Then the lights come on and some naked ladies are dancing around and Fat Mike keeps telling Applejack to close his eyes. Applejack's father doesn't care. For fuck sake. Let the boy see what his future holds. At least these are the good kind of whores, he says, the obvious kind. Greg Goodyear wins on a raffle ticket and he goes into the office behind the bar with one of the naked ladies. Applejack's father tears his tickets into tiny little pieces and drops them in the ashtray. For fuck sake, he says, I can't win for losing. Not even a fucking blow job. He finishes his beer and picks up Applejack and grabs his handmade pool stick and dismantles it, sheaths it, knocks his chair over on purpose.

Applejack goes piggyback once they get outside. Then he sits in
the bed of the pickup with his dog Nanook. It's his favorite to ride
like that. When he closes his eyes he can smell the swamp and the
pickle shop and the candle factory. He can smell the tannery and the
train tracks and the tall rows of forever corn. He can still smell his
daddy's neck.

Nanook barks. There's a strange car in the yard. Applejack's father
tells him to stay put. Let's see who this is, he says. He reaches under
his seat for his pistol and he goes inside the house where some lights
are already on. Applejack can see his mother and Jim the Barber in
the kitchen eating sandwiches, like he's watching it on television.
Applejack's father enters the screen and hits his mother upside the
head with the butt of the gun before she sees him. Then Jim the
Barber stands up and wipes his mouth as though he has time for
that and then he disappears behind a flurry of fists. Then Applejack's
father slams closed the storm door and tells his son to shut up that
goddamn dog. For fuck sake, he says. What is wrong with him now.
His hands are bloody, his T-shirt is torn. They drive up into Conway
and Ashfield and along the back roads where Applejack's father likes
to clear his head. Applejack clears his head, too. Then they stop at
the Ashfield Lakehouse so his father can make a bit of money playing
eight ball. It's mostly bikers in there. Applejack goes outside and
throws rocks at the ducks and spreads his arms out and does the
airplane, running like that, and Nanook bounces alongside him.

MAY 22, 8:23 a.m.

Stavros and the Selectman sat across from each other at Stavros's desk in the Castaway Lounge. The glass top was arrayed with to-go containers from the diner. The Selectman leaned over a warm plate of food—kielbasa, stuffed peppers, eggs—and got after it pretty good for a guy in his predicament. He had showered and was wearing his rumpled suit. His face was fucked up, his nose swollen, blackening around his eyes.

Stavros watched the Selectman eat. Jesus, he said. Nice to see you haven't lost your appetite.

The Selectman looked up and wiped his mouth with a corner of his napkin. A man's got to eat, he said.

Yeah, Stavros said. I guess a man does hey.

The Selectman heard something different in Stavros's tone and he paused mid-chew to cock his head at the Greek, really considered him, and then shrugged his shoulders and shifted his focus back to the plate. The Selectman's fork stabbed at a sausage, trimmed the fat off a chunk of kielbasa, then pushed it between his greasy lips.

You really are something else, Stavros said.

I'm worried about the cops.

Ah shit, that's not a thing to worry over.

The Selectman grunted his approval.

You know these boys out here, Stavros said. Ain't exactly bending over backwards.

Good. I hope so.

And I think we'll disappear her all right, he said, but he wasn't convinced.

That was really something, the Selectman said. Your boy Rodney there.

Stavros didn't respond.

With the chainsaw, the Selectman said. He really seemed to be enjoying himself.

Stavros pictured the look on Rodney's face when the chainsaw had run out of gas and he whipped the musclehead with the telephone cord, a child who'd just been told there's no Santa Claus. Yeah, he yawned as he rubbed his eyes with his thumbs. Well.

I mean Jesus Christ. That took some effort.

The kind of effort, Stavros said, that don't come cheap.

The Selectman put his fork down atop his plate. Well, shit, he said. Now here it comes.

Stavros put his finger in his ear and wiggled it around.

Now what the fuck are you talking about, the Selectman said.

I'm talking about remuneration.

That's a big word for a fucking immigrant.

All that shit at the hotel, Stavros ignored the dig. You said so yourself.

But I paid for the party.

I'm not talking about the party. I'm talking about the above and beyond shit.

Above and beyond what.

Come on, Stavros said. Money talks and bullshit walks.

Jesus, the Selectman said. This feels like a shakedown.

So you were never here, Stavros said. We all get amnesia and everything.

Even that Woods, the Selectman said. I'm worried about that fucker.

Yeah hey that might be a thing we got to keep an eye on.

More than one eye, I expect.

Stavros held his upturned hand out and rubbed his thumb against his fingers.

Again, he said. This is what it comes down to.

You think that will do it.

Yessir. I do. Because it always does.

Are you shaking me down, the Selectman said, you Greek fuck.

Stavros laughed but not as though he was having a good time. The Selectman had heard the laugh before and it made him uncomfortable.

You know how these things work, Stavros said. You of all people know goddamn well.

Stavros pushed back from the desk like to stand up, but the Selectman motioned for him to wait. He was working vigorously on his teeth with his thumbnail, then with his tongue.

You got a toothpick or something, the Selectman said.

Yeah, I usually got some in here hey.

He opened his top drawer and rummaged for a box of toothpicks and as he did so the Selectman saw the chrome-plated .45 and he stared at it for a couple heartbeats and it made him sweat, the sight of it and all that it promised, and his forehead really beaded up as he suddenly realized the shit he was in, the kind of people he was being forced to deal with. All those filthy fucking whores and the backwoods badass and this fucking clown. The muscled-up cokehead with the chainsaw. Stavros found the toothpicks, handed one to the Selectman, closed the drawer, and stood up.

Got to cut myself a new asshole, he said through a grimace.

He farted as he turned toward the private bathroom in the back corner.

All right, the Selectman said. But when you get back give me a figure.

A figure, Stavros said over his shoulder.

Yeah, the Selectman said. So we can do like you said hey.

Stavros stopped and turned to face the Selectman.

What happened to the shakedown, he said.

You're right, the Selectman said. I do know how these things work.

Stavros turned away and headed to the bathroom in a big rush, passing wind.

CHAPTER FIFTY-FOUR

Bored teenagers admit to making the crop circles, but believers are still coming from across the county to check out the supernatural phenomenon that has taken place in Charlie Smiaroski's fields. It's giving meaning to them. Meaning from the meaningless. Making sense of the senseless.

The television is on mostly for background noise, but Applejack and Suzanne hear the interview from the mattress and they each get up on their elbows to watch.

Two pimple-faced fucks vying for attention, cutting each other off with answers to obvious questions. The interviewer is a girl Applejack recognizes from high school. Anita something. A real wallflower back then, but look at her now. Glamorous. And those goddamn kids. They should mind their own business and leave adult things alone. If even one man ditches believing in something from outside this hellhole, those boys should be made to eat his shit. Suzanne puts her head on the pillow, stares at the ceiling.

We got to get out of here.

What.

Everybody thinks I made it up hey, she says. And that I'm crazy.

Yeah, well. Fuck everybody then.

She turns her head to look at him, still listening to the television. There's a montage of clips of the kids putting forth platitudes.

We were bored.

There's nothing to do around here.

We saw it on a show.

How to do it.

We got some planks from a construction site.

My dad had rope.

We couldn't believe the big deal everybody made.

We were like, oh man.

But we're tired of these nutjobs.

Martians or whatever.

It was just us.

Just kidding around.

There's no aliens.

The segment ends and Applejack chucks a can of Bud at the screen. Fuck those fucking kids and the horse they rode in on. Maybe flying saucer stories anywhere in the world start out as pranks, but the buzz can develop into something bigger and people come alive who've been sleepwalking for years. Like a gang of Maine lobstermen watching a hurricane crash in from the Atlantic and deciding let's party before we die.

Applejack could stomach that Peanut being hauled off by a spaceship. Her spirit somehow beamed up, right out of that dirty motel bathroom, leaving the shitbag Selectman and everybody else behind. Maybe she got to wink and nod and turn away from the glass-eyed dicks and just slip out the back, Jack. He likes to think so anyhow.

Suzanne puts her hand on his shoulder. A penny for your thoughts, she says.

He looks at her. And then away.

Boy Country's Jack Russell kills a chipmunk. The dog is called Huckleberry or Huck. Huck whips it around and snaps its neck like they do. Applejack is drinking a cold beer and sitting with Suzanne on the bumper of the International with Elvis on the tape deck singing "Love Me Tender" full blast. Huck gets blood everywhere, prouder than shit about what he's done and Applejack tells him he's a good boy. Then he puts the dog in the back of the truck and Suzanne jumps in the front, and Applejack drives out to the crop circles and he does donuts around them, belting out Elvis, digging up the field and spitting chunks of grass and mud and cornhusk all over the place as they watch the night sky for shooting stars or a strange blinking light or some other sign of that poor little girl.

The river is running hard under Cheapside Bridge and Huck bites Boy Country's ankle a little bit. The dog doesn't want him to jump. He is maybe the only one. Boy Country can hear water down there slapping around against the hard rocks. There are mosquitoes and fireflies. He stands on the cement railing with his arms straight out and he tries to balance himself against the wind that is sneezing off the Berkshire Mountains. It is like he's walking on a tightrope, which is hard to do with his bum leg. He sees the moon and it looks to him like a piece of cheese. He smells mountain ash and tamarack. Then Applejack gets out of the International and shines a big flashlight on him and Huck goes after his ankle, too. How long you gone to stand there like that, Applejack says. He helps his friend down and lets him sit in the front seat of the pickup with the dog squirming in his lap.

I'ma take you home now, Applejack says. Then I'm not gone to see you for a little while.

MAY 22, 8:25 a.m.

Jill and Nick sat together at a table in the Castaway Lounge. Nick's leg was going a mile a minute and he kept looking out the window. Jill had her head in her hands.

Wish they'd hurry up, Nick said.

Jill looked like she would blow at any second. She eyeballed him between her splayed fingers. What the fuck, she said, can them two do for us. She reached over and grabbed his leg. And will you stop with the fucking leg.

Nick looked at her all hangdog and such.

Applejack gets us out of shit, he said. That's what he always does.

Hate to break it to you, she said, but your hero can't save us this time.

Fuck you say.

You know what they're talking about in there, she said. Stavros and that sick fuck.

No, Nick said. What.

How to get rid of us, she said. Because we seen too much.

Bullshit. I didn't see shit.

You saw all that blood we cleaned up didn't you. She indicates the trash bags piled in a corner of the room. You saw Rodney going to town with his fucking chainsaw.

Jesus Christ. Wished I didn't.

Then you saw plenty, she said. And you're deep in it now.

Jesus.

They made sure of that.

You're making it sound like I done something wrong.

I'm not making it sound like anything.

Jesus, girl, Nick said.

I'm just saying we don't have time to wait for Applejack and them.

Well, Stavros says I got to dump that shit anyhow.

Fuck you and those bloody towels.

Can't you at least wait for that, Nick said. So we can figure something out.

I don't know I can do it, she said. We got to make some moves.

CHAPTER FIFTY-FIVE

The local police cruiser has a green Opel pulled over on the side of the road under a flickering streetlight. Gumball lights on the cruiser spinning. Letorneau is standing near the driver-side window. Mercier positions himself on the other side of the car as he shines his flashlight in and around the backseat. The beam falls on a black suitcase. Letorneau sees it and asks Bob the Fag if he's going on vacation or something.

That's right, Bob says. I'm going to the lake for a couple three days.

But the truth is he doesn't know where he's going yet and might not know until he gets there. That fucking Applejack did a number on Sambuchino and it's only a matter of time before they run into each other, Bob figures. So time to get fucking gone.

Letorneau checks his license and registration.

Bob the Fag is nervous but also pissed off at the inconvenience and blinded by the cruiser's high beams reflecting off his rearview. Fuck, he says. Can't you turn that shit down hey.

Where's the fire anyhow, Letorneau says.

Don't you know who I am.

I see your name right here, Letorneau says. Robert William Moss.

But you know damn well who I work for.

Sure I do. Are you bragging.

Bob the Fag shakes his head. I got shit to do, he says. If we can move things along.

Yeah, Letorneau says. You bet there, buddy.

He hands the paperwork back to Bob the Fag and goes around the vehicle to meet up with his partner. They walk together toward the back of the car, stand by the trunk.

What you think, Mercier says.

That man's an asshole hey.

But he's been one his whole life. Why stop now.

And queer as a three-dollar bill.

There ain't no law against that.

Maybe there oughta be.

All right, Mercier said. Go easy on that shit now.

I just don't get it.

Don't get what now.

How a man can be with a man like that. You know.

Well, that's not for you to get.

What you mean.

If that don't float your boat.

Fuck you say.

It's just pussy on a stick to some fellas, I guess.

Letorneau makes a face like he just sucked on a lemon.

Tell him slow down, Mercier said. And go on to wherever the fuck.

With all his pickle-smooching buddies.

Mercier shakes his head and clicks off his flashlight.

Letorneau returns to the car and Mercier heads to the cruiser. At the same time, Scotch's brown van passes slowly in a northbound direction, his dogs going absolutely nuts inside. Then the van backfires, startling Mercier and Letorneau, and they each turn and clumsily reach for their sidearms—not a smooth transaction in either case, as neither cop has had to draw down much in this town.

MAY 22, 8:42 a.m.

An overripe sun peeked over the top of Sunsick Mountain as a blanket of mist formed above the tree line. Applejack drove the limousine, concentrating on the road. Hoyt fiddled with the radio. They each smoked, an El Producto cigar box on the seat between them. Nick's truck flew by going in the opposite direction on Route 5 and 10.

Jesus Christ, Hoyt said.

Must be heading to the reservoir, Applejack said. To dump the rags and shit.

Like a bat out of hell, though.

Yeah hey, Applejack said. That's one way to get noticed.

The stretch of 5 and 10 was a narrow two-lane. A plump bullfrog rested about at the halfway point in crossing the road, trying to return to the small bog on the other side. The scene was lazy and quiet. Then there was a rumbling in the distance, getting louder and closer. The limousine was in the wrong lane. Hoyt looked at Nick, motioning for him to pull over and stop, yelling but Nick couldn't hear over the din of the engines. He stared straight ahead, concentrating on the road, ignoring his friends—then he looked over at them and arched his eyebrows, issuing a subtle challenge, it seemed to Hoyt.

He looked at Applejack. What the fuck, he said.

What's got into that boy.

Hoyt looked up to see an eighteen-wheeler from Harold C. Kocot's coming fast in the opposite direction, blasting its horn. A tense chicken scene played out. Then Applejack changed lanes at the very last second. Nick veered just as the big rig passed, and then the pickup came to a smoky halt in the dirt parking lot just before the sun-blasted picnic tables of Tom's Famous Footlong Hot Dog Stand. Applejack readjusted his rearview mirror and drove on, smiling, leaving Nick red-faced behind him.

Applejack sat on the cement wall at the edge of the reservoir and Nick and Hoyt stood below. Nick's pant legs were rolled up, but nonetheless he was wet to his waist. His shoes and socks were on the ground a few feet away. He was out of breath. They all three looked out at the water. Applejack and Hoyt were still smoking their cigars. Nobody talked. A series of air bubbles rose from the depths a little ways out.

How deep is it out there, Nick said.

Deep enough, Hoyt said.

Not as deep as the shit we're in hey, Applejack said.

Think them rocks'll do the trick.

It's just bags of rags, Hoyt said. They'll be fine.

Well, Nick said, I don't like leaving Jill back there with them.

Applejack rubbed his head.

I'd be more worried about them others, he said. That one can take care of herself.

The boys clucked.

Nick picked up his shoes and socks and looked at Hoyt and Applejack and then turned away. Hoyt watched him walk back up the access road where his pickup was parked next to the limousine at the chained-up gate. Applejack stared out at the water.

So much for keeping you away from trouble hey, Hoyt said.

No shit.

Sorry for that.

Nobody's fault, Applejack said. It seems to follow me.

Well, Hoyt said. I got to get the limousine back or Larry will pop a nut.

Oh right. You got a funeral or something.

Want me to dump you at the club first, Hoyt said. Or what's the plan.

Sometimes, Applejack said, you don't need a fucking plan.

Hoyt looked up at Applejack as he watched the last of the air bubbles pop.

CHAPTER FIFTY-SIX

The Selectman is driving his Ranchero, speeding south on Route 5 and 10, drunk and hugging the center line. It's past two in the morning. He's thinking breakfast, but first there's another hunger to satisfy. He hasn't been to the Lounge since that night in May so Stavros sounded surprised to receive his call. The Selectman's wearing a shabby suit from another fundraiser at the Four Leaf Clover in Bernardston. He removes his clip-on tie and tosses it to the backseat, undoes the two top buttons of his wrinkled shirt. He tilts the rearview mirror so he can see his reflection and he tries to fix his hair then checks his teeth, which are crooked and yellow. And the space where Applejack kicked one out. He has long understood that his is not a handsome face and he must reach out to women from some other place—usually the same place he keeps his credit cards. There's a tape of polka music playing and he's humming along. Then he pops the tape cassette out and replaces it and Tom Petty croons "American Girl," and the Selectman sings along however off key, cranks up the volume and bangs on the steering wheel with both hands.

The Selectman and Suzanne sit at one of the small tables next to the main stage in the Castaway Lounge. Seeing as he hasn't been to the club in a few months he feels funny about it. Returning to the scene of the crime, Stavros called it. But despite his awkwardness he appears pleased with himself. The sleeves of his shirt are rolled up just below his elbows. Suzanne's faraway look says she's somewhere else, thinking up a plan maybe.

Alone at last, the Selectman says.

Yeah hey, she says. And then there was two.

Nobody around to fuck with us.

We got the place to ourselves. Stavros's out back counting cash.

Counting what cash.

From the weekend.

The Selectman leans toward Suzanne, puts his hand on her knee, speaking softly.

I guess you heard what happened a while ago, he says. With that other girl.

What's that now.

Don't get smart with me. Stavros told me you know.

Sure he told me, she thinks, and Applejack did too you sick twist. That's why I'm here right now—tonight's not a money thing.

But what she says is, All right, then, maybe I did hear some shit.

I'm all tore up inside, the Selectman says. About that whole damn thing.

Suzanne points her bottle of beer at his chest and fake smiles her teeth. No judgment here, she says. That's why everybody comes back.

Well I just want you to understand, he says. It was a damn accident.

Like this whore gives two shits about anything other than getting paid, but it feels good to break the silence, to talk about what happened even in the vaguest of terms. He's been quiet for so long and a little talk won't hurt now. That's his mindset. He keeps his hand on her knee and at first it looks like she might knock it away. But instead she puts her own hand on top of his, strokes the unkempt white fur on his forearm ever so slightly. Like stroking a lost dog.

I know, she says. Don't worry.

Well, so can't we be friends. You and me.

Yeah, sure, Suzanne says. And maybe we already are hey.

I like the way that sounds.

She gently removes his hand from her knee and stands up.

Wait right here, she says. I got an idea.

Suzanne struts toward the dressing room with the Selectman's eyes glued to her ass the whole way. She's really working it as she disappears around the corner, knowing she's got him now. Before heading to the dressing room she detours to Stavros's office, sees the stack of bills on his desk, hears the bathroom fan. Voices from the radio. He's nodded off for sure. Right on cue, she thinks, and checks the clock on the wall, quietly jams a chair-back up under the knob of the shithouse door to slow the old fucker down. Just in case.

What she and Applejack talked about.

The best time to shoot a mountain rooster is when he's courting a hen, is how he had put it that night out in the field, looking up at the stars. So setting a pussy trap for that sick fuck Selectman and getting Stavros too in one fell swoop.

The Selectman waits alone in the quiet room, sipping brown liquor and smoking a cigarette from the pack Suzanne left on the table. After a few minutes he hears footsteps and there she is wearing a hat with a Massachusetts State Police patch on the front, a tiny blue bra and matching thong, a black belt with handcuffs, a black water pistol that almost looks real, and a pair of the Gestapo-style boots favored by the troopers. She looks in her fucking element now, he thinks.

Suzanne goes over and messes with the jukebox until "I've Always Been Crazy" starts to play and then she turns her attention to the Selectman, makes her way toward him and he smiles, snuffs out the smoke on the bottom of his shoe.

Oh shit, he smartasses. It's the po-leece.

Coming to get you, she says. Heard you been real bad.

He laughs and Suzanne sings a few words.

I've always been crazy, but it's kept me from going insane.

She stops short of him and grabs a chair, drags it to center stage, making a real production out of it. On the platform now, she makes it clear she knows her way around a stripper pole. Then she points at the Selectman and crooks her finger, beckoning him to join her. He figures what the hell. Hops up on the stage and gets comfortable in the chair that she has positioned against the brass pole. Suzanne moves around his perimeter, she doesn't really need music, oozing rhythm and sex appeal. She opens his legs with her left knee, leaning into him, brushing her tits against his face. The Selectman closes his eyes and breathes in her perfume, the archetypal stripper fragrance. She puts her knee into his crotch and pushes against him, causing the old chair to move a bit and it creaks.

You all right, she says.

The Selectman opens his eyes.

Yeah, he says. I'm all right now.

She rubs against him some more.

This day ain't turning out half bad, he says.

He doesn't see it coming. How could he. She has him in such a fucking state, putty in her hands. He doesn't even think the handcuffs are real. But before he can react she has his wrists clamped together behind him around the pole. Once he realizes what's happening he pushes her away with his shoulder and tugs at the bracelets, but it's no use.

Stop fucking around, he says. Come on.

Suzanne falls when he shoves her back. She sprawls splay-legged onto the stage and manages herself into a sitting position. She laughs at him. He kicks at her but she's beyond his reach. Laughing at him still. The Selectman is not used to being laughed at.

Got yourself a situation, she says.

I'm not into this tying-me-up shit, he says. Undo me.

You'll be undone soon enough.

What the fuck, he says. Then over his shoulder and louder, Fucking Stavros, he yells.

Can't hear nothing, Suzanne says, when he's shitting a brick.

The Selectman snorts.

The fan on in there and the radio and everything, Suzanne says.

The Selectman slumps, tired of yelling and struggling against his cuffs.

He'll be in there a full hour, she says. Falls asleep on the can all the time.

Fuck me then.

Not in this lifetime.

You are nuts hey. It's true what they say.

Maybe, but it's just you and me now for a little bit here. Like you wanted.

Suzanne goes behind the bar and grabs a bottle of Cutty Sark and a couple of glasses. The Selectman struggles some more with the handcuffs but he can tell it's no use. Fuck me, he thinks again.

I'm truly sorry what happened, he says. I'm guessing now she was your friend.

Good guess, but nah, Suzanne says. She was just another girl.

Then why all this.

She keeps her back to him, ignoring his stupid fucking question.

Truly sorry, he says. It was a hell of a thing.

She fills each glass to the halfway mark.

But nobody killed her, the Selectman says. You got to know that.

He pauses for her to say something but she stays quiet on the matter.

It was a accident. And besides, that other one drugged her up.

Suzanne faces the Selectman and squeezes her face into a tight mess. But you're the one raped that poor girl when she was out cold, she says. And then bashed her fucking skull in.

You weren't even there. You don't know shit about it.

I know enough hey.

She takes the toy gun out of her holster and puts the barrel in her mouth, pulls the trigger and puts her head back and gargles, takes the plastic pistol out and says yum yum. Then she points it at him, sprays the front of his pants so it looks like he pissed himself.

Well look there, she says. I guess accidents can happen.

He regards the mess in his lap for a moment and then looks back at Suzanne.

What is that, he says. That's not just water.

The hard stuff. I hear it's flammable.

Suzanne laughs and sprays him again. She puts the toy gun on the edge of the stage beside her Pall Malls and picks up the book of matches.

I better be careful with these hey, she says.

Think about what you're doing, he says. Before you go and do something stupid.

Suzanne approaches the edge of the stage and slides one of the glasses toward the Selectman, but of course he can't reach it even though it stops at his feet. His fear switches to anger. He gets like high and mighty with her, showing his true colors again.

You fucking cunt, he says. You're gone to pay.

No, Suzanne says. Always on the house during private sessions hey.

She laughs, crooks her elbow, and throws her drink back in a single motion. He kicks the glass that she poured for him and sends it flying, making a mess.

See now that's just rude, Suzanne says. You got no class.

You cunt.

Call me cunt one more time.

Cunt. Fucking crazy redneck white trash cunt.

She pours another drink for herself, more whiskey in the glass this time. The Selectman is struggling again. Suzanne gets up on the stage and moves around him, taunting him now. She lights a cigarette and blows smoke rings in his direction. She drinks directly from the green bottle. The Selectman fumes. Suzanne is really feeling the alcohol and throwing caution to the wind. She gets a little too close and he kicks at her and just about connects with her hip as she tries to turn away. A bit awkward in the big boots, she stumbles off the stage and falls to the floor. She goes down ass first, but there is a resounding thud when her head makes contact, and she lays there motionless. From his position, the Selectman can barely see her lying there, one of her knees sticking up.

Jesus Christ, the Selectman says. Get the fuck up here and take these cuffs of me.

Nothing.

Say something to me, you redneck cunt.

Silence.

Here we go again, he says. He can hardly believe his shitty luck.

The Selectman jerks at the handcuffs and looks up at the spinning ceiling fan.

Stavros sits on the can in the narrow bathroom. Some talk show on the radio. A fan drowning out any background noise. An old issue of *Penthouse Magazine* open and face down across his lap. His face is intense, growling through clenched teeth. His eyes are closed tightly. Beads of sweat freckle his large forehead. He's not feeling well. The stress is getting to him. This life, he thinks. I got to make some motherfucking changes. A cigarette dangles from one side of his mouth, a thin tube of ashes built up on the end of it.

CHAPTER FIFTY-SEVEN

The Selectman is slumped in the chair at center stage, done in. Suzanne is out cold. The front door opens and throws a thick shaft of light onto the Selectman and he turns his head awkwardly away from it, wondering where the fuck it came from. Looks like headlights of some kind. The door closes after a few seconds and he blinks, trying to adjust his eyes to the interior darkness. A blurry figure stands before him.

Who's there, the Selectman says. Who in fuck is that.

He blinks his eyes and the blurry figure begins to come into focus for him.

Stavros, the Selectman says hopefully.

Nah, Applejack says. It's just me, you sorry sack of shit.

The Selectman knows the voice. He closes his eyes thinking this is just what I need, then opens them. Get these fucking cuffs off me boy, he says. Please.

You tried to get me, Applejack says. But look who got got in the end.

What end. This shit ain't over, boy.

Applejack uses his open hands to box the Selectman's ears so his head rings like a fucking dinner bell.

Holy shit that hurts, the Selectman says, whining.

Applejack looks around and finds Suzanne on the floor where she hasn't moved a muscle. He goes to her, checks her vitals and sees she's okay, or going to be when she comes to. He returns to the Selectman, who's got fingers in his ears like to pop a bubble. Applejack is not smiling.

Your fucking nightmare just got worse, he says.

Boy, the Selectman says, withdrawing his fingers. I know what you're thinking.

No, Applejack says. You don't by a long shot.

She just fell. Plain and simple.

Applejack goes to Suzanne, picks her up and makes his way to the door, kicking stacked chairs and tables aside. She comes to in his arms, looks up at him.

Hey there, my handsome man, she says.

What you doing, doll.

Oh you know, she says. Fixing things like we talked about.

All right. But now you got a goose egg on your head.

Yeah hey, I guess I got careless. Caught in the moment and all.

Ah, but we live a careless kind of life, don't we.

Take me away from it, will you. All this.

Promised I would.

Yeah, you did.

Applejack shoulders the door open and outside a sharp crack jolts Suzanne and she clings to his neck. Scotch's van pulls into the lot, dogs barking, and Applejack just about smiles. Well I'll be damned, he says. If it ain't one of God's true soldiers.

The Selectman has given up. No fight left in him. Then the front door is flung open, bathing him in the slow-sinking smuggler's moon. He winces, assumes it's Applejack.

Always took you for the smart one, he says. Now you come undo me, boy.

Whoever it is moves closer to the Selectman, slinging his hands and arms like feeding chickens. The Selectman tries to make sense of it and makes Chink eyes and sniffs.

What the fuck, he says.

And then he hears sloshing and splashing, and he smells gasoline.

His eyes adjust again and the figure becomes clear, a man he doesn't recognize. Who the fuck are you, the Selectman says.

Scotch ignores him and continues pouring unleaded gasoline from a red plastic container onto the stage around the Selectman. He's smoking half an El Producto cigar.

What the fuck you doing, the Selectman says.

Scotch doesn't say a word, very businesslike. On a mission from God.

The Selectman squirms and with a burst of adrenalin calls for help at the top of his lungs. But he's quick running out of breath and energy. You're looking at cold-blooded murder motherfucker, he says.

Scotch finally makes eye contact. Put the Devil back in hell, he says, and then he goes back to work.

What the fuck. I'm no devil, boy.

The Selectman is in pain, sweating, his eyes are bloodshot and he's panic-stricken. Off the chair now, standing. Whipping his head left and right, choking and gagging, he pukes in his mouth and swallows it back but that only tastes worse and so more comes out and hits the floor with a splat. He slides down the pole to his knees.

Applejack appears in the corner of the room, and the Selectman sees him.

That's right, Applejack says. Send that devil back to hell.

The Selectman tosses his head away from Applejack, snot flowing, and simply says no. This last word coming out in a whisper just as Scotch strikes a match.

CHAPTER FIFTY-EIGHT

The sound of a toilet flushing. Stavros washes his hands in the small sink and regards his face in the cracked vanity mirror hanging on the wall. He splashes cold water on his cheeks, more or less refreshed from the little snooze, dries his hands on his shirt. He tries to open the door that leads into his office but it won't give. Must be stuck, he thinks. Jiggles the knob, leans with his shoulder. His next thought is he's being robbed, all that money from the weekend left out in the open. What a fucking idiot. The Selectman and Suzanne are having a little session and they wouldn't be hard to overpower, especially if they got caught in the middle of it. They're not going to stop somebody looking for a big payday. But who's got balls enough, he wonders. Banana Nose comes to mind. Fucking shutting me down for good finally, Stavros thinks.

After three tries he kicks the door open, and the chair goes flying against the opposite wall. The cash is on his desk in a neat little pile, untouched.

What the fuck, he thinks. If not the money, then what.

Smoke is pouring in from under the door that leads to the bar and dance floor. Stavros takes two steps and puts the flat of his hand against it and pulls back immediately, burned. Fuck me, he says. Whether it's accident or arson, Stavros believes in signs. It's time to get far away from this place.

Moving fast now, he goes to his desk, opens the top drawer, gets his handgun, his favorite pea shooter, blows on it like to get the dust

off, checks the chamber, and sticks it in his belt. Looks again at the
tidy little pile of money. He stares at it for a few beats and then takes
what he can fit in his pocket. He's going after another handful when
an explosion just on the other side of the wall scares the shit out of him
and he thinks, fuck, I got money enough to last me a while, to get me
to Florida or somewhere like that. He spins and stumbles, hauling ass
to the other door that leads to the parking lot.

Hell of a way to go, he thinks.

He removes his false teeth and underhands them beneath the
desk, hoping that will be evidence enough for the dumb fucks that
he's dead in the club, or at least hold back the hounds until his trail
goes cold. Then he's startled by a horrible noise, this time almost
human, under the roar of the fire. Who the fuck, he thinks, but then
doesn't give a shit and quicksteps the hell away and out through the
emergency exit into the nearly empty lot. His Cadillac in its usual
spot. The Selectman's red Ranchero. Then he hears the sound of small
dogs barking and fussing, and he sees Scotch's van under a tree. The
Econoline's headlights click on and flash at him once and then twice.
Some kind of signal, but he doesn't know what it means or who it's
meant for.

Or maybe he does. Son of a bitch.

Bastard saw I didn't die, he thinks.

He nods his head at the van as it inches toward the street. Wishes
he was closer, had a clean shot at the driver. Damn it.

Stavros slowly backs away from the burning building, his fiery
empire falling, and toward the edge of the thick woods surrounding
the property. When he gets to the first line of trees he stops and turns
and reaches a hand into the thicket, peers in as though looking past a
curtain set to drop on his third act. Then he steps into the foliage and
disappears with a rustle and a snap of twigs. Branches creak in the wind
as the dense wilderness swallows him up.

Applejack emerges from a pocket of dark. Standing alone in the middle of the parking lot, he'd been watching the building burn but he's now looking at the spot in the foliage where Stavros disappeared. One problem I might never see again, he figures. Then a loud bang catches his attention and he looks toward the swinging back door of the office. It blows all the way open again and slams against the side of the building. He goes to look, thinking could some poor soul be trapped, maybe one of the dancers had been in there with that Greek fuck. Flames just starting to lick under the still-closed interior door.

Nobody there.

A good mess of cash on the desk, though.

He's considering snatching some of that fucking blood money when he hears his name and turns his head toward the voice coming from the gloom. Stavros's voice, but Applejack can't yet see him. He blinks once and then twice. There's a flash like from snapping a photograph and Applejack makes out the Greek's toothless smile for an instant in the light of it and then he feels something hot tear at his chest. The impact of bullet on bone spins him around so he takes a knee, and then he hears the gunpowder crack.

CHAPTER FIFTY-NINE

At sunup, barely visible from Stillwater Road, the police cruiser is parked under a canopy of trees. Windows up, engine off. Whippoorwills calling. The cops are napping with their seats reclined. Letorneau is in the passenger side with his hat over his face. His snoring is loud and getting louder. Mercier stirs and opens his eyes, looks at his partner, annoyed. He considers shaking the bastard awake but decides to let him rest. Mercier tries to settle back in his seat when something catches his eye. He leans forward, peering out the windshield, squinting. He reaches his right hand over and shakes Letorneau.

Letorneau starts and stretches. What the fuck, he says.

Something's burning.

Sorry, Letorneau says. That one slipped out.

No, Mercier says. Something's really fucking burning.

Letorneau takes the hat from his face and sits up, groggy. He rubs his eyes, looks at Mercier, follows his gaze and his eyes widen. Out past the bug-splattered windshield black smoke is filling the sky over the tree-lined horizon.

Oh shit, Letorneau says.

I can't even think what all's over there.

Probably just some old tobacco barn.

The Greek's place.

Nobody over there at this hour. Daylight and all.

We should go at least make sure.

Ah shit, Letorneau says. We *should* do lots of things.

He checks his watch, turns on the two-way to see did they miss a call.

Guarantee it's just some yahoo burning leaves without a permit.

He reclines in his seat and puts the hat back over his face.

Mercier shrugs his shoulders.

One hell of a pile of leaves, he says.

Then Scotch's van passes slowly, going south, dogs barking, and it backfires.

God almighty, Letorneau says. He needs to get that shit fixed one day.

CHAPTER SIXTY

The Castaway Lounge has been reduced to smoldering piles of embers and several charred columns of cinder blocks. All that's left in evidence it was ever there is the new sign out by the road. A fire truck is in the lot and several beer-bellied volunteer firefighters wander around. A high-pressure hose is extended from the truck and pooled on the ground, dripping a bit of water from the end.

The men are taking turns cracking wise. Always heard these girls was hotter than hell, stuff like that.

Laughter.

Letorneau and Mercier are sitting in the police cruiser at the edge of the parking lot. They scan the lot and see Stavros's Cadillac in its usual spot. The reeds behind the Caddy are flattened where another car had been parked, but it's not there anymore. They get out of the cruiser. Mercier sits on the hood, removes his hat and scratches his head. Letorneau approaches the firefighter who appears to be in charge.

Hey, you, Letorneau says.

Sorry to wake you, Whitey smartasses.

What's doing.

Same shit on a different day. He indicates the ash piles that used to be the club.

Fuck happened here.

Well. There was a fire, see.

Letorneau spits over his shoulder and kicks up some dirt. Everybody's a comedian, he says. I mean, what you make of it.

Whitey laughs. It'll maybe take a while to sift through all this shit, he says.

Maybe Stavros was going for insurance or something.

Maybe. The safe bet is on *or something*.

Letorneau spits again. That's lots of maybes, he says. Well was anybody in there.

Ah shit, Whitey says. Too early to call that.

Stavros's car over there.

Right.

He wouldn't typically leave it there.

Not typically.

But then Stavros never did run a typical place.

Crunching gravel turns their heads toward Nick driving the Selectman's Ranchero with Applejack's ATV loaded in the back, all covered in red mud, and Jill is sitting right up against Nick—they're both wide-eyed as they take in the scene, trying to look in shock. He pulls alongside Letorneau and Whitey, cranks down his window. Whitey shakes his head and whistles some bird call. Letorneau leans in to address Nick.

Hey.

What the fuck happened here, Nick says.

I'll ask the questions, Letorneau says. What the fuck you driving, boy.

Oh it's just my new ride, Nick says.

Jill coughs.

You're not so slick as you might think, Letorneau says.

Nick doesn't say anything in response to that and Jill quiets down, too.

Well, Letorneau says. Then who exactly is this here with you now.

He's looking across Nick at Jill and she smiles at him and he removes his cap and shows his teeth right back at her, pretty as she is. He's wondering would this one like a shot at the title. Nick knows what he's thinking, recognizes how Jill can twist a man up. The way she has had him all twisted up like a pretzel since they were just little kids.

This here is nobody, Nick says. Far as you're concerned.

Jill looks away and pretends to cough again.

All right, asshole, Letorneau says as he puts his cap back on his head. Just account for your whereabouts.

My what now.

This is for the record, boy.

What record.

Come on now.

Oh, all right. I worked all day, then I stopped over to the Brook.

You don't even know what day I'm talking about yet.

Doesn't matter, Nick says. That's about every day now.

How many beers you have at the Brook then.

A couple, three.

Smartass, Letorneau says. Like I could give a fuck about that.

Nick closes his eyes.

What I'm talking about, Letorneau says, is this fire right here.

Nick opens his eyes and looks at the cop.

Shit, he says. I'm no burner.

Letorneau waits for him to continue.

You know me. That's not me.

I know you, all right, Letorneau says. You saying you didn't do it.

I didn't do it.

But maybe you know who then.

I don't know shit, Nick says. Probably faulty wiring.

Electrical, you say.

Sure. Or whoever did it over to Anthony's maybe.

He's trying to plant some kind of seed in this cop's mind, like Jill told him to. She's got a good head on her shoulders, this one. Get these boys chasing a wild goose.

Damn, Letorneau says.

A personal vendetta against such clubs, Nick says, sticking to the script. I don't know.

Letorneau thinks about that. Somebody sure did put a wick to a titty bar a couple towns over. Damn if this here isn't but the work of some kind of serial arsonist. Simple as fucking that. Goddamn the state police and their meddling ways. He likes the idea of gumming up their conspiracy theories and maybe solving this case on his own.

He looks at Nick, really lets his eyes rest on him now.

Well, shit. You practically took up residence here.

So what.

I'm just saying. Lucky you weren't inside when it happened.

Lucky.

Yeah, funny how that works. Luck.

Nick doesn't say anything else. Letorneau stands up straight and removes his cap and scratches his scalp, spits over his shoulder and squeezes the brim of his cap once and then twice, puts his hands on his hips, and sticks his bare head back inside the window. He gives a wink to Miss Nobody, really feeling his oats with this one.

Where you all headed anyhow, he says to her.

Just taking a little ride, Nick says. Down the road a bit.

Letorneau pulls his head out of the window. Whitey barks instructions at his men who are taking turns pissing on the smoky piles. Nick puts the car in drive and pulls away just as a two-tone blue, four-door Buick cuts into the lot, maybe unmarked but police written all over it. A woman with a white collared shirt and mirrored sunglasses behind the wheel, her head on a swivel as she tracks Nick and Jill's unhurried departure.

CHAPTER SIXTY-ONE

The sun is low in a cloudless sky. Acres and acres of water smooth as glass. A bird's-eye view of the reservoir would reveal a majestic scene, classic New England, the Town of Stillwater, the rugged hills, the fields, the surrounding country. Whole towns died for this reservoir, so Boston could drink clean water. Dana and Enfield, Prescott and Greenwich, all drowned slow under a rising manmade tide. But that was a long time ago and the drowning of the Swift River towns was not a unique event. Happens every damn day all over the world. Somebody's always thirsty for something: drugs, booze, money, sex, power, a fresh start. One man gets a bellyful while another has his blood drained out.

Suzanne pulls onto a mud bank, opens the door and gets out of the truck. Applejack squeezes his eyes against a raging in his head and heart and lungs. Suzanne goes around to his side, opens his door, and holds him up—she places her hand over the rose-petal stain on his shirt, that mortal corsage, and she talks in his ear.

Does it hurt real bad, she says.

He shakes his head no. But how's your head, he says. That lump.

My head's fine, she says, touching where it's tender and set to bruise. Then she checks the oily rag he's pressing against the hole in his chest. Soaked right through, she says. We got to get you seen.

Applejack shakes his head again and tries to smile at her. When he breathes hard it sounds like a liquid is filling him up and then he coughs and spits pink onto the floor.

Shit, Suzanne says. It got your lung too.

Just nicked it maybe.

Jesus.

Nah, it'll be all right, he says. Let's just ride around for a while more.

You been shot bad. This ain't just a scratch or something.

I don't know.

She lets out a long breath and he launches into another coughing fit.

Well, she says when he settles down, where to then.

You know what. Just till we run out of road. How about that.

Out of road, huh.

One of his favorite things to do in simpler times, take to the back roads with no particular destination in mind and no rush whatsoever to get there.

We ain't done that in a while, he says.

Yeah, Suzanne says. That what you want.

I think so.

That's how you want to do this.

He looks at her and holds her there in his eyes as long as he can.

All right, she says.

Just don't leave me, he says, taking her hand, squeezing maybe too hard. Maybe not hard enough.

Something new in his voice she hasn't heard before.

He shows her some teeth again, more grimace than grin.

Never again, she says. Not for a single fucking minute.

Suzanne drives with Applejack at her side. After a while he's motionless but for his body adjusting to the rhythms of the road, his eyes closed, and she heads west on the logging trail alongside the water's edge. She stops the pickup at an intersection.

Applejack uses his strong hand to apply pressure to his gunshot wound and his love leans over and soft puts her lips to his temple and just rests them there for a spell.

Applejack opens his eyes half mast and then slow closes them again. His finger-curled hand falls down to the seat.

A boulder is set back from the road and nestled among woodchips and purple and yellow flowers, a memorial of sorts to the towns that decades ago disappeared to make way for this giant water hole, cut to a smooth face, words etched into it talking about how reservoirs are trade-offs, and like all such deals they are never easy, never perfectly fair. The horizon is a jagged sawcut, tall pine trees lording over this land for a thousand years. Suzanne checks the gas gauge and figures she'll drive as long as she can on a full tank, windows all the way down so she can breathe in the day and make her peace with God or whoever the fuck and then she'll follow her man to someplace just beyond those pines.

Suzanne has at no time been a church girl, but on a teenage dare she once stumbled, high as a kite, into a funeral at St. Matthew's where she encountered an old priest who after a bit of small talk shared what she guessed to be his unconventional views of the afterlife. Maybe death is just a creaky door on an old barn, he said. We hesitate to pass through the dark passage because we don't know what's inside. Maybe bats will come down from the rafters and get tangled in our hair, and rats will shadow-scamper up the legs of our trousers. The big door will slam shut and lock behind us and a hay hook will fall from above and go into our neck. That's what we think dead is about so we do everything we can to avoid it and keep it closed up in that barn. Perhaps we understand we don't have a choice, and that we might even cross that threshold not so loudly when our time does come. That's if there's a chance that on the other side there are no rats and bats, no falling hay hooks, only a single white swallow that flutters in the window backlit by the setting sun and it lands soft on our shoulder and we're done with dying just as easy as that.

CHAPTER SIXTY-TWO

There's the manmade pond out back where William and Honey can swim if they want. Reeds and cattails skirt the bank and bullfrogs warble in unseen pockets of dark. Everything is August and hot and William already caught a bucketful of catfish to fry. William's daddy goes to get the Remington 28. He bought it cheap off Tyrone Hatfield over to the Rod and Gun Club and he wants his son to see it. William smokes most of his Marlboros anyhow. Honey watches him sideways, sticks out her tongue.

Then they sit under the weeping willow where William's daddy's view from the shack is blocked. William drinks the old man's Jack Daniel's and he puts his finger inside Honey until she smiles and closes her eyes like almonds. Dawn through the canopy of deciduous trees is random pastel swirls of tangerine and strawberry today. They hear the old man staggering down the path toward them, kicking loose stones and snapping dry twigs. They separate and William fixes himself. Honey dives into the water.

William's daddy doesn't know that William knows.

But William smelled his daddy on Honey the other day and so she told him about dancing and taking off her clothes at that awful joint and carrying on with his daddy since Thanksgiving. All this starting up even before William had met Honey at the Franklin County Fair. It near to fucked up his head like so he'd never get over it. That his daddy had been messing with his girl all along. And that she kept the shit up for so long.

William had asked her why, but she didn't even know the answer anymore. So they fucked in the Silverado and hatched this half-baked plan together. The great escape is what she called it.

He got me under his thumb, is what she said. Cut off the hand and there goes the thumb.

So now William's daddy stands before him, swaying a bit.

He shows William the blue barrel and the pump action and brags of breaking birds, standing too close to his son. His breath smells like fifty years of living wrong. He tells William that the grip reminds him of putting his hand on the waist of a pretty girl and he smiles over to Honey, in what he thinks to be a seductive way, when he says it. He shoves the gun at William and William holds it and says a couple agreeable enough things so his daddy will shut the fuck up already. There are lawn chairs with rusty piping on the dock and William's daddy sits in one and it bows beneath the weight of him.

Then William hears him snoring. The old fucker's been up all night drinking again.

William sets down the gun and swims to where Honey is resting on a cool gray rock. He splashes her and she acts mad. They tongue kiss sloppy like eating an overripe peach and she looks over William's shoulder at his daddy and lets out a long breath.

So we gone to do this, she says in William's ear.

William tells her he doesn't know yet. She rubs on him for a while to get him in the proper frame of mind, a warm breeze and a bit of her ginger hair in his face. Honey's green duffle bag is already packed. He figures they'll take the Silverado up north to Derby or wherever and it'll be a week before anybody misses his daddy, and at that point he can torch the fucking truck in a barren field beneath the moon. Honey rests her head on his chest. Then she goes for another swim, giving him some space and time to think.

William swims back to the dock and picks up the rifle.

He checks the chamber.

He plants his feet.

Puts his cheekbone firmly down on the stock.

Squeezes one eye shut until his daddy is in his sights.

He eases his elbow just a cunt hair to the left.

Then something distracts him, up the bank and through the trees where Sand Gulley Road wraps around Bull Hill, and he lowers the Remington to his side and tries to focus on what could be a passing car but it's simply too high and away from where he pictures the blacktop. Could it be the lights of a crop duster flying low. Not over in the trees like that, and it's too close to be any normal kind of aircraft under typical circumstances. Honey is behind him because he can feel her hand on his shoulder, her breath on his neck.

What the hell, she whispers.

They stand there waiting and watching in silence.

Until that silence is broken.

Branches crack and an American-made engine whines just before dying.

A mud-caked International bursts through the tall pines, its undercarriage casting a shadow upon the dry dock and spreading around William's daddy still asleep in that chair, a blackened beast from the ether that wants to swallow him whole, the pickup truck descends: tires spinning slow motion, rusted leaf springs creaking, the whoosh of a heavy metal body vaulting through warm summer air. Faint music and somebody singing like, it's getting louder and for certain a woman's choked-up voice, and William closes his eyes so he can make out the words: *Love me tender, love me sweet, never let me go.*

CHAPTER SIXTY-THREE

Stavros asks the pretty girl for coffee. Stavros. Nobody calls him that anymore, but it's still how he thinks of himself. He's a thousand miles away from that life now. Outside he stands on the corner holding his Styrofoam cup and a newspaper. A car engine revs and somebody shouts his name. Staffon Stavros, the voice says. He looks up, of course, because how could you fucking not. And as he does so two strong sets of hands pin his arms to his sides and guide him to his knees. He tries to turn his head, to see who has such a hold on him, but Cornfed won't allow it. Dumb as a couple stumps but loyal as dogs, the voice from the car says, only closer to him now.

The author would like to acknowledge the talented team at Dzanc Books, especially Steven Gillis and Guy Intoci for their unwavering support and encouragement. Also, Sonny Brewer for taking a first run at this book.